W9-AGB-062

MURDER IN THE

QUEEN'S BOUDOIR

MURDER IN THE QUEEN'S BOUDOIR

Amy Myers

This first world edition published in Great Britain 2000 by
SEVERN HOUSE PUBLISHERS LTD of
9–15 High Street, Sutton, Surrey SM1 1DF.
This first world edition published in the U.S.A. 2000 by
SEVERN HOUSE PUBLISHERS INC of
595 Madison Avenue, New York, N.Y. 10022.

British Library Cataloguing in Publication Data

Myers, Amy
    Murder in the Queen's boudoir
    1. Didier, Auguste (Fictitious character) - Fiction
    2. Cooks - Fiction
    3. Detective and mystery stories
    I. Title
    823.9'14 [F]

    ISBN 0-7278-5561-1

Typeset by Palimpsest Book Production Ltd.
Polmont, Stirlingshire, Scotland.
Printed and bound in Great Britain by
MPG Books Ltd, Bodmin, Cornwall.

Author's Note

The adventures of Miss Moberly and Miss Jourdain at the Petit Trianon in 1901 are well recorded. Having written full accounts of their experiences both for private use and in letters to family and friends, they then spent some years researching the history of Marie Antoinette and the Petit Trianon. Without revealing their true names they published *An Adventure* in 1911, which set out their experiences, the results of their research and their conclusions from both. They have been the subject of controversy ever since. Their two foremost critics at the time, from the Psychical Research Society, changed their minds when the ladies revealed their true identities as Principal and Vice-Principal of St Hugh's Hall, Oxford, and after examining their original documents. New editions of the book appeared at intervals up to the 1950s, bringing both fresh criticism and stalwart defence. In 1957 Lucile Iremonger published her excellent study of evidence for and against the truth of the ladies' story under the title *The Ghosts of Versailles*.

In 1906, when this novel is set, Auguste Didier did not of course have the benefit of later research and had to rely on his own experiences.

The gardens at the Petit Trianon have changed greatly since the days of Marie Antoinette, and differ today from their appearance in 1906. I have followed the old maps, save that the outbuildings of the Petit Trianon French Garden, from which the ladies observed a cottage woman shaking a cloth, include here a car museum, as I believe they later did. This was entirely to please Tatiana, and does not affect the plot.

A. M.

Prologue

1901

"**D**amned weird thing."

The Hon. George Ladyboys' voice from his dressing room was muffled as he struggled into his nightgown. Winifred, poised with one foot on the floor and one in the bed, eased her plump body onwards, and was somewhat surprised when George appeared through the doorway that he did not seem eager to follow suit. They had been married for only two years and the sight of her rounded body usually sent him into ecstasies of excitement; it was a panacea for all damned weird things that disturbed her husband's ponderous way through life.

"Ghosts," George announced from the end of the bed. "Do you believe in them, Winifred?"

"Certainly," she replied vigorously.

There was a pause. "I never knew that. Rum thing, marriage. You'll be interested in that letter I had this morning then."

"From a ghost?" She gave a bark of laughter to jolly him out of this train of thought. There must be nothing rum about their wedded life; the past had been so deeply buried in order that the flowers of bliss could continue to flourish above it in unsuspecting tranquillity.

1

"No. From Annie Moberly. Principal of St Hugh's Hall, Oxford, for ladies. Distant relative. Mentioned her before."

So he had. Winifred had lodged in her memory every member of George's impeccable family as far as second cousins thrice removed and back as far as 1746. Her cut-off date was to ignore the unfortunate 6th Earl of Stratton who had lost his head for romantically, but unwisely, deciding to fight for Bonnie Prince Charlie. Winifred's knowledge repaid the hours she had pored over the family tree before she was admitted to the Ladyboys name. It had been a passport at which she had clutched eagerly after she had first met George in France.

George, now sitting bolt upright in bed, disregarded, to her astonishment, her hand on his thigh. "Says she went to the Petit Trianon at Versailles with some Oxford friend, and they walked straight into Marie Antoinette and half her court."

"Remarkable, George," she replied sleepily, abandoning hope of marital bliss. Ghosts, even guillotined queens of long ago, could wait.

"Why don't we take a trip to Paris to see if we run into them too?"

She was suddenly fully awake once more. "No, George," she said firmly. "Bournemouth is much more suitable, and there are just as many ghosts, I'm quite sure."

George Ladyboys said no more. A wistful, unfulfilled longing to return to the scenes of his bachelor days clung obstinately to the back of his mind as the years passed.

One

"The truffles in the stuffing for the *Poularde à la Roi* – I have *forgotten* to put them in, Mrs Jolly."

The walls of his kitchen closed around him like a prison cage. *Forgot* was not a word known to the vocabulary of Auguste Didier, master chef, and his cry of anguish brought his staff to an appalled standstill, even the usually unflappable Mrs Jolly.

"Don't you worry, sir," she replied, though her shock was evident. "I'll drop more curry powder in the sauce; His Majesty will never notice."

"He *always* notices," Auguste muttered. In an hour's time a royal banquet must be served to His Majesty, perfect in every detail and suitable for the inaugural meeting of the Amis de l'Entente Cordiale held at His Majesty's request, and Tatiana's enthusiastic agreement, in their London Queen Anne's Gate home, on 10 June 1906. *Forgot* indeed. This was professional ruin; he would never cook again. He would devote himself to being merely Tatiana's husband, distant relative to the British, as well as Romanov, royal families. And after this evening it would indeed be distant. Auguste stared at the chicken poaching merrily on the gas stove, wondering if even now he could plunge in to rescue it and adjust the stuffing.

"No, Mr Didier." Mrs Jolly had obviously read his mind. "I'll do them truffles up quick as anything *à la Piedmontaise*."

"That is a Francatelli recipe, not a Didier." Oh, the humiliation.

"If it was good enough for Queen Victoria, it's good enough for her son," Mrs Jolly retorted with impeccable logic.

Seeing the staff holding their breath instead of their cooking knives, Auguste bowed his head in defeat. His Majesty had been quite right to refuse him permission to cook when he married Tatiana, save under strict exceptions. He would resign his paradise kitchen to Mrs Jolly completely. He was lost, the dish was lost, the evening would be a disaster.

There was no doubt about it.

Auguste's heart thudded like a herb chopper on a board. Seconds ticked by into minutes, minutes into the moment when the royal Daimler would draw up, the royal chauffeur open the door, and the royal feet be placed on the royal running board. The arrival of the Queen of Sheba might have been more ostentatious, but the arrival of King Edward VII could beat it for inspiring sheer terror. Auguste shivered. It wasn't only the meal that boded ill for the evening. There were the guests to be reckoned with. The mere fact that it had taken hundreds of years to achieve an Entente Cordiale between Britain and France must surely suggest that there were difficulties in basing an evening on a mixture of French and English people, and this would not change, despite the fact that Auguste Didier was chef and host.

"He's here," Tatiana said at his side, for once nervous herself, as they waited at the open doorway. The diamonds in her tiara seemed to be winking at Auguste in mockery in the June evening sunshine. It was only with difficulty he had persuaded her to wear it. His Majesty (Cousin Bertie on less formal occasions) liked ladies to be appropriately dressed, and Tatiana's preferred mode of apparel for her working life at her motoring club rarely featured tiaras.

Here! The word struck like the knell of doom. Oh for a star-trap to open up beneath him and whisk him from the stage of public view. It didn't happen, and Auguste prepared for the worst.

The royal feet were advancing towards them, and Charlie, Mrs Jolly's son, who was their temporary butler, managed an impressively deep bow in spite of his girth.

"Tatiana, my dear." Bertie beamed as Tatiana curtseyed, and then turned with somewhat less of a beam to her husband. "Auguste!"

Majesty must be in benevolent mood, if he was being addressed by his Christian name. Auguste decided to continue fearing the worst, for benevolent moods, like still sunny days, could switch all too quickly to sudden storms.

The tramp of their footsteps as they escorted their guest of honour up the main staircase to the drawing room sounded to Auguste like the roll of the drum on the way to the scaffold. Tramp, tramp, and step nearer. Awaiting them were eight guests, of whom he had met only one, Louise Danielle, before. And *that* ensured trouble, even if the truffles had been in their appointed place.

The doors to the drawing room were flung open, and the guests revealed assembled in two lines, for all the world as if they were about to launch into dancing the 'Sir Roger de Coverley'. Above them the cherubic gods and nymphs on the painted ceiling looked down in high glee on what was undoubtedly going to be great sport for them, if no one else. Perhaps it was his own fraught nerves that gave Auguste a sudden impression that there was a taut web of tension spun between these guests that could not wholly be explained by Bertie's presence. He pulled himself together for his duties as host.

"Lady Harper, Your Majesty." Auguste had never met her ladyship, but had been looking forward to doing so. Mirabelle Harper was French, and the widow of Sir John Harper, who must have been much older than she, for she seemed only in her mid-thirties – though age was not what one first thought of when you were privileged to look upon those calm blue-grey eyes and that classically curled golden hair. The silken skirts swished as she rose from her curtsey, and the eyes gazed steadily at Bertie as though they shared an intimate secret. She was an elegant *sauce aux mirabelles*, Auguste decided, the perfect complement for the pork of an elderly husband, flavoursome, sweet and perfectly blended. It could, however, become suffocating if too much was taken. "I am honoured, Your Majesty." Her voice was low and musical, and every diamond shone on cue, to complete Auguste's impression of an exotic canary.

"Mr Jacob Fernby." His Majesty would of course already know the most fashionable portrait painter of the day, who had hopes of winning Mirabelle's hand. He too was a sauce, but a lighter one, of *écrevisses* perhaps – or should it be *à la provencale*? Yes, a strong sauce with strong tastes underlying it, Auguste decided. The touches of grey in his light-brown curls only enhanced the artist's good looks. Jacob was as classically handsome as the Greek gods he had come to fame in portraying. Now they had been abandoned for the god of society, although somehow his portrait subjects, male or female, all acquired a noble, classical mien.

"Madame Alice Gaston and Monsieur Pierre Gaston."

Tatiana nudged him, and he was hastily recalled to his duty. His wife smiled at the Gastons, for all the world as if there were nothing she would rather be doing than entertaining Cousin Bertie's guests.

Following dutifully behind, Auguste felt sympathy for Alice, who was the youngest present, though she looked eager rather than nervous. Her mass of fair curls and china-blue eyes gave her only a superficial resemblance to Mirabelle; she was a child *ingénue* to Mirabelle's *grande dame*. She was English, but her husband Pierre, in his early to mid-forties, was French. They lived, he knew, in Paris, and he promptly dubbed them *sole au chablis* (light and slender) and lobster bisque (heavy with, perhaps, hidden depths). It occurred to him, however, that sole was not always so simple to prepare as its resulting texture suggested.

Rapt by his pleasant analogy, Auguste began to relax.

"Mr and Mrs George Ladyboys, whom of course you know, sir." Roast beef and Christmas plum pudding, Auguste decided happily. As a fellow member of the Marlborough Club, His Majesty must know George Ladyboys well, and he stayed, so Tatiana said, at his Leicester seat every so often.

Robert, Comte de Tourville, was another old friend of His Majesty, although anyone less like the stolid George Ladyboys would be hard to imagine. He was an ortolan, a bird of passage through the fashionable season, a man of charm and culture – and also, of course, French, though Auguste had not met him before. Now that he had, he was not sure he warmed to him. He appeared to use his charm like a sauce, not a stuffing. However, His Majesty approved highly of him – naturally enough. It had been Robert in the 1890s who had introduced Bertie, then Prince of Wales, to the Moulin Rouge, according to Tatiana.

And that brought him to Madame Louise Danielle, Robert's long-term and, he gathered, long-public mistress, married to an apparently acquiescent politician husband; she could not be more than about thirty-five, but looked older. If Alice was the sole, then Louise was the pike, for all her dark glossy hair, seductive dark eyes, and olive skin. This quenelle of *brochet*, the most predatory fish in fresh water, was hidden by its charming sauce Nantua. He had seen Louise once during her years of fame at the Moulin Rouge, and no one who had done so had ever forgotten La Dervicheuse, as she had been known far and side. She had taken great care later to become 'respectable' through marriage, but if the sauce were omitted, the quenelle would taste the same.

"Such a pleasure," Louise purred in her deep throaty voice, casting a look round at her fellow guests, then fixing those dark eyes on His Majesty, "to meet so many old friends here."

Auguste trembled. He knew full well that Bertie disliked being reminded of the old days – especially if His Majesty had been intimately concerned in them. He'd known it all along. This evening would lead to disaster.

"Not quite up to your usual standard, Auguste," Bertie barked jovially. "The curry sauce was a shade too hot. The truffles *Piedmontaise* were excellent though. You can do that one again."

Auguste smiled politely, seething inside. Almost the most annoying thing about Bertie where food was concerned was that he tended to be right. Publicly criticising your host's cooking, however, hardly seemed the best way of promoting amity between Britain and France – especially since His Majesty himself had insisted on Auguste's cooking, in preference to bringing his own chefs.

"Ladies," Tatiana had picked up the danger signals, "shall we retire?"

Tatiana disliked this English custom, practical though it might be for those wishing to escape after dinner without embarrassment, but this evening she appeared only too eager to conform. Auguste could not blame her. Conversation had been dominated by Louise who, while following protocol in waiting for His Majesty to initiate all topics of conversation, had nevertheless managed to turn all subjects to her own advantage. Tatiana had had enough. All very well, but wifely duty also covered supporting husbands, not leaving them to the mercies of His Majesty.

By the time Auguste judged he could decently suggest they rejoin the ladies in the drawing room, and the footmen, who had obediently squeezed themselves into formal full livery for this event, flung open the doors, he was glad to see that Tatiana looked relieved to see them. She was well used to handling parties of difficult ladies for her motoring club, but any group with Louise Danielle in it could not be easy, and it had been obvious at dinner that there was even less love lost between Louise and Mirabelle than between most women. Tatiana had met Louise in Paris, and had remarked that she regarded every moment spent solely in female company as a waste of time. Robert adored her, her husband adored her, half the men in Paris still adored her, but she preferred to spend her energy on captivating the other half. Now, with the doors opened, her boredom could vanish and the throaty purr return.

As His Majesty entered, Louise rose gracefully to her feet, obviously intending to move straight across to him. Whatever her plan for taking command of the rest of the evening, as she had at dinner, she was forestalled. Mirabelle had no intention of letting her do so. She walked calmly to

Robert's side, announcing in defiance of any protocol at all: "Ah, the gentlemen have returned. There shall be nothing of this ridiculous English custom when we marry, shall there, Robert?"

Every detail of that moment remained imprinted on Auguste's memory. It was worthy of a painting by Jacob Fernby: *Society Shocked*. Louise remained quite still, like a cat about to pounce. The count said nothing, his face drained of expression as he stared not at Mirabelle but at Louise. Jacob's changed from shock to barely suppressed anger, and Alice Gaston was the only one who beamed at the announcement, clapping her hands in childish excitement.

After a moment Louise drawled, "Congratulations, Robert. And to you too, dear Mirabelle, after all your hard work."

"I too congratulate you," Jacob said quietly. "You deceived me into believing you loved me." Mirabelle smiled, his accusation leaving her unruffled.

Robert, Auguste was interested to note, quickly regained his usual composure, after his initial shock at Mirabelle's choice of timing.

His Majesty cleared his throat. "When's the wedding to be, Robert?"

"Nothing is decided, sir. Our plans are still under discussion."

"Mine also," Louise retorted offhandedly. "Pray don't allow any ghosts from the past to spoil your happiness, however."

Before Tatiana could intervene, having seen the black cloud descending on Bertie's face, George Ladyboys galloped to the rescue remarking hastily, "Talking of ghosts, I know a splendid story about Versailles – I think you'll all be interested."

"No, George," Winifred cried in vain, as there were murmurs of relieved interest. Even Bertie seemed only too pleased to ignore his royal prerogative, as this new subject was introduced. Or perhaps it was due to the brandy that Charlie Jolly, bursting out of his rarely donned livery, placed in his hand.

Louise was not so amused. "Not," she yawned slightly, "the old story about Marie Antoinette haunting the Petit Trianon?"

George flushed, as there was a squeal from Alice. "Oh, how lovely. Did you know I am descended from Marie Antoinette? I am very like her, am I not, Pierre?"

"Yes, my dove." Pierre smiled indulgently at his wife.

"You all know the story then?" George's disappointment was obvious.

"There was a book published twenty years ago of these old tales," Robert laughed. "It sells very well – to the credulous."

"My mother comes from an old Austrian family." Alice was not to be deterred now. "I am descended from the Dauphin. It's not true that he died in Paris; he escaped to Vienna. I *know* he did."

George ploughed doggedly on. "This ghost story took place only five years ago. The lady Principal of St Hugh's in Oxford, Annie Moberly, and her prospective Vice-Principal, Eleanor Jourdain, became lost in the grounds of Versailles while they were trying to find the Petit Trianon château on a hot August day. They wandered up a lane by the Grand Trianon château, took a pathway leading round the back of the Petit Trianon gardens, branched off it and, realising they were lost, asked two johnnies they took to be gardeners the way to the château. They ran into other oddly dressed fellows, but eventually arrived at the rear of the building. A lady was sketching in the garden, dressed in exquisite but old-fashioned clothes, and then a young man came rushing out from the adjacent chapel to direct them round to the proper entrance. There

11

they joined a big wedding party and thought no more of it, until they compared notes some time later and agreed the place was haunted, not least" – George waxed enthusiastic – "because not all the characters were seen by both ladies. The woman sketching, for instance, was only seen by Miss Moberly although they had passed quite near to her."

"A hot August day, you say," Robert observed languidly.

"My husband," boomed Winifred loyally, "is convinced, as they were, that they had walked back into the time of Marie Antoinette."

"The past is such a fruitful area for investigation, is it not?" Mirabelle purred to the room in general, but no one appeared to agree with her, for another silence greeted her comment.

"Do you believe in ghosts too, Mrs Ladyboys?" Auguste asked, determined to resurrect this reasonably non-controversial subject.

"I do, Mr Didier." Winifred leapt eagerly at his conversational gambit. "Does Your Majesty believe in them?"

"I understand we've a few wandering around Windsor. Herne the Hunter, for instance." Bertie glared at Auguste, obviously remembering a time when that ghost, becoming all too real, had managed to get himself murdered.*

"*English* ghosts are more solid, sire," Robert laughed. "Ghosts seen in broad daylight by ladies not in their native land and unaccustomed, dare I suggest, to drinking wine with luncheon, are altogether different."

"That is hardly applicable in the case of Miss Moberly and Miss Jourdain," George replied stiffly. "As the heads of an Oxford college, they can hardly be so impressionable as you suggest."

* See *Murder with Majesty*.

"My parents knew Bishop Moberly and his daughters. Your Miss Moberly is the seventh child, and they told me she is always having strange experiences like that," Alice offered brightly.

"That," Jacob pointed out, "is as much proof for their experience being genuine as against. We artists—"

"*Pourquoi?*" Pierre interrupted belligerently. "The story is rubbish. There are no such things as ghosts."

"Oh." His wife looked disappointed. "I should so like to have met Queen Marie Antoinette. Though of course Mr Fernby has a point." She bestowed an admiring glance on Jacob.

Jacob smiled patronisingly. "Psychic experiences are only possible for the special few who have the gift. Miss Annie Moberly, perhaps, is one of them."

"Poppycock!" said Mirabelle spiritedly. "I am sure, Jacob dear, your theory is good, but those who know Versailles well would wonder why out of all the thousands of people who visit it, many of whom must have psychic powers, Queen Marie Antoinette should have chosen to haunt two English ladies that day."

"Quite," Alice said eagerly. "I cannot see why Her Majesty would manifest herself to strangers in preference to her own family."

"That is quite simple." Winifred, after her earlier reluctance to let her husband talk, now seemed only too eager to do so herself. "These two ladies were there on the tenth of August, the anniversary of the massacre at the Tuileries and the day when Louis the sixteenth and Marie Antoinette were forced to submit themselves to the National Assembly."

"So why choose that day to haunt the Trianon?" Mirabelle laughed, exchanging a merry glance with Robert.

Louise saw it, and quickly switched camps. "Very simple,

for those with any sensitivity, Mirabelle dear. Let me explain. On the tenth of August, in the midst of the horrors the Queen was enduring, she was remembering her last day at the Trianon, which was the fifth of October 1789. There she had spent her happiest days as queen. The poor lady tried to blot out her fears at the Assembly by remembering happier times, and it is the sheer force of her emotion on that August day that has imprinted itself on the Trianon. The legends support its being on an August day that the apparition is usually seen."

"This ghost appears to have a most confused social diary," Mirabelle said lazily.

"What about another brandy and soda, Didier?" His Majesty was giving the clearest possible indication of discontent and, as Auguste summoned the footman, Tatiana tried to pour oil on Bertie's troubled waters.

"How interesting," she declared brightly. "Your Majesty, my husband and I have taken no sides in this story, but four of the remaining eight seem to be sceptical of Miss Moberly's and Miss Jourdain's story, and four to believe in it."

Auguste relaxed at this non-contentious observation by his wife. Bertie was drinking his brandy, and would in a moment speak of something new. All might yet be well. The evening might even go down as a qualified success. His hopes were immediately dashed as George Ladyboys, red-faced with wine, port, brandy, and the unaccustomed position of centre stage, said, "Miss Moberly and Miss Jourdain are *English*. Of course I believe their story. So would anyone with a head on their shoulders."

"Unlike poor Queen Marie Antoinette," Robert sighed. "I'd wager you a thousand English pounds they invented the whole thing."

"*Invented?*" George was offended. "I'll take your wager. Two thousand that they didn't, sir."

"Very well." Robert shrugged. "I'll wager you that on the tenth of August this year not only will the ghosts of Marie Antoinette and her court not be seen at Trianon, but that we can prove your two blue-stocking ladies couldn't have seen any either."

"How will you do that?" Tatiana asked, intrigued.

"We'll both go to the Petit Trianon on that date," Robert said after a moment's thought. "Are you on, George?"

"George never refuses a bet," Bertie assured him from much experience, "and it's not often he loses one. I'll back him myself," he added with relish.

George galloped after the fox without a second thought. "Your wager is on, Robert," he roared.

"You said you weren't a betting man," Winifred wailed, shocked at this new George.

"It isn't a bet, Winifred. I'm quite sure about the outcome."

"You'll need witnesses," Auguste rashly pointed out.

"We'll all have to go there." Mirabelle laughed. "Won't that be nice, Robert?"

"Oh, yes, do let's," Alice cried excitedly.

"There are no such things as ghosts, Alice," Pierre reminded her curtly.

Robert's eyes were on Louise as he answered. "*Magnifique.* Your Majesty, if you would honour us with your presence, I can arrange for us all to dine and lodge in the Petit Trianon itself. It would make a remarkable occasion of what I fear would otherwise be a damp squib of an afternoon."

"All?" cried Winifred in horror.

"Why not?" Pierre roared with laughter. "Scared you *will* see ghosts?"

From the horrified look on Bertie's face, Auguste saw that he realised he had boxed himself into a corner. Unfortunately His Majesty glanced up at that moment and saw Auguste studying him. His face darkened, but he only said, "Delighted, I'm sure, Robert."

Winifred, ignoring Pierre, attempted a last appeal. "It won't work, Robert. Suppose no ghosts turn up? There may not be a medium among us, and George would lose unfairly."

"We will encourage them to do so. Is that not sporting of a mere Frenchman?" Robert laughed. "We will retrace the route the ladies took, to prove they were in the gardens of 1901, not 1789, all the time and the people they saw *were* merely gardeners and other visitors. Provided the dead Queen doesn't honour us with a visit, that will win me the wager."

"Agreed," snarled George.

"Somehow I believe I shall win," Robert said complacently.

"We could dress up," Alice said, inspired. "That would encourage the ghosts to appear. Not that I believe in them, of course. I'll play—"

"Why, yes," Louise interrupted. "Dear George. What a splendid wager. We will each take the role of one of the characters in the story, I will encourage the Queen to appear by playing her myself."

George beamed at the compliment, but the corners of Alice's mouth took a downward plunge. "But Marie Antoinette was *my* ancestor." No one was listening, intent on the hidden battle between Louise, Robert and Mirabelle.

"I feel, Louise dear," Mirabelle drawled, "that you might be over-eager for the Queen's ghost to appear."

"Unlike you, sweet Mirabelle, I *never* cheat," Louise retorted. "Nevertheless, it would be more fitting if I play her, will it not, Robert?"

The gauntlet had been thrown down, and there was a hush as everyone awaited his reply. "Perhaps, Louise, in this instance Mirabelle is right."

"But that's not fair, Robert," wailed Alice.

"Dear child, life never is." Louise threw back her head and laughed. "Very well. Monsieur and Madame Didier must take the parts of the two ladies, follow their route, and greet the people they greeted. It will persuade the ghosts to emerge while we have tea. Do you trust our hosts, gentlemen?"

There was an instant murmur of agreement. Appalled, Auguste glanced at Tatiana. Was she thinking, as he was, that it would be the height of folly to be drawn into this charade; it seemed clear to him that there was far more than a wager involved. He would invent an alternative engagement – now!

"I regret—"

"Splendid idea." His Majesty nodded approvingly.

Auguste reeled from the shock of having been personally included in this horrific fantasy. The Entente had ceased to bear any resemblance to Cordiale for him. The regal eye fell on him thoughtfully. "Ah, Auguste," he added. "That was a good dinner this evening. Don't worry about that curry powder. As you're going to be at the Petit Trianon, you can cook the lunch and dinner. Tea, too, if you like."

"Your Majesty is too kind." Were those lying words coming out of *his* mouth?

If His Majesty commanded his services as a chef, he had to obey. This was one of the conditions, the worst, on which he had received the royal permission to wed Tatiana.

He would never cook *Poularde à la Roi* again. It had all been the fault of the stuffing.

Mirabelle reflected on the events of the evening and her own part in them, as Jacob drove her back to Claridge's in his new Royce motor car. "*Not* over ten miles per hour, please, dear Jacob. You know that is the safe level for dust protection." Jacob was a dear, and she was only too well aware that he had been intent on becoming dearer still. She had been a widow for two years, and that was long enough in his opinion – and hers too. Jacob had served his purpose, however, and this evening she had taken a vital step in her plan to marry Robert. She could deal with the slight threat that Jacob posed. Robert had been a widower since Hélène's death six years ago and, she supposed, she should be grateful to Louise for keeping him single for so long, and also for having a husband in the best of health, which had prevented Robert from marrying her.

It was time to think of the next step, and so little did Jacob now figure in her plans, that she was surprised when he said, "I cannot believe you are serious about marrying that man."

"But I am, Jacob. *Très serieuse.*"

"He loves Louise, and you, I had thought, loved me."

"You are a dear, dear friend, *mon Jacob*, but my heart has been Robert's for a long time. As for Louise – you are surely mistaken. She is a married lady, after all." Mirabelle's voice was reproachful, and Jacob brought the motor car to an abrupt stop outside the hotel.

"You have deceived me, Mirabelle," he said simply. "Do you not believe in nemesis dogging your footsteps?"

She laughed. "No. Nor any ghosts of the past. Are you hoping Marie Antoinette will appear so that you can paint her portrait? That would help your ambitions, would it not?"

"There are other ghosts." Jacob was trembling with anger, but kept his voice quiet.

She glanced at him. So he hadn't forgotten. "Ah, you think of Hélène."

"Don't we all?"

"You idolised her too much."

"Of course. But now I am thirty-four, then I was twenty-one."

Mirabelle too was thirty-four, but unlike Jacob she had left her earlier life far behind when she married in 1898. She had not forgotten it, however, nor the information she had gathered since. Knowledge was power. She was on the point of achieving what she had most wanted from life, and no one today connected Lady Harper with Mathilde Plevinne, singer at the Jardin de Paris. No one but those who were closest to her then: Louise, Robert – and Jacob.

Pierre and Alice Gaston took a horse-drawn cab back to Alice's parents' Mayfair home where they usually stayed when in London.

"You're very silent, Pierre," Alice ventured at last. "You're not cross with me, are you, my great big growly bear?"

"Of course not, my love." Pierre, shaken by the surprises of the evening, had other matters on his mind, wondering if and how he could turn the situation to his advantage, or whether it would work against him. Who would have thought it after all these years? One thing was sure. Alice must know nothing about it. He'd been married five years now, and the source of the wealth that had made it possible for him to marry into such a high-class English family must remain his secret, and not his only one.

Ghosts indeed. Whatever happened on 10 August, it was only seeing the living reminder of what lay so deeply buried that would concern him at Versailles: Louise Danielle.

Louise chose her moment to speak carefully. She had made it

clear that as Robert had brought her here this evening, he would also be escorting her home, engagement or no engagement. She would spend the night with him too, she decided. Rage battled with bewilderment. If Mirabelle Harper had had any money she could perhaps have understood it, but she did not. Louise had no doubt that for all his superficially light manner, Robert was as passionately devoted to her as ever. She was supremely confident that he was hers to command, and would remain so.

"And when, my love," she said at last, "you take me in your arms tonight, will it be me or your fiancée you see?"

If she had expected excuses, explanations, protestations of love, she was disappointed.

He laughed, which nonplussed her. "Yours, *ma mie*, if I were fortunate enough to be able to embrace you tonight. But I cannot."

"You are mine, are you not, Robert?" There was still no doubt in her mind, but he owed her confirmation.

"My heart is yours."

"And your head too, I trust. You will not marry that woman, Robert."

He did not reply.

"If you do," Louise continued pleasantly, "it will be difficult for me to decide."

"What?"

"Whether to kill sweet Mirabelle or you. A *crime passionnel*," she purred, "how tempting."

"Bournemouth, George. We'd booked to go to Bournemouth in August." There was a note of desperation in Winifred's voice.

George was apologetic, but firm. Indeed, he seemed almost

excited. "Couldn't do anything else, bunnykins. A gentleman can't turn down a wager in company."

"But I don't have to go to France, do I?"

"I'm afraid so, now His Majesty's going. He'd have your head off if we insulted him. And mine."

At the moment that seemed to Winifred a reasonable price to pay. "I could explain to him about Bournemouth," she suggested hopelessly.

He stared at her. "You do really believe in the two old girls' story, don't you? You're usually the first to back me up."

"Of course, George," his wife answered dully. "All the same, if no ghosts appear and we can't prove the story is correct . . ."

"Everyone will be laying odds on it now. We can't back out. Anyway, we can afford it," George said reassuringly.

Perhaps he could. Winifred, however, could not.

Auguste looked at the remains of the dinner, always a salutary experience, and he never omitted to do so. The clearing-up could provide as many helpful hints as the preparation, even if not so enjoyable.

"How was it, sir?" Mrs Jolly asked without much anxiety. She ran his kitchen like the East End pie shop where he had discovered her; it was orderly, precise, she kept standards up, and footmen and butler (especially her son) in their places. A dinner for His Majesty would be like her pies: each one a model of perfection. If she didn't take a fancy to a dish, nothing could make her cook it; if she did, one could rely on it.

"His Majesty enjoyed the truffles *Piedmontaise*."

"Oh dear. As bad as that, sir?" Now she was worried.

"Not on account of the food, Mrs Jolly." Auguste hesitated. "Do you believe in ghosts, Mrs Jolly?"

"Yes, sir. I had one in my pantry at the pie shop. An old sweep, he was. Will that be all? Everything's in the larders now."

Left alone, Auguste stayed a few moments to enjoy the peace and certainties of his kitchen. Even ghosts seemed acceptable here, and Le Petit Trianon a long way off.

He went upstairs to find Tatiana already in bed, and bent over to kiss her.

"*Mon brave*, your ordeal by torture is over," she said, returning the kiss with enthusiasm.

"In two months it begins again."

"Perhaps the ghosts of Marie Antoinette's *cuisiniers* will emerge to help you," Tatiana suggested sleepily.

"Or her executioners."

She shot up in bed. "Don't joke about it, Auguste. It's bad luck," she said fiercely.

"You can't really think these ghosts will appear?"

There was a short pause. "I am Russian, Auguste."

"I know."

"And there are those in my family who have had unusual experiences."

Something in Auguste's stomach, stronger even than the curry powder, churned energetically.

"I am afraid, Auguste, that I, too, am probably a medium."

Two

"*Non!*"

To be greeted by this! It was too much after crossing the Channel on a steamship where all the world save he and Tatiana seemed to be *en vacances*, followed by a long uncomfortable train ride to Paris in which every speck of dirt from the steam engine had seemed intent on seeking out the window behind which Auguste Didier was cowering. And now this terrible sight!

Robert idly flicked away a ladybird which had the temerity to land on the carnation in the buttonhole of his immaculate morning coat. Kriegck of the rue Royale did not intend his designs to include red-spotted ladybirds. "Did not the incomparable chef Alexis Soyer invent a portable stove to cook a superb dinner on top of a pyramid?"

Auguste glared at him, momentarily bereft of words at this effrontery. Soyer had died many years ago, but his reputation lived on to bedevil his successors. "Monsieur Soyer," he eventually managed to reply, "did not have to produce on a pyramid several meals fit to set before His Majesty King Edward VII."

"Nevertheless—"

"*Non!*"

The Petit Trianon, in the grounds of the Château of Versailles just outside Paris, was an elegant and pleasing mansion, and Auguste did not begrudge Queen Marie Antoinette this delightful retreat from the pressures of life at Versailles, where she could indulge her preference for the simple life. Simple her tastes may have been in theory but, he noted, they demanded extravagance to satisfy: apart from redesigning the house from the days of Louis XV and his mistress, the Comtesse Du Barry, a theatre had been built, a Chinese ring game installed in the gardens, Louis XV's carefully planted gardens had been uprooted and redesigned, machinery had been installed to convert the boudoir into a mirror room to provide some diversion, and in the grounds a whole mock village had been built in rustic style, where the Queen might enjoy to the full her simple country life. And then there were the kitchens!

No doubt in the pre-Revolution times of Marie Antoinette, before the mob had been allowed to roam at will through the gardens, before the contents of the house had been sold and before the house had become a common inn for some years, these kitchens had been a miracle and a joy in which to work. There was the trifling disadvantage that the service block was a considerable way from the main house, and that, so far as Auguste could see, the food had to be transported either out into the road and through the main château courtyard, or along a lengthy path round the chapel, past its own courtyard which lay behind it, then into a reheating room provided by Louis XV (highly necessary) and then, at last, into the château. Once upon a time this route had been a covered passageway, Auguste gathered. It was so no longer, but was open to the elements. His Majesty's *potage* was going to become extremely watery if it rained.

Auguste's imagination peopled these kitchens with liveried

24

servants and chefs and superb delicacies laid out on every side. The room in which he stood had been devoted, he was told, to cold meats. He had visions of the place humming with delighted chefs as they recreated their masterpieces of aspic of fowl *à la Reine*, potted pheasants, fillets of sole mayonnaise, galantines, tongue, all providing a riot of colour and ingenuity. Next to this kitchen had been one devoted to soups and *entremets*; vast tureens of stock would be simmering, delightful sauces, vegetables, salads – a whole regal array of small dishes to tempt the appetite and balance the meats. Next to it had been a large kitchen devoted to the *grandes entrées*, a majestic room with chimney and ovens as befitted its importance. From here would emerge – surely he could still smell them in the air? – pies, timbales, casseroles, *chartreuses* of vegetables, meats and fish, miracles of pastry, dishes of venison, poultry, game, fish, soufflés – everything to reflect the chef's art.

Nestling next door had been a small kitchen devoted entirely to special patisserie to be served as *entremets*, and next to that the great kitchen devoted to the roast meats – ah, the aromas. Perhaps roasts were the epitome of the art of cuisine, not *entrées*; did not his former *maître*, Monsieur Escoffier, claim that it lay in simplicity, not showy contrivance? The last of the kitchens had been devoted to sweet patisserie, delicate and sumptuous morsels to set before a queen. In addition to the kitchens, there had been larders, a wine-glass store, bread, pastry and wine-service rooms, a silver store, a room for cooking utensils and a dining room for the servants.

What promise, what riches lay within the world that ran this household. There was only one problem with it. Every single room was empty. Empty of fires, ovens, utensils, cooking pots and, worst of all, empty of any food. In each room stood a bare wooden table and, as a munificent gesture, a pile of logs in the hearth ready for open fires. The tables were, he admitted, wonderfully scrubbed but this was hardly compensation.

"*Non*," Auguste repeated with simple dignity. Then, in case his point was not sufficiently made, it came out in a screech, "*Non, non, non! Jamais!* I am a chef, not a soldier *en bivouac*."

Robert did not seem to be taking him seriously. "For banquets held here nowadays, the food is cooked in the Grand Trianon, and brought down to be kept hot. I imagine that is what my chef has planned for you." Even his bored voice trailed off, however, at the look on Auguste's face.

"For *you*, monsieur, I would all too willingly agree," he snarled in reply. "For His Majesty, I will not."

A compromise was finally agreed. By ten o'clock on the following morning, 8 August, three of the disused kitchens in this service block and one usually set aside now in the Petit Trianon as a serving room for food brought down from the Grand Trianon would be fully equipped. Robert's own kitchen staff and footmen would be at Auguste's command. He would have forty-eight hours to prepare luncheon, tea and dinner for the King of England, and he would need every one of them. Usually he began his preparations at least four days in advance. It was not an auspicious start.

If the ghost of Queen Marie Antoinette did condescend to appear, she would undoubtedly have that of Alexis Soyer at her side, smirking at his unfortunate successor's plight.

"Monsieur Bollée is a brilliant man." Tatiana remarked. "The new car at the works has four cylinders and is chain driven, and forty-five horse power. It is true it is expensive, but we could afford—" Tatiana broke off from the glowing description of her visit.

"What could we afford?" Auguste asked wearily.

Tatiana eyed him. "It was not important, I'll buy it, and I'm sure you'll like it."

Her long-suffering maid Héloise seized her opportunity. "Madame was referring to Madame Cadolle's new corset which allows room for madame's beautiful hips." She tugged energetically on the less amenable Grand Corset Louis XV, and Tatiana was silenced. Given her way, all corsets would be flung to the winds and the entire female population clad in knickerbockers, and it was Héloise's task to reconcile her mistress's quaint opinions with the rules of polite society, as led by her remote cousin the King. Two years previously, Auguste had been much amused that his wife was wholly in favour of a new gentlemen's club in England which vowed never to marry a corseted lady. It had taken Her Majesty Queen Alexandra to whisper in her ear that this was unwise.

They had been spared the ordeal of sleeping in the château: perhaps the bedrooms too were equipped merely with a scrubbed table. His Majesty and those of the guests needing accommodation were lodging in the Hôtel Trianon, adjacent to the château grounds, since Bertie had refused point-blank to sleep in the Queen's bedchamber in the Petit Trianon, and for once Auguste had sympathised. It would be unnerving to sleep in the room where the last famous royal head to touch the pillow had landed up on the guillotine.

"It's not that I am afraid of ghosts, of course," His Majesty had explained to them a little too quickly.

"Naturally not, sire."

"There are no such things. Seeing ghosts comes from over-indulging in rich food. I never do."

"Naturally not, sire."

Auguste was delighted he wouldn't have to cook His Majesty's breakfast of poached eggs, woodcock, chicken and fish, plus a large dish of kedgeree, in case he fancied anything more substantial. Even Bertie would not expect Auguste to take over the hotel kitchens – would he? Hastily, he casually mentioned that he and Tatiana would stay in her Paris home in the Russian quarter near the Arc de Triomphe.

"What is wrong?" Tatiana asked him anxiously, wriggling into her black silk dress with considerably less dexterity than she displayed under one of her beloved motor cars.

He explained, and received a giggle in reply, which was hastily suppressed when she saw his baleful look.

"Chéri," she said soothingly, "not even Bertie is going to notice a few flaws in the meals, there'll be too much excitement."

"Ghosts?" In Auguste's view, tomorrow afternoon, which was to be spent prowling the gardens in fancy dress, and searching for non-existent eighteenth-century phantoms, promised only boredom – had it not been for his premonitions about his own role in it. In addition to having to prepare luncheon and tea, and supervise tomorrow evening's dinner, he had to retrace the route Miss Moberly and Miss Jourdain claimed to have taken five years earlier. That *sounded* very straightforward, but in a wager on which His Majesty had betted heavily against their host, he could foresee problems arising. Moreover, he would be alone on his trek, since Robert had realised they were two people short of the number required to fulfil all the roles needed for this pantomime. Tatiana had offered to play both characters, before Auguste could appeal to her better nature.

"No, if only it were so simple," Tatiana replied.

"Tell me." Auguste had a feeling he was not going to like this.

"Robert married Mirabelle a week ago."

Auguste's premonition had been right. The news was stupefying, if true, and boded ill for the morrow. "He didn't tell me. I thought Robert was devoted to Louise, and that the engagement was only to save Mirabelle's face. We must have been wrong, and he married to *escape* Louise. Unless of course Mirabelle has money."

"You are cynical, Auguste. There's worse. Louise got wind of the wedding and turned up at the church door, furious, threatening to kill both of them or at least Mirabelle. She seized hold of her, ripped off her hat, stamped on it, and started work on her dress. She tore one sleeve off and was ripping off the bodice by the time Robert managed to pull her off."

Worse and worse, even though he had a glorious picture of La Dervicheuse in mid-battle. "What happened then?"

"Her husband arrived in their motor car, and she promptly calmed down, and sobbed on his chest."

Auguste had never met Bertrand Danielle, but devoted to his wife as he was said to be, he felt the reputedly austere politician was even less likely to appreciate being sobbed on than to see his wife distraught over another man. "And what," he asked with trepidation, "is happening about Friday and the ghost hunt?"

"Robert, I'm told, explained to Louise's husband that in view of what had happened, he must ensure that Louise did not attend. Mirabelle was delighted. No opposition to her playing the Queen now." Tatiana paused. "And there's another problem too. Poor Jacob has taken Mirabelle's defection badly."

In Auguste's view his pride would be worse affected than his heart. That gentleman took himself far too seriously.

"The last I heard he was threatening to challenge Robert to a duel in the Bois de Boulogne, and if Robert refused, he said he would slaughter both of them. In the heat of the moment, of course," Tatiana added hastily.

"Does Bertie know about all this?" A Bertie upset was apt to be a Bertie who took it out on anyone around not exempt under the rules of social etiquette. Remote cousins by marriage were not exempt.

Tatiana smiled at him comfortingly. "Not yet. Won't it be exciting?"

"Alouette, gentille alouette . . ."

Auguste hastily stopped his sudden outburst of song. It was somewhat indelicate to warble about charming little skylarks when their brother quails, ortolans, and woodcocks lay before him, legs in the air, stuffed and ready to greet His Majesty.

Auguste had toured the whole château now and it was clear that regardless of the rumoured state of his finances, the count had spared no expense in preparing for the King's visit. Last century the Petit Trianon or La Maison, as the Queen had called it, had been restored to resemble as closely as possible the house that Marie Antoinette had left so abruptly, but some features had gone for good. The gardens had changed, the ring game had vanished, and so had the machinery for the mirrors in the boudoir and – to Auguste's relief – the famous *tables volantes*, Louis XV's grandiose scheme by which machinery on the ground floor sent up tables ready set with food to the waiting diners above. (Even *his* royal purse had given out, and the scheme had been only partly put into service. In Auguste's view, the diners should be despatched down through the floor

30

to greet the chef's cuisine in its most perfect condition, rather than the food risk the perils of being elevated on tables.)

Marie Antoinette's bedchamber now looked as perfect as once it had been. The count had had mirrors temporarily installed on the two outside walls of the boudoir next door so that if the Queen's ghost should happen to turn up after all, she would feel completely at home. As Bertie had declined the honour of sleeping in the bedchamber, Robert and, Auguste presumed, Mirabelle were to take advantage of it themselves. Marie Antoinette had made sure she slept alone, by only having a single bed in her chamber, but Robert had installed a temporary extra bed.

Nor had Robert spared expense over the kitchens, after Auguste's outburst. They were now fully equipped, save for the trifling absence of a *daubière*, and since *daubes* did not appear on the menu, even Auguste was forced to concede this was immaterial. The menus – ah, yes! Another cause of friction. Instead of Auguste being permitted to select the menus, Robert had conceived the notion that he should base the menus for the luncheon on one served to King Louis XVI and Queen Marie Antoinette, and for the dinner this evening on those for a *grande fête* held for the Swedish King and his entire court in 1784. The Swedish monarch had been honoured by a service of 407 dishes, not to mention those provided for the court and leading officials. Auguste's glazed eye had run over *petite matelote mêlée au blanc*, *dindon gras* – a never-ending list, all to be achieved in a matter of two or three days. Fortunately, Robert's enthusiasm waned when Auguste pointed out the cost, and it was finally agreed that a dinner menu based on the menus of specialities served to the Queen and His Swedish Majesty would suffice.

The menu on which today's luncheon was based consisted of two soups and twenty *plats*, of which eight were *entrées*, four roasts and eight *entremets*; it was obvious therefore that their Majesties had been dining alone for this was not a banquet menu, either in quantity or choice. Whoever their chef was, he should be ashamed of himself, Auguste fumed. Noodle soup, saddle of mutton with macedoine of vegetables, vol au vent, beef, wild rabbit fillets with turnips, breadcrumbed chicken wings, *coupé de veau à la crème*, blanquette of turkey, skewers of rabbit livers, salmis of partridge, quails, *campine*, chicken, *halbrans*. When Robert flourished the actual menu cards before him, Auguste's eye had run quickly over the *entremets*, fearing the worst. It stopped when he saw *beignets de blancmange*. "*Non.*" This time he kept the word to himself. What he served would be *à la Didier*. No fried blancmange would appear on *his* table.

Alice Gaston tucked the white kerchief into the bodice of her coarse-spun dress with distaste. The dress was quite hideous. She should have been playing Marie Antoinette, not a fourteen-year-old cottage girl called Marion. She had cheated a little, using silk for the kerchief, fichu and cap, and conceded that she did look rather fetching. Perhaps that was why gentlemen always seemed attracted to maids. Not Pierre, of course, who was above such things.

Pierre bustled in from his dressing room in their Paris home in the boulevard des Capucines, and Alice struggled to find words of praise. He was dressed as one of the two uniformed officials, whom apparently the two ladies in 1901 had taken to be gardeners, but had later decided were guards at Marie Antoinette's court. The three-cornered hat, greenish uniform jacket and breeches looked quite distinguished, but Pierre's *en bon point* figure was ill-suited to it, bulging out in front like a drum before a bandsman.

"*Chérie*," she carolled fondly, "you look so handsome."

Pierre did not answer immediately. He was far too busy staring at his Alice, suddenly transformed by the little cap and the simple dress. Then he observed, "If you had a little lace apron too, my dear, and the skirt even shorter—"

"What do you mean, Pierre?" Alice was taken aback. There was nothing in the account they had been sent of what the ladies had seen to suggest lace aprons.

"You look charming as you are, of course," he said hastily.

Alice dimpled, back on safe ground. "Do you think anything will happen today, dearest?" She had every intention of making sure something did happen. Pierre should be proud of her.

He burst into jovial laughter. "You aren't expecting the phantom of Marie Antoinette to appear, are you?"

"Of course not." She giggled. Pierre was convinced there were no such things as ghosts, but she harboured a little wistfulness to think that others believed it possible her heroine might appear. "I meant poor dear Louise." Alice had been pleased to hear of the marriage, for Jacob was extremely handsome and would have been wasted on that terrible Mirabelle.

Pierre wrenched his thoughts away from Alice's ankles, memories of the previous evening at the Folies Bergère (a gentlemen only party) clearly in his mind. "Even if the Queen is hanging around, she may not choose to come out, so Robert's money is safe. Poor Fernby if anyone. That young man fully expected to walk into Lady Harper's bed."

Poor Jacob, indeed. Given the slightest opportunity – or making one – Alice decided she could do a little to cheer him up. Pierre was a good *husband* – but not romantic, a gourmand rather than a gourmet in the marriage bed. As

Mama said, however, that was only to be expected of gentlemen.

"Don't waste your time feeling sorry for Louise," Pierre added viciously, snapping in his collar studs one by one. "She's broken enough hearts in her time." One of them had belonged to his brother. He had killed himself three months later, and La Dervicheuse had not even bothered to come to the funeral. She had been seen lunching at Maxim's instead. He was almost sorry she wouldn't be present today, for eventually there must be a reckoning. Moreover, Winifred Ladyboys *would* be present, and although he burst into sudden loud laughter, as he thought back to past times, there was no denying it could be very awkward. He turned his mind to pleasanter thoughts: Alice in a very short maid's skirt – or rather out of it. No, he shouldn't do that. Alice was his wife, and moreover was far too refined and diffident to indulge in such practices.

George Ladyboys cleared his throat. He felt ridiculous in this black sombrero hat and cloak. He was playing the man the ladies had seen at the mysterious kiosk, and therefore was supposed to look sinister; however, he was most uncertain what His Majesty would say if he looked sinisterly at him. George had been striving to retain the sort of attentive, amiable expression that came so easily to him when he and HM were chatting in armchairs at the Marlborough Club, and which here seemed impossible. Winifred had insisted he shave off his moustache 'to look the part' as that blasted nancy Count de Tourville had suggested. That made him feel sinister all right. He could run this sword right through him given half a chance. He supposed the fellow couldn't be a nancy as he'd just married for the second time, but he behaved like one.

Everyone knew he'd never really got over the death of his first wife, the ethereal dancer, Hélène Mai, but if you asked George Ladyboys she had died of boredom, not consumption.

Someone had said Louise had been Robert's mistress, but he couldn't believe it. Not Louise. She was wasted on Robert. What's more, it would be a betrayal of him, George, for it was obvious Louise still cared for him as she'd supported him in the wager. Because of that row over who was to play the Queen, Louise wouldn't be coming today, according to the blasted, supercilious Robert, and all his plans for a quiet romantic word with Louise had been ruined. One day Robert would get what he deserved.

He stared at his face in Winifred's mirror. He *looked* sinister too, without his moustache. Naked, open and evil. He suddenly cheered up. "You're very quiet, Winifred."

Women were odd creatures. Bring them to Paris and all they wanted to do was scuttle back to Bournemouth. He had never thought that Winnie would take to it so much when he took her there on honeymoon.

At least he never called her Winnie, his wife was thinking. That was the old life. Winifred set her apart, gave her status and dignity, even when struggling into this revolting bodice to play a cottage woman. She didn't like this role at all, she was not nearly old enough to play Alice's mother. Winifred knew she should be grateful to George, but this was one time when she wished she was not such a loyal wife. She had vowed never to return to France and with Pierre of all people present, this was the worst possible thing that could happen. George would never back out of a wager, however, so that was that. She tried to look on the bright side. Pierre was married too now, and wouldn't want that disconcertingly silly girl to know about his previous life.

"I was thinking about ghosts," she improvised quickly. "You are sure we'll see some, aren't you?"

"I certainly hope so, old girl."

Winifred rather liked being called old girl, for it gave her a comfortable settled-down feeling that nothing would go wrong with her marriage. She paid close attention to what George was saying.

"I'm not going to lose that wager. My only worry is that with so many sceptics prancing around, the cosmic energy may be too disturbed for the Queen and her retinue to appear."

Winifred looked at George. He really did seem serious. She believed in ghosts because George did, but why did George? He was stolid, middle-aged and matter of fact. Perhaps he merely believed Miss Moberly and Miss Jourdain's story, though that came to the same thing.

"I've been doing some reading," George announced somewhat shamefacedly. "Catherine Crowe. *The Night Side of Nature*. Ever read it?"

Reading? *George?* Odder and odder. The *Field* magazine was usually too weighty a tome for him to get through.

"I'm afraid not, George, but I will." It was strange how little one could know about a husband. Nevertheless, if he believed he was developing an interest in psychic experiences, so must she. She concentrated all her considerable willpower in the vague direction of Queen Marie Antoinette. *If you're listening, Your Majesty, would you* please *materialise this afternoon?*

Having sent this plea, it occurred to her that the lady might appear with her head cut off. Or was that Anne Boleyn and the Tower of London? It would be very messy, even in a ghost. She pursued this worry for some time, for it saved her thinking of what might happen if Pierre took it into his head to be awkward.

Dressed as George was, he looked as though he could be capable of anything if things got out of hand. Winifred almost wished Louise would be there, so that in the mayhem that would surely ensue Winifred could quietly be overlooked.

"We shall show them, shan't we, George?" She beamed, reverting to her usual jolly self, and her husband reflected once again how fortunate he was to have found practical, down-to-earth, sensible Winifred for a wife. She could always make him laugh; easy enough, he supposed, for she'd nothing to worry about.

In the Queen's bedchamber in the Petit Trianon, Mirabelle put the finishing touches to the only attractive ensemble among the allotted costumes, a long-waisted, short-skirted dress which showed her ankles delightfully, with a cream skirt, pale-green bodice and white fichu. A picture-book white hat crowned her golden curls.

"How ridiculous," she turned large adoring eyes on Robert, "that Louise thought she could play Marie Antoinette. The Queen was fair like me." She fluffed her hair over her forehead, placed the hat over it, and admired the effect.

"You look beautiful, my love." Robert came to her, placed his hands on her shoulders and kissed her cheek.

"*Merci*, Robert." She giggled. "And you, my precious, my beloved, are too . . . well, not beautiful, but *soigné. Très, très soigné.*" She pirouetted around the room, as he watched her with devoted eyes.

"You are the Running Man, Robert," She laughed. "That's what Mr Ladyboys' silly old ladies have named you, isn't it? Well then, run after me."

Obediently, swishing the cloak round his shoulders, and tipping the large hat over his eyes, he leapt after her.

"Grrrrh!" he growled. "Here comes a nasty old ghost to gobble you up."

Marie Antoinette needed little catching for this fate, and squealed in delight as he rained kisses on every exposed millimetre of skin. "Oh, Robert," she said contentedly, "we are happy now, are we not? After all our years of waiting."

Robert, his head buried in the Queen's fichu, agreed with muffled voice.

"You don't miss Louise, do you?" she asked wistfully. "I know queens have to put up with their husbands having mistresses, but somehow, Robert dear, I don't think I'd like that very much."

Robert sat up. "Miss her, kitten? I miss her tantrums, certainly. And her cruelty, her vulgarity. And I am grateful to *le bon Dieu* for taking her from me and giving me you." He paused. "And He has given me you, hasn't He? No lingering regrets for your artistic Monsieur Jacob Fernby?"

Mirabelle laughed, preening herself. "Poor dear Jacob. He will recover."

"Do not ignore his hurt, Mirabelle. It could be dangerous."

She glanced at him to see if he were serious. "Like you," she said, laughing. "Without your moustache you are a big white bear."

"He has actually challenged me to a duel." Robert frowned. "I gather he has some quaint ideas about swords at dawn."

Mirabelle was very alarmed. "I will speak to him."

"Don't. If there is no duel, he could use other methods more dangerous still."

"Not," said Mirabelle contemplatively, "while I am here to keep you safe. My beloved." She bestowed one of her sweetest smiles on her new husband, but for some reason it failed to console him.

*   *   *

Jacob Fernby dressed for his role as the Chapel Man, as those old women termed it, with some care. He had hated his barber shaving off his moustache, for it took with it the entire persona he had carefully built up over the last twelve years. Away went the 34-year-old suave, artistic, serious portrait painter, and back came the naive, socially uncertain, but passionate, boy who had haunted the Paris nightclubs in search of sophistication, the boy who had been spellbound by the artistry of Hélène Mai, and – the wound still festered – been laughed at and rejected by Louise Danielle. He had spent much time in banishing that callow youth, and it was annoying to see him still written into the face in the mirror, hiding under the moustache with all his weaknesses. Marriage to Mirabelle would have been the last nail in the callow youth's coffin; now she, just as Hélène and Louise, had been taken from him, and he had a shrewd suspicion why. Robert should answer for them all; it would give him the greatest satisfaction to plunge a rapier into his opponent. Not to *kill* him, of course, for that might have unfortunate repercussions for himself. It needed something far more subtle.

His first reaction had been not to come here today. How could he watch Mirabelle on the arm of another? Then he had realised he was trapped. His Majesty would be present. If ever his ambition to paint the Princess Victoria were to be realised, nothing but a sudden attack of cholera would be reason enough not to appear. Very well, he would attend. He would play this ridiculous Chapel Man – and in compensation he would make his presence felt.

No ghost of a dead lover, he, this afternoon.

"Shall we go, Auguste?" Tatiana, dressed half as the woman

seen by Miss Moberly waving a white cloth out of a cottage window, and half in greyish-green knickerbockers, appeared in the doorway of Kitchen Number 2 where Auguste was attending to the liaison of eggs and cream for the *lentilles fricassées (à la Didier)*. Even in his distraction Auguste registered that this was hardly the usual dress for a lady to greet the monarch in, and there was no doubt Bertie would notice.

"What, my love, are you wearing?" he asked faintly.

"It's very sensible." Tatiana was defensive. "I'm playing a court guard, and the woman with the cloth. As only her top half appears, I can wear both costumes."

"A gardener is hardly likely to wear a bodice and fichu with a decolleté neckline."

"In that case I shall wear the long uniform coat over it during luncheon, and not offend Bertie."

"Or," Auguste said firmly, "a skirt over the trousers."

"What inspiration." Tatiana kissed him, and produced a skirt from behind her back.

"You have been mocking me," he said, resigned. "It is not fair to mock a chef who still has to battle with *attelettes de foies de lapereaux*."

"*Ma mie*, it will all be splendid."

But there, Auguste was convinced, she was mistaken. Luncheon might be as perfect as he could make it, tea would – or should have been – simple rustic fare laid out for the 'ghosts' at La Petit Hameau lakeside, Queen Marie Antoinette's rustic village. Unfortunately, there was no such thing as simple where the King's stomach was concerned.

His Majesty's idea of a simple picnic could be a vast heap of hampers filled with his favourite delicacies such as pigeon pie, or it could be a large marquee filled with all the hot and cold dishes he would expect at Buckingham Palace plus a staff of twenty or so to serve it. For luncheon, tea and dinner, Auguste would do his best. The rest of the day, however, was out of his control.

Through the large gates of the Petit Trianon a splendid carriage could now be seen about to turn in from the allée des deux Trianons. There was an immediate stir in the group awaiting its arrival. Robert and Mirabelle were to the fore in the courtyard, with George and Winifred, Alice and Pierre, Jacob, Auguste and Tatiana ranged behind them by the entrance. Looking at the group, Auguste decided he was the only sane member of it, clad as he was in a respectable lounge suit and not a motley attire of old-fashioned dress. Thank goodness that it had been Bertie himself who had decreed at Goodwood this year that formal frock and morning coats were no longer *de rigueur* and that bowlers might replace top hats. Today the King was wearing his favourite white bowler, which was a good sign.

Tatiana looked as bulky as if she were wearing a crinoline, Mirabelle as if she had leapt off a mantelpiece full of Dresden shepherdesses, and the men as though they were musketeers on their way to rescue the Man in the Iron Mask. And the King of England was approaching. He only hoped someone had reminded Bertie that his fellow guests would be in fancy dress, or the Trianon would be responsible for a few more beheadings.

The coachman reined in the horses. Liveried footmen sprang to open the doors, and Auguste waited for the heavy foot of royalty to descend. When it did, the heavy foot was daintily clad in little pink satin boots.

"*Bonjour*, Robert!"

From the carriage descended not the King of England, but a guillotined Queen of France. Identically clad to Mirabelle, but instantly recognisable with her dark eyes and complexion, despite the fair wig, Louise Danielle had come to join the festivities. In the stunned silence, it was Mirabelle who found her voice first.

"What," she shrieked, "are *you* doing here? *I'm* Marie Antoinette."

"My dear," drawled Louise, "I decided I could not let His Majesty down, and though my poor heart still aches for Robert, it was my duty to force myself to come." She dabbed at her eyes with a dainty lace handkerchief.

"Then you can turn round and go home again," Robert declared.

"Oh, Robert." Louise's face crumpled as she threw herself into his arms so unexpectedly and forcefully that he collapsed on the gravel with Louise on top of him.

Even as George, the nearest, rushed to help, Mirabelle forestalled him, tugging at Louise and succeeding in pulling her off, whereupon Louise flung herself into George's only too willing arms.

"His Majesty!" shrieked Auguste, seeing a familiar Daimler had arrive. All eyes had been elsewhere.

King Edward VII was even now emerging to greet the assembled company, followed by Caesar, his favourite fox terrier. Fortunately, royalty is trained to ignore mishaps, even the spectacle of two strangely dressed ladies apparently fighting with his host.

"Ah, Auguste," His Majesty said, as his eyes fell on a safe target for his displeasure. "Don't forget the truffles today, will you?"

Auguste managed a sycophantic laugh, and received in exchange an icy glare. His Majesty had not been jesting as he had assumed. What *had* he done with the truffles?

*   *   *

Auguste staggered from the grand dining room through to the Queen's boudoir. It was the end of his career. Never, *never* would he cook again, never subject his art to such an ordeal, although perhaps for Tatiana he might prepare an occasional *velouté d'homard*. His banquet had been superb, perfection, cuisine at its very best. The *blanquette de dindonneau* had exquisite creamy delicacy, the *halbrans* had been pink and tender, the sole *purée d'oignons* had just the right balance of sweetness and piquancy, even the *entremet* of fried blanc-mange (*à la Didier*, with sorrel and brandy) had been well received.

What was the use? It had all gone for nothing, his pearls cast before swine, on this disaster of a day. It was not that there had been any unpleasant scene over luncheon, for the presence of His Majesty had prevented that; underneath the bursts of polite conversation that stabbed the atmosphere like hatpins, he had sensed so many undercurrents that the table had been like his patent digester – the whole thing might blow up with the greatest of ease.

Indeed, His Majesty, Auguste considered, had been the most civilised person present, apparently sublimely unaware of the tension Louise's appearance had created; Louise was complacent; Robert silent; Mirabelle made repeated unsuccessful attempts to sparkle with gaiety and not rage; Jacob looked as though he would like to strangle Robert, while making the most of his position next to Louise; Winifred, whenever protocol permitted, maintained a babble of ghostly tales; George was for some reason glaring at Jacob; Pierre at Louise; and Alice appeared to be sulking. Only Tatiana was paying any attention to the food – save, of course, His Majesty, to whom Auguste was warming greatly. Bertie was not so bad after all. However, his approbation alone could not recoup Auguste's reputation in his own eyes, nor would dinner this evening, since it had to be left mainly in the hands of the count's chef, a gentleman who seemed to be considering whether it was worth upsetting the stomach of the King of England merely in order to thwart Auguste Didier. They had had words on the correct presentation of the *oeufs à l'oseille*, since Monsieur Grospied, as Auguste privately termed him, strongly resisted the need for pressing the braised sorrel through a tammy.

The Queen's boudoir would at any moment become the gathering point for the guests to assemble, having put the finishing touches to their costumes for the afternoon, and to listen to Robert run through the programme. Everyone had been supplied by George Ladyboys with a copy of Miss Moberly's and Miss Jourdain's account of their first visit, and Auguste, at least, was still nervous. It was not the thought of the ghosts that troubled him, so much as fear of getting lost. After all, if those ladies had really seen what they claimed, the whole of the gardens had changed in over a hundred years. Suppose he *did* stray back into 1789; he might never find his way out, and be condemned to cook fried blancmange for the rest of his life.

His anguish, writ large on his face, was reflected all around him, with the two walls with windows in this small corner room now enlarged with the help of the mirrors. Robert had improved on Marie Antoinette's architect; his temporary mirrors did not merely cover the windows of this corner room; they extended over the walls also so that the two met at right angles. As a result, two Auguste Didiers gazed back at him as he entered and others appeared the closer he came to where the plates of *croquignoles* shaped like fleur-de-lys and English roses were placed on a table set in the angle of the corner. These biscuits too had appeared on the royal 1784 menu and one, reflected in the mirror, had caught his eye as less than perfect. Three footmen were already standing to attention, ready to hand coffee and patisserie round, and just as Auguste was fumbling for the offending *croquignole* and becoming confused between the mirror image and reality, he realised that His Majesty was entering. He endeavoured to pretend that all was well, thankful that Bertie was not such a connoisseur of patisserie as of truffles.

His Majesty looked round at the multiple images of himself. "At least I'll notice any assassins you've provided for me, Auguste."

Auguste smiled politely. Bertie was perpetually under the impression that as a garnish to solving murders, he had taken to arranging them as well. At least His Majesty was now in good humour.

Had Robert not been so eager to display his expertise in re-fashioning the Trianon for His Majesty, he might have reflected that this boudoir was hardly large enough to seat eleven guests at ease and, save for Bertie, the guests preferred to stand, which hindered the footmen as they brought round coffee cups and Auguste's precious *croquignoles* from the table. Thanks to the mirrors, the room seemed full of Marie Antoinettes in large picture hats. Both of the Queens had chosen to sit – or, to be more precise, Mirabelle had chosen to hold court from a chair at the corner table, and Louise had promptly decided to follow suit at the other side of the table. With great bravery, Jacob drew up a chair and placed himself between them.

Auguste caught glimpses of them through the crowd, and wondered what, if anything, they had to say to each other. Perhaps nothing, for in an obvious attempt to avert more trouble, the company seemed set on individual forays to aid Jacob avert trouble. This did not help the problem of space, as guests and footmen manoeuvred themselves round the room like macaroni in boiling water. What, Auguste wondered, was boiling in this pan today? It would soon be starting, because it was already a quarter to three, and he was almost glad when Robert made his way to His Majesty's side (since this was the only part of the room where any space could be obtained) and announced that in ten minutes they would all disperse to their appointed positions.

"Mr Didier, our well-known detective, will walk round the grounds following the path of Miss Moberly and Miss Jourdain. He is more accustomed to finding murderers than ghosts, and so I am most honoured that he is our umpire today."

"Umpire?" It came out as a cry of anguish, so great was Auguste's shock.

Robert looked mildly surprised. "But of course. We need one, and are all, save His Majesty and yourself, engaged in re-enacting the scene. How can we also be aware of ghosts passing? It is you, Monsieur Didier, with your sharp eye, who must tell us of such happenings, as well as determining whether Miss Moberly and Miss Jourdain are truly describing paths and buildings which no longer exist. Do you not agree, George?"

George Ladyboys looked more doubtful than Auguste could have wished, but nodded reluctantly. "You wouldn't prefer to do it yourself, sire?" he asked His Majesty hopefully.

The royal face beamed. "I'm betting on you, George. You know that. Can't be umpire too."

"His Majesty is going to Le Hameau, on the far side of the grounds, to await our arrival for tea," Robert pointed out.

And to sleep off luncheon, thought Auguste irreverently.

"Robert, *ma chéri*." Mirabelle had been fidgeting and now found her moment, "there is a little problem. We have *two* Marie Antoinettes. I feel we should make it clear to everyone, including dear Louise, that *I* shall be playing Marie Antoinette sketching on the lawn."

Auguste waited for battle to begin, but when it did, it did not take the form he expected.

Instead of La Dervicheuse snarling in fury, Louise gurgled in womanly understanding. "Of course, dear Mirabelle. That is your right as Robert's wife. I would never dream of anything else."

"Excellent," Robert said, obviously relieved to have got away so lightly.

"If only I had thought to bring my jewels," Louise sighed, "and a change of dress, I could have played the Comtesse Du Barry, poor Marie Antoinette's greatest enemy."

"And formerly a notorious whore," Mirabelle retorted sweetly.

"I shall repair to where the old grotto used to be, according to the old legends," Louise continued, as though she had not spoken. "The queen is often spotted sketching there, and moreover," she added, "I do believe that means I shall be close to where Robert is stationed. We can keep each other company, and talk of happier times."

Mirabelle opened her mouth to speak, but Robert spoke first. "Delightful as that would be, Louise, I would remind you that for the Queen to be seen in the close company of her courtiers would not be proper. We shall meet at our rendezvous at Le Hameau at four o'clock instead."

Louise shrugged. "That would indeed be delightful. Very well, I shall go to Le Hameau with His Majesty. We too can talk about old times – *oh*!"

"What is the matter, Louise?" Tatiana asked anxiously.

"You look as though you have seen a ghost, my dear," Mirabelle said, all mock concern.

"Something like that," Louise managed to reply. "It's these mirrors – I thought I saw . . . no matter."

Puzzled, Auguste found himself thinking of Miss Moberly and Miss Jourdain's account of their visit. It had been a hot sultry August afternoon, but as they had entered the Petit Trianon grounds, the air had suddenly become oppressive and heavy, full of the threat of thunder. It seemed to him that today it was happening again, even before they had left the house – and not even the cuisine of Auguste Didier would be able to avert the menace.

Three

B ravely, Auguste faced the truth: suddenly he did not want to be alone. How ridiculous. Nevertheless he suggested to Tatiana as casually as he could, "*Ma mie*, we could perhaps walk together as far as the Musée des Voitures."

This was housed, together with the *gardien's* quarters, in a building on the corner of the lane by the Grand Trianon which Miss Moberly and Miss Jourdain had mistakenly taken five years earlier. Had they continued along the broad allée des deux Trianons, it would have led them straight to their objective (and saved Auguste Didier much anguish). The present use of the building explained much, to his mind, of why he was being deprived of Tatiana's company for his march in the two ladies' footsteps. Her allotted task of shaking a white cloth out of the window at her husband would leave Tatiana time for her favourite pursuit of admiring motor cars, both before and after her secondary role of court guard (or, as the ladies had at first assumed, gardener).

Tatiana glanced at him. "We can walk to the *musée* together, and there you will have to wait for a few moments before you set off."

Auguste was suspicious. Had she arranged for Monsieur Renault or Monsieur Bollée to be present in person to sell them yet another new car?

"I must be calm and receptive to encourage the ghosts," she added.

"Please do not encourage them too much."

"*Non, chéri.*"

"I suppose it would not be possible to suspend your supernatural powers for the afternoon?"

"No. However, they very rarely become active," she reassured him. "And as we agreed that the ladies might have been mistaken on the route they thought they were following, you have nothing to worry about." They had pored over the sketch map Miss Moberly had sent George Ladyboys, studying it in conjunction with a map of the gardens in 1898 together with that drawn in 1783 by Richard Mique, Marie Antoinette's architect-cum-garden designer.

As Tatiana disappeared inside the *musée*, all his misgivings flooded back. He felt hot, he felt abandoned, he felt apprehensive. The August heat on this still day choked at his nostrils and dulled his senses. He waited, fidgeting, for five minutes, as Tatiana had instructed him. Had she been seduced by an early Renault and forgotten all about him? No. To his relief, her familiar, if oddly dressed, figure appeared at an upstairs window vigorously waving her white cloth. She was real, she was solid, she was no ghost.

Now the flag had dropped, he was under starter's orders, the race was on. As a temporary reprieve, Auguste took his time walking up the lane. It was at the next corner that his ordeal would really begin, for that was where Miss Moberly and Miss Jourdain had both felt the atmosphere change from an enjoyably overcast, slightly breezy August afternoon to an atmosphere of depression and mounting gloom. He could understand that – he felt it already.

The Trianons and their gardens had been closed to the public for the day, in view of His Majesty's presence, but behind Auguste the main gardens of the Château of Versailles echoed with comfortingly normal sounds. There would be mothers and nannies with children, and gentlemen strolling, discussing the affairs of the day, dotting the broad avenues and wandering among the trees. The fountains would be playing, the classical statues gazing calmly down at the crowds, and glasses clinking at the delightful café of La Flottille.

As he walked on, the voices were increasingly distanced by the warmth of the still afternoon, and Auguste began to regret even the one glass of wine he had permitted himself at luncheon to fortify himself for it added to the heaviness of the atmosphere, robbing him of stamina. He consoled himself he had only to walk for a few hundred yards, and he would once more see Tatiana, this time in her garb as the green-uniformed guard. She would have sped from the museum through the gardens of the Petit Trianon up to the point where it had been agreed by both sides in the wager that the officials guarding the entrance to the gardens while the Queen was present would have stood.

August was a strange month, he reflected. Gone were the delicate perfumes of early summer and the warm luxuriousness of July; August beat down relentlessly, proclaiming, 'Here am I, your bastion before the winter'. It seemed airless as he turned on to the path towards the rendezvous point; the atmosphere sucked at his vitality. A heat haze seemed to shimmer over the dusty gravel, although there was no sun. The crunch of his footsteps seemed an intrusion in this silent world. To his right the end of a building came in sight at right angles to the path. This must be the *logement* where the ladies turned to the right seeking guidance, but could find no one.

"Courage, mon ami, le diable est mort." He recited this to

himself several times, as he forced himself along the path to the point where there would be a division of the ways, and where the guards would be. He found he was almost running. Trees bordering the path seemed to leer at him, luring him onwards into their dark embrace. The path was rising as Miss Jourdain had said and ahead there was indeed both a garden and several paths to choose from. His footsteps seemed to slow without his authority, as though some physical barrier was opposing his progress.

What had he to worry about (save losing Bertie his bet by not spotting any ghosts)? Auguste asked himself feverishly, but the answer 'nothing' failed to materialise. His eye fell on an old plough. Obviously Robert had done his work well and provided the correct stage props described by the ladies to encourage the ghosts to return home. Now he was at the junction, there were more old buildings, and a sense that there were people within them. A little further on, if he looked to his right he should see Alice and Winifred, in their peasant dresses and white kerchiefs tucked into their bodices. To his relief, there was no sign of the cottage the ladies claimed to have seen at this point, but he *could* see Alice and Winfred. Never had he been so glad to see the stalwart figures of two Englishwomen. He waved cheerfully at them, and Winifred solemnly passed her jug to Alice, just as Miss Jourdain had reported. Alice looked a remarkably adult fourteen-year-old, but at least she was of the twentieth, not the eighteenth century.

Ahead of him he should find Pierre and Tatiana in their greenish-grey guard uniforms – and there they were, standing, just as Miss Moberly had described, by a wheelbarrow. No ghosts so far. He opened his mouth to ask them which way to go to the Petit Trianon, but sudden panic gripped him. *This was not Tatiana*. One was definitely Pierre, but the other one was not only also a man, but not one he recognised from the party. Under the three-cornered hat was a face he did not immediately know, though it had some vague familiarity to it.

"You're not my wife," he blurted out.

"La Maison" – Auguste remembered this was Marie Antoinette's name for the Petit Trianon – "lies that way, monsieur," was all the answer he received.

His stomach knotted up, as though he had had sudden doubts about the freshness of the oysters at luncheon. The man was just playing his part, wasn't he? That mechanical dead-pan voice must be intended to recreate the ladies' experience. The man looked solid enough, and yet . . . No, it was merely that glass of wine confusing him. He must play his part and walk straight on. Tatiana must be absorbed in the motor-car museum, and had sent someone else to play her part. The new Bollée should be hers, if only she would appear *now* to reassure him. But there was no one; nothing but the silence of the undergrowth and trees.

Which way was it? The map of his route, once so clear in his mind, vanished, and he picked what seemed the direct route to La Maison. There seemed no sight of it, however, though he knew it must be close by. Suddenly, ahead of him, shrouded by bushes, he glimpsed the comforting figure of George, sitting stolidly by a circular wooden columned structure. (The count had been very thorough indeed to erect the ladies' 'kiosk' just for the day.) True, George was wrapped in a black cloak and had a large sombrero hat on, but the evil-faced Kiosk Man of the ladies' description, whom they were now convinced was the Queen's friend the Créole Comte de Vaudreuil, was most definitely not inside them, despite the pock-marks George had laboriously painted on his face.

Feeling very foolish, Auguste called out to himself, "Which

way shall I go, I wonder?" as the path divided. The ladies had been so repulsed by the man's appearance that they had not asked for help but had discussed the matter between themselves.

"This way," yelled a voice in his right ear, making him cry out in alarm.

"I say, that's cheating!" George shouted indignantly from the kiosk. "You're in the wrong place."

Robert stroked one end of his moustache, twirled his cloak around his shoulders, and pulled his own sombrero over his eyes like a stage villain.

"I am the ghost of the Comte de Vaudreuil," he intoned gravely.

"No, you're not. That's me." George came bustling angrily up to them.

"My dear George, you appear to be running, yet you're not the Running Man. I am. Or is it Jacob?" Robert sighed. "*Mon dieu*, I do hope we have not frightened the ghosts away for ever. What can I do to make amends?"

Auguste's dislike for Robert increased. "Return to the script?" he suggested curtly.

He received a mock bow for his pains. "*Mesdames*," Robert obeyed meekly, "*il ne faut pas passer par là. Par ici . . . cherchez la maison.*"

Auguste obediently turned to the right, leaving the Running Man hopping neatly up and down on the path to imitate more pounding footsteps. The effect was spoilt by Robert's mocking laughter.

Hesitating as new junctions presented themselves, Auguste walked along in what he assumed was the direction of La Maison. It was at this point that the ladies claimed to have crossed a rustic bridge, with a high green bank on the right over a tiny stream, which ran down to a small pool on their left, and this was the chief point of present-day divergence from their story, for no such path now appeared to exist.

He stopped, as an insidious thought was refusing to vanish. What would have happened if he had taken the path the Running Man had forbidden? Nothing, he told himself hastily. It would have brought him either to the main bridge over the lake by the large *Rocher* rock, or on to Escargot Hill, where the remains of an old grotto lay. Or would it have brought him face to face with the Paris mob storming their way through the Versailles grounds? What was it Miss Moberly had said about the point where he had turned? 'Nothing will induce me to go to the left.'

Auguste tried to pull himself together. He was here on a scientific investigation; the path to the left was irrelevant; what was relevant was whether the path he was on had ever had a bridge over a green ravine and a stream, and this one did not. Everything had changed since 1789; the carefully constructed *montagnes* that harboured the Queen's grotto had been destroyed years ago, and now only mounds and rocks remained, thick undergrowth and trees. It occurred to him, reluctantly, that there might be something to support their story, and in theory ghosts might still frequent the site. It was nonsense of course, but he must look.

As soon as he clambered down over the rocks from the path, he began to feel uneasy. The afternoon became more oppressive, prickles stood on his spine like an *oursin*, and he had a sense of no longer being on his own. Of course not, he told himself valiantly, either George and Robert must still be nearby, or it was his imagination.

And yet . . . and yet . . . he felt he was a pawn in a game he did not understand. Every instinct in him began to cry out that he should return to the path, but he refused to be a pawn any longer. He must take control of the chessboard, beat this force of inertia that had once again settled around him. He would search this wilderness for ancient paths, remains of grottos and bridges, then proceed to the château – and eventually Le Hameau and afternoon tea. Oh, how far away and how blissful that now seemed.

He could hear the sound of trickling water. It ran over a huge rock that seemed as large as the one by the Rocher Bridge. It must have been hidden from him earlier by bushes or the top of a mound. One side of it, covered with moss and ferns, gaped open, and inside was the beginnings of a stone staircase. Inexplicable dread seized hold of him. Had he come by mistake to the Rocher Bridge after all? He must have done, for this rock bore an uncanny resemblance to it. He knew there was no way he was going to climb those steps. He edged away, working his way out into the open air again, where fears seemed less ridiculous, and round to the far side of the rock, giving it a wide berth as he scrambled through thick undergrowth. As soon as he had worked his way completely round, he would regain the path.

He began his journey, and feeling braver he glanced up – and froze. Surely those were columns up there amid the ferns, and a bench constructed from the rock? From where he was, the folds of a woman's pale-pink dress were just visible, or was it just a trick of the light? Could it be possible? Had he walked straight back into the Queen's Grotto? Was the Queen of France, guillotined well over a hundred years earlier, sitting not on a stool by the terrace where Mirabelle would undoubtedly be but here in her beloved grotto, where legend had it that a courtier had come rushing to warn her of the approaching danger in October 1789?

He could not see her face – *and he did not want to*. If
the *thing* came closer to the edge and looked down at him
would he see the gash round her neck? Would there even be
a face there? He turned abruptly, plunged back the way he had
come, scrambling over fallen rocks, pushing bushes aside, to
regain the rightful path. Suppose he came face to face with the
courtier, the ladies' Running Man, on his way to the Queen?
But no one came. 'And no birds sang.' Keats' La Belle Dame
Sans Merci had appeared on such a day. The heaviness and
sense of decay were surely more than an August day and one
glass of wine could cause. There was evil lurking here; he
could almost smell it.

Ça suffit! Auguste told himself furiously, trying to breathe
calmly, as at last he reached the path to the right again.
This would wind round towards the house, and he would
see Mirabelle sitting by the terrace. Trees seemed to be
preventing him seeing it yet, and, he remembered, with a
lurch of his stomach, that the ladies had said that tall trees as
well as Marie Antoinette's ring game, a large wooden structure
enclosing a merry-go-round, had blocked their view. The Jeu
de Bague had long since vanished, however, and although trees
still remained they were spaced out, so that La Maison must
surely be visible above or between them.

She was there! He came upon the house much quicker than
he expected, and seated on a chair on the gravel beneath the
north front terrace was a Marie Antoinette who caused him
no qualms at all. Auguste had a fleeting thought that it might
be Louise, not Mirabelle, but dismissed it. Mirabelle would
never be dissuaded from her role. In the eighteenth century
this had been a rough meadow, part of the Queen's carefully
designed and much beloved English Garden, and the ladies
claimed to have seen the long grass growing right up to the

terrace wall instead of the modern gravel paths. He had no doubt however that it was a flesh and blood Queen who sat there now with her sketchbook, her large white hat perched on top of her fair curls.

"I'm me, Auguste," she called out gaily and unnecessarily.

"*Enchanté*," he replied fervently, as he ran towards the north-west corner of the house. Mirabelle sat to one side of a large rhododendron bush, since this was now covering the spot where Miss Moberly claimed to have seen the Queen. Auguste suppressed with some difficulty an urge to peer under the bush in case a ghost were perched in the midst of it. Left to himself, he might have done, but with Mirabelle's mocking gaze upon him, he ran round the wall bordering the French Garden to reach the stairs to the west terrace, since, to his relief, he could see no sign of the steps up which the ladies claimed to have climbed at the corner of the north terrace. From the far side of the terrace he peered down into the *cour d'honneur* as had Miss Moberly and Miss Jourdain.

Jacob, the Chapel Man, ran up the steps to him, since he was unable, as in Marie Antoinette's time, to rush along an extended terrace linking the chapel to the house. He had been disappointed at being deprived of his dramatic entrance into the story through the chapel door, but Robert had informed him that he had no intention of restoring the chapel, its stairs and passageways merely for an afternoon. 'What about the kiosk?' Auguste suddenly thought uneasily, as Robert had not mentioned this as one of his embellishments for the day. He decided to stop thinking about it.

"Seen any ghosts?" Jacob laughed. This was against the agreed rules of the wager.

Auguste returned to the script, ignoring him. "I should be obliged, young man, if you would show me the way out."

Jacob shrugged, and dutifully escorted him down through the French Garden and out into the avenue that would bring him back to the front of the Petit Trianon and the main entrance. He disappeared again so quickly, Auguste wondered uneasily if he was hurrying to see Mirabelle, and whether he should follow him. Jacob, after all, had threatened to kill not only Robert but his bride as well, although they were probably merely words uttered in the heat of the moment and not meant seriously. He decided to follow his prescribed route as far as the main entrance to the château. The courtyard was deserted save for Robert's landaulette, and his tour was now over.

What should he do? It was only three thirty, and tea at Le Hameau would not begin until four o'clock. Afterwards, the whole party would walk the route, in the hope – or otherwise – of ghost-spotting. That, thankfully, would conclude the festivities for the afternoon, the guests could change into respectable clothing and Auguste could return to his rock of life, preparations for dinner.

Where would he find Tatiana? Was she still likely to be in the car museum? Or could she, it suddenly occurred to him, be in a medium's trance, lying somewhere unconscious as, against her will, she summoned up ghosts from the past? Nonsense. He had seen no ghosts, he convinced himself. This time he would walk through the French Garden towards the Grand Trianon, not along the main avenue. All was pleasantly normal with red geraniums lazily sprawling in the sunshine, and the perfect proportions of the French Pavilion gracing the midway point. "I do not believe in ghosts," he told himself happily, as he set off. He was halted by the sound of quarrelling female voices behind him and, curious, he walked back towards the entrance to the English Garden, where Mirabelle sat. The rhododendron bush obscured his view but Marie Antoinette was obviously

59

quarrelling with someone, and it was a woman. Two Marie Antoinettes perhaps? It was quite possible with Louise on the rampage.

Louise – with great relief, Auguste recalled that Louise had first said she might go to the grotto. Perhaps she had changed her mind about entertaining His Majesty and had gone for a tryst with Robert at the grotto. It had been *her* he had seen, and now she was with Mirabelle on the lawn. He dismissed the small matter of the grotto having been destroyed by Louis XVIII last century, by telling himself he had merely mistaken his route.

A private quarrel between Louise and Mirabelle was no affair of his, he decided. They were not ghosts, and that was what he was here to seek. He resumed his way to the museum, which he found still open, as Robert had suggested His Majesty might enjoy looking round it, To his surprise, however there was no sign of Tatiana, and the *gardien* had not seen her for some while.

Auguste tried to subdue anxiety with common sense. Nothing could have happened to her here, despite the unexpected appearance of a replacement second guard, who had seemed faintly familiar to him. The unwelcome thought occurred to him that he had been looking at reproductions of pictures of Marie Antoinette's court and officials recently. In sudden panic, he decided to take a detour on his way to Le Hameau to pass the spot where he encountered the guards. Perhaps Tatiana might be there?

She was not. But on his way he passed Pierre in the middle of what seemed an animated conversation, to say the least, with Winifred, presumably on their way to Le Hameau for tea, though he had the impression he had interrupted urgent business rather than a gentle stroll.

"Monsieur Gaston, have you seen my wife?" he asked anxiously. "She was meant to be playing the second guard with you, but when I passed by earlier, someone else was with you – a man."

Pierre looked surprised. "You sent a substitute. Don't you remember?"

Auguste's heart plummeted. "I did?"

"*Mais oui.* When he arrived, he talked as though I knew about it. He was dressed for the part, so I assumed the plan had changed."

"Who was it?"

Pierre laughed heartily. "Perhaps he was a ghost." Then seeing Auguste failed to appreciate the joke, he added weakly, "Did you not recognise him?"

"There you are, Pierre," Winifred said jokingly, "you've acted with a real ghost. Now George will win the wager."

"Nonsense." Pierre was irritated. "That's just like you, Winnie. You've always had an imagination as big as your—" He broke off and Auguste tactfully went on his way towards Le Hameau. When he looked round, they were not following him. No matter. This time there were no running footsteps, or any sign of Robert or George. It looked innocent enough. He would soon be at Le Hameau, where he would find tea and Tatiana. No ghosts, no evil atmospheres, only the clink of bone-china cups on saucers and the satisfying crunch of the well-made cucumber sandwich.

Le Hameau was *jolie*, he decided, not *belle*. *Belle* was for sights which were of this world, which drew man and nature together in accord; this village with its carefully reconstructed rustic Norman cottages round an artificial lake, its mill, its dairy, its pigeon house, had no life of its own. It was to be looked at, admired and played in. For Marie Antoinette, as was the fashion of the day, it was her dolls' village, a playhouse where she and her ladies could dance, dine, laugh and sing. The Queen's House, a large cottage with a wooden gallery and a wonderful view over the lake, was, for all its outward simplicity, furnished with the most elegant furniture, the huge dining room could entertain a hundred or more guests, and a battery of servants and stores were well hidden from outward view to maintain the rustic semblance. Here Marie Antoinette could retreat even further from the reality of her position as Queen of France than she could at the Petit Trianon.

As in any fairy tale, however, this village had a dark centre, Auguste remembered. When Miss Jourdain came back for her second visit the following year, 1902, she again claimed to have had psychic experiences, this time at Le Hameau, and the surrounding grounds. On this occasion, her recollections were of music and voices and silken dresses brushing gently against her, nothing very dark, but worthy of the pleasure this place had given the Queen who demanded her 'time off'.

But one can never truly escape. On 5 October 1789 the Queen had had to return to Versailles, only to be dragged to Paris to face a cruel death a few years later; a white-haired old woman at thirty-eight, forsaken by all save one devoted lover. Even her son, the Dauphin, had betrayed her. "He escaped to Vienna. I know he did." Auguste recalled Alice's excited voice. But that was another legend. There was no evidence for it, it was merely Alice's dream.

He was lucky, for his dream *had* been realised. He had married Tatiana. It was true that his image of finding her by the fireside, eager dark eyes turning as he entered the room weary after a day's toil, had vanished, as she was underneath a motor car most of the time, but he would not have it otherwise.

Murder in the Queen's Boudoir

The afternoon was still warm, and the reflections of the timbered buildings in the water of the lake were unruffled by breeze. It was oddly silent – for Auguste had expected to see the company gathered by the far lakeside for tea. He glanced at his pocket watch. Five to four. Odd. Where was everyone? He could see only two figures, one of which was undoubtedly His Majesty, and presumably the other was Mr Sweeney his private detective, and His Majesty was a stickler for punctuality. One question to his great relief was answered, as a third figure emerged behind the other two – it was Tatiana, dressed in her peasant woman's bodice and skirt.

He hurried round past the impressive Marlborough Tower on the side of the lake, with its landing stage, fishery and dairy. As he passed the dairy, he remembered uneasily that legend held that this was haunted by the Queen, who used to play at dairymaid using the produce from the Le Hameau farm a little way away. No doubt the farm, too, had been tidied and prettied up for the Queen's delight. No cow pats for that dainty foot. The animals probably had strict instructions only to exercise their natural functions at certain times to avoid any such embarrassment.

As he rushed by, however, he felt an irresistible impulse to peep inside – just in case. To his horror, there inside, her back to him, was a familiar short cream gown, green bodice and white hat. The Queen was not alone, however. Was it King Louis XVI embracing his wife? His heart beating audibly, Auguste looked again – and relaxed. It was Jacob in whose close embrace Marie Antoinette nestled, and though it posed several interesting questions, at least this lady could be no ghost. It must be Mirabelle, clasped in her former lover's arms.

Outside the Queen's House, the tables were laid out, and the liveried servants were tending them. Tatiana was chatting to Bertie, and for once Auguste took pleasure in this familiar scene.

"Ah, the ghost hunter!" Bertie actually looked pleased to see him. His rest must have done him good. "How's my bet looking?"

"I give my verdict at six o'clock, sir. We still have to perambulate the route again after tea." Did one get guillotined in England for refusing to answer a question from the monarch? Fortunately Bertie took it in good humour. "Just make sure I win, or I'll have your head chopped off."

Auguste gulped, and ventured on a neutral, "Is no one else here yet, sir?"

Bertie frowned, and ostentatiously studied his Albert watch. "It's four o'clock," he replied. That was answer enough.

"Where have you been, Tatiana?" Auguste tried to sound nonchalantly interested, but he must have failed for she looked at him in some surprise. "Here," she replied.

"But you were going to play the second guard."

Even more surprise. "You asked someone else to do it. I ran round into the gardens as planned, but there was another man there as well as Pierre. He told me you had asked him to play the role, so I thought you had forgotten to mention it. I didn't mind – I went back to have a look at the early de Dions in the museum, then I came here. Bertie and I have been chatting about old times."

"Old times?" This sounded ominous.

"Bertie used to visit us in Paris, and he even took me to the Moulin Rouge once. Papa would not have been pleased."

"Hmmm." Bertie cleared his throat, a sign that he was not overpleased either. Old times for him were best forgotten. "A special performance, Tati. I would never have taken you to the regular show."

"No." Tatiana laughed. "I remember once going with Robert into the Moulin Rouge gardens to hear Le Petomane performing on the little stage inside the plaster elephant. I was entranced."

His Majesty was clearly shocked. Entertainment which consisted of a fellow making so-called music by control of his anal muscles was not a matter which ladies should discuss, even Tatiana. It was for private enjoyment by gentlemen only. "I thought this English tea of yours began at four?" He glared at Auguste.

"Yes, Your Majesty. Whenever you wish. It is planned as an informal optional buffet, which must be why the other guests have not yet arrived." Was it? He had no idea. Where were they all?

"I'll begin now."

An English tea in a Norman *hameau* adjoining an English garden. That had been Auguste's plan; willingly endorsed by their host, Robert. Perhaps he too had been a little carried away by his dreams. What could be better than an August afternoon on an English lawn or river bank and English tea, a light repast of infinite possibility, like a summer's day itself. Scones, sandwiches (not popular with His Majesty), patisserie, jellies, trifles – and the pleasure of seeing ices emerge from their metal *bombes*, moulded into the shape of the fruit with which they were flavoured. Today it was peach, decorated with slices of the fresh fruit.

The *pièce de résistance* this afternoon would be a chantilly swan, based on the lightest sponge cake, moulded in meringue and surrounded by a web of spun sugar. This had caused Auguste great anguish, for the spun sugar, a last-minute task, was beyond his eagle eye to control. Moreover it was not yet here, he suddenly realised, and he ran into the Queen's House to investigate. There was no sign of it, but he was informed it would arrive shortly. Short of walking back to collect it personally, there was nothing he could do and, fuming, he returned to the party which had now grown larger.

Tatiana was talking to George whose sombrero still adorned his head, although the black cloak had been discarded to reveal some very odd black costume trousers. He seemed somewhat subdued. Winifred arrived from the other direction with Pierre, flushed from hurrying, but there was no sign yet of Jacob, Alice or Mirabelle. Nor, he realised, of Louise, who had earlier declared her intention of entertaining Bertie here. Unless it had been Louise in the dairy with Jacob, of course. In that case, where was Mirabelle? And Alice, come to that?

Five minutes later, he hurried back into the Queen's House to see whether the swan had arrived. To his relief it was just being carried in by Robert himself, who bore it igno-miniously in a large washing tub since the hamper Auguste had set aside for it had apparently been used for some-thing else – typical of Monsieur Grospied, Auguste thought viciously, as he flew to his beloved swan, still awaiting its spun sugar.

"Knowing how precious this is to you, Auguste," Robert said gravely, "I volunteered to drive it here in my motor car when the chef explained it was urgently required." As Auguste gratefully took it from him, he continued, "I'm worried about Louise. Have you seen her?" He looked strained, and no wonder with Louise on the rampage undoubtedly plotting her revenge.

"I hoped you might have persuaded her to leave."

"If only I had. But Louise is not a persuadable person. I

thought I saw her going into the Petit Trianon, but could not find her. Isn't she here?"

"I'm not sure if I saw her," Auguste began cautiously, as they walked outside. "I saw in the grotto one of the Marie Antoinettes, and Mirabelle was quarrelling with a lady who could have been Louise."

"No, it couldn't," Bertie suddenly rumbled. "Must have been a ghost you saw. Louise was here with me. That wins my horse the race, doesn't it?" He chuckled, either at his joke or the excellence of the cucumber sandwiches. "You saw a ghost."

Auguste suddenly found he had no appetite for his *petit éclair*.

"All the afternoon, sir?" Robert asked doubtfully.

"She was *here*, though not all the time with me. She said she was tired, so I sent her off to have a sleep in the Queen's cottage. Thought it a little odd, knowing her, but you know what women are." Bertie managed a half-hearted laugh.

Auguste knew what Bertie was too. It was more probable that it had been Bertie dropping off. Tatiana offered to check the Queen's House, but emerged five minutes later to report. "There's no sign of her there."

"There must be," Bertie announced gruffly. "That's where I sent her."

"She might still be with your wife, Robert," Auguste said, "if it was she I heard quarrelling on the lawn with her." Too late he remembered this could not be so. Mirabelle had been firmly embracing Jacob Fernby.

"I haven't seen Mirabelle either," Robert said with foreboding.

"I've lost Alice, too," Pierre announced cheerfully, as a footman refilled his glass. "Not a sign of her."

The champagne cup, an alternative to tea, was proving popular, and worries over details like lost wives were dispelled in the general bonhomie. Even Auguste relaxed, his puzzlement over seeing Jacob arrive about 4.30 but with still no sign of Louise or Mirabelle forgotten. It was generally agreed that the ladies might have retired for a 'nice chat' as Winifred suggested. It seemed very unlikely to Auguste, since a nice battle royal seemed more probable, but the champagne cup was very pleasant. Just a little too much champagne in it, perhaps, but it was distancing worries wonderfully. There was only one more hour of his ordeal left, then everyone would gather to hear his verdict and settle the wager. After that it would be time for what he did best: supervising and serving the grand dinner at eight. A dinner would once more be cooked in these beautiful kitchens, to surpass even the grand dinner at the fête served to the Comte de Haga in April 1784. That name was part of a masquerade, too. Just as Marie Antoinette played at dairymaid in Le Hameau to escape the responsibilities of monarchy, Gustavus, the King of Sweden, adopted the name of the Comte de Haga after the château near Stockholm that was his own 'Petit Trianon'. It made a charming picture, Auguste thought, all the monarchs of Europe laying aside their crowns to play together. Perhaps Bertie, when the eyes of the world were not on him, became a Punch and Judy man, or a shrimp fisherman.

He decided to stroll round the lake before rejoining the tea party, to luxuriate in the details of the menu ahead of him, and the programme that as master chef he must check. There were the herbs to be decided for the *fines herbes* sauce to accompany the *sauté de filets de lapereaux*, the *concombres à l'Espagnole* to supervise, the German sweet sauce for the *Poulets à la Reine,* and a hundred other delightful tasks. All his life he had prepared food *à la Reine*, without considering its origin, and now that he could cook for the Queen herself – no, the *King*, he corrected himself. Louis XVI. No, *Bertie*. His mind must be cloudier than he had realised.

Auguste felt as though he were in a Charles Perrault fairy tale walking past these immaculate, over-pretty, unused cottages – save for one set back on his right where the *gardien* lived. He almost expected a mechanical dove to fly out from the pigeon loft, timed to emerge every half hour. There was nothing save the chatter of the group at the tea tables behind him, echoing over the still waters of the lake, past the landing stage by the Marlborough Tower and past the dairy. Summoning his courage he peered inside once more, but whether Jacob had been embracing a ghost or a woman, it was empty now.

By the time he rejoined the party, Pierre was obviously becoming worried about Alice's absence, claiming she would never abandon tea with His Majesty in favour of a chat with Louise and Mirabelle. He was conducting a heated argument with Winifred in a low voice in order not to disturb His Majesty, in which, by mistake, Auguste found himself involved.

"You must have seen her, Winnie. You were acting with her. She was with you. What have you done with her?"

"Nothing." Winifred hissed. "Alice went off as soon as Auguste had passed us at about ten past three."

"Then where is she now?"

"Perhaps with the second guard that you sent, Auguste," Winifred cried in self-defence. "I don't see him either."

"I did not send a second anybody. Tatiana was to play the part with Pierre."

"He said you sent him," Pierre pointed out belligerently.

"*Non.* I am the chef." Auguste was beginning to get tired

of Pierre's large angry face close to his. He was responsible for the food on the table, not in the grounds. No, that wasn't right. His mind was still confused. They weren't really guards or court officials. Or was this mysterious second guard a second ghost?

"She must be with the other ladies," Winifred maintained stalwartly.

Pierre turned purple. "If she's with that *poule de luxe*, I'll murder her."

"Who, Pierre, your wife or Louise?" Auguste asked with interest.

Pierre glared at him. "My apologies, Auguste. I am naturally concerned. I have no liking for La Dervicheuse, and Alice knows it."

La Dervicheuse. Odd how often that name still cropped up, but Auguste reflected this was understandable since many of those in this group had first met when Louise was at the height of her fame.

"While we are walking the route again," he said placatingly, "perhaps some of us could search for the ladies."

"And dear Jacob," Winifred pointed out. "He seems to have vanished too."

"And the second guard," Pierre added.

"Did I hear my name?" Jacob emerged from the Queen's House where the retiring rooms were situated. At least that only left three – four? – vanishing persons. Auguste tried to grapple with the problem and gave up. In an hour's time he must give his verdict as to whether he had seen any ghosts that afternoon, and he had not the slightest idea what that verdict should be. Moreover it was a verdict in which His Majesty had a personal interest.

"Let us go," Robert said impatiently. "We'll go to the Petit

Trianon itself; that's where they'll be. I'm sure that's where Louise went."

"She was *here*," Bertie rumbled.

"Perhaps she left while you were dozing, Your Majesty," Winifred suggested tactlessly.

"I never *doze*, madam."

Everyone (save His Majesty who returned to the Petit Trianon by motor car) took the quickest route back to the main house past the island of the Temple d'Amour, a part of the gardens that Auguste had not yet seen. The gardens had long lost their charm for him, however, and as they approached the house he longed for the serenity of his kitchens. He still had the whole route to traverse again, he remembered, and his heart sank as they approached the north terrace to ascend the steps to the house.

"I'll go inside," Robert said. "You search—"

"No," Auguste cried. "Mirabelle's still there by the terrace wall – and—"

His voice died away as he got a clearer view. His feet no longer seemed under his control as they propelled him towards the sprawling figure. Marie Antoinette was no longer sketching. She had toppled from the stool on to the gravel by the rhododendron bush, and her hat had fallen to shield her face and the gore that must lie beneath it. By her side stood another Marie Antoinette, a bloodied carving knife in her hand. She looked up at the noise of their arrival.

"She's dead!" Alice shrieked. "Oh Pierre, she's been guillotined."

Four

"No, Robert!"

After a moment's aghast pause, Auguste's hand restrained the count from rushing to the crumpled figure on the gravel. "I will look for you." No one else present would know what to do save he, reluctant though he was. The police at the Préfecture must be summoned, but Robert would not wait until then to confirm the terrible truth – that it was Mirabelle whose head lay beneath that large, once spotless, white hat. Even from several yards away, the red stains told their own story.

Robert swayed for a moment, but as Auguste ran towards the body, he threw himself at Alice, gripping her tightly by the free arm. "What have you done, you English bitch?"

Pierre seemed rooted to the spot, and it was George who came to free her with a feeble, "Take it easy, old chap."

"It wasn't me!" Alice shrieked at her husband. "I didn't do it."

"The knife," stuttered Pierre. "What are you doing with it?"

Alice looked down at the knife, as though surprised to find it in her hands, frowned, then began to examine the blood smeared on her creamy-white skirt. "I must change," she said distractedly. "My gown is ruined."

"Not yet. I will tell you when you may do so," Auguste said firmly. He had to leave the body to take command: Alice, it appeared, had murdered one person with that knife, and to upset her could be disastrous in her present state. "Shall I take that horrid knife away, Alice?" He spoke as matter of factly as he could. "And perhaps you could take her arm, George. She may faint with such a shock." George obediently obeyed, but he looked close to fainting himself, with his eyes fixed on the figure on the ground.

Alice made no move to stop Auguste taking the knife from her with his handkerchief, as his friend Chief Inspector Egbert Rose of Scotland Yard would have done. He wrapped it carefully round. He did not recognise it as one of his own, but it could be one from the equipment supplied by Robert's household. Alice's fingerprints would be on it and, if by any chance she had not been the murderess, there might even be other prints on it. The art of lifting fingerprints from objects was still in its infancy, but he knew from Egbert that the courts were increasingly impressed with such evidence.

His head, which had cleared from the effects of the champagne cup faced with the atrocity before them, began to spin once more with complexities. Was it Mirabelle or could it be Louise who lay there? And why was Alice suddenly in Marie Antoinette's costume?

"Tatiana," he said quietly, aware that she was at his side, though trembling with shock, "please go to La Maison and telephone the Sûreté Générale. Ask for Inspector Chesnais. If he is not there, then Monsieur le Préfect in Versailles." The last time he had seen Inspector Chesnais, he himself had been under lock and key at the Inspector's order, but this was no time to hold grudges. If only Egbert were here now. Never had Auguste dreamed he could be in his native

France, yet longing for the solid comforting presence of an Englishman.

Robert seemed in two minds as to whether to accompany her, but Winifred took Tatiana's place in trying to steady him, or perhaps to steady herself, while Pierre and Jacob stood together, white-faced.

Auguste had always been squeamish about blood but as no one in the group questioned his authority, he must remain with the body. Or was it that he was the outsider, the joker in society's pack, who could be relied upon when the rules evaporated? Once that large white hat was removed – no, he would not make matters worse by imagining what he would see: they were quite terrible enough on their own. Gingerly he edged the hat away from the head, and all the tea and champagne inside him fought to rise up in his throat together as it slid to one side.

"Who is it?" croaked Jacob.

Underneath were the fair curls of Mirabelle, which no longer tumbled and danced but were matted with blood from what was obviously a deep gash across the throat. Blood had soaked the white fichu tucked over the green bodice, and spattered the bushes, gravel and stonework. Gingerly he felt for a pulse, although there was no doubt at all that she was dead. There was nothing, and he shook his head as he glanced up and caught Robert's eye.

Robert gave a howl of anguish, then moaned, "Mirabelle," as he shook off Winifred's well-meant comforting arm. "Keep hold of that woman, George," he shouted. "She's a murderess, she's mad – my Mirabelle."

"Alice could not kill a chicken," Pierre blurted out, "let alone your wife, Robert." As a husband's defence it was inadequate, but at least he now moved protectingly towards her.

"I didn't do it. I *didn't*." Tears streamed down her face once more.

"Then what are you doing in that dress, Alice?" Winifred asked.

"I only wanted to play the Queen too," she sobbed. "After all, she is my ancestor. I arranged for my maid to have it ready in the *gardien's* cottage, and I changed immediately Auguste had passed us. I wanted to surprise you all."

"You succeeded," Pierre muttered.

"Where is Louise then?" Winifred cried.

"You haven't murdered her too?" asked George, perhaps alarmed at his responsibilities as prisoner's guard.

"No," wailed Alice. "The gown is *mine*. I had it made. Don't be cross with me, Pierre, please. It was expensive."

Pierre had other things on his mind than household bills. "Louise – of course – she is to blame," he exclaimed with relief.

"Your wife is here; she was found holding the knife, and there is blood on her dress," Robert retorted, as Alice looked down again in dismay at the smear of blood on her skirt.

Who better to blame than La Dervicheuse, however, whose act, if Auguste remembered correctly, included a knife which she twirled with dextrous ability. And who had more reason to wish Mirabelle dead? His mind began to grapple with the ramifications of there being three Marie Antoinettes, but he decided to leave this until later. All that mattered now was the dead body at his feet, and any evidence that the ground around might reveal, and he went to inspect it more closely.

Tatiana was quickly back with them. "The Inspector will be here in an hour, and the police from the local Préfecture any moment." She paused. "Is it—"

"Yes, *ma mie*." Auguste told her gravely. "It is Mirabelle."

Gently she laid a hand on Robert's arm. "Come inside. This is no place for you."

Auguste seized the opportunity. "I would like you all to go into the château, please, and remain together until the police come. They will need to talk to us all."

"What more do they need to know than that the knife was in that woman's hand?" Robert moaned. "I will not sit in the same room as my dear Mirabelle's murderess."

"Very well." Auguste thought quickly. "George, you take Alice and Pierre to the ante-chamber at the head of the stairs, and everyone else can gather in the *salon*."

"George may be needed elsewhere," Tatiana said quietly. "One of His Majesty's detectives could sit with Alice."

The truth hit Auguste like a steak mallet on an entrecôte. How could he have forgotten that in the Petit Trianon Bertie must be waiting to blame yet another murder on Auguste Didier, since Tatiana would obviously have notified him? Waiting for Inspector Chesnais suddenly seemed the easier option.

The Versailles police arrived first and, finding him alone with the body, did their best, firstly to arrest him, and then to escort him to the Petit Trianon under armed guard. They only desisted when he informed them that he was not only acquainted with Inspector Chesnais but a relative of the King of England who would be seriously annoyed if his cousin were convicted of murder.

He was greatly relieved when Chesnais at last arrived from Paris with his team. Auguste had not taken to him on their previous meetings, but now he appeared a saviour. A short man, with piercing eyes, Chesnais had an air of laissez faire and bonhomie, of being a man to whom the working day was provided merely to work up an appetite for luncheon and dinner. While Auguste did not altogether disapprove of this attitude, in a policeman it was disconcerting. Unfortunately it was also deceptive, as Auguste well knew. Chesnais' face conveyed nothing as he looked at the body, talked quietly to the policemen and then finally turned to Auguste.

"*Monsieur l'agent* tells me you handed the knife to him, Monsieur Didier," he commented lazily after greeting him formally. "A similar crime to the one over which we last met."

Auguste sighed. "I took the knife from Madame Gaston, who was found standing by the body with it in her hand. There are many witnesses to this, Inspector, including le Comte de Tourville."

Chesnais looked disappointed, as though he had hoped all his previous suspicions about Auguste to be vindicated at last. "*Le pauvre.* I have spoken to him already, he is distraught over the death of his wife." A short pause. "Why is everyone in such strange attire?"

"To encourage the ghosts." Auguste expected Chesnais to look surprised at this truthful answer, but the immaculate whiskers did not stir.

"Ah, of Marie Antoinette, I presume. It is the time of year when she is said to walk these grounds, though I have heard she generally wears pink. This poor lady is in cream and green. A small point perhaps." He looked down at the terrible reality of the nearby corpse, by which the doctor was now kneeling.

"It is for a bet, Monsieur l'inspecteur," Auguste explained, struggling to put Chesnais' casual mention of 'pink' from his mind. "Some of the party believed the ghost of Marie Antoinette would appear and some did not."

"And now the Comtesse de Tourville has been murdered by this Englishwoman. She must surely be mad."

"At first sight that appears so."

"At second sight also. I believe our mutual friend Inspector Rose would agree that to have a knife in her hand and be standing by the body is evidence enough," Chesnais remarked drily.

"The blood already seems to be clotting and that helps confirm her story that she had just arrived to find the countess dead, and picked up the knife in shock." Auguste proceeded to explain the afternoon's programme and the rendezvous at Le Hameau, while Chesnais listened attentively.

"Was the countess present at Le Hameau or Madame Gaston?"

"I don't know," Auguste confessed unhappily.

"And why is that? Too much tea, perhaps?"

"No. I – er – caught a glimpse of one Marie Antoinette, but I did not know that Madame Gaston was also dressed as the Queen. She too has fair hair, but her allotted costume for the afternoon was that of a fourteen-year-old girl."

"Why did she change roles?"

"She claims she wanted to surprise her husband. She believes she is descended from Marie Antoinette."

"Why could you not tell which queen it was?"

Auguste decided on full disclosure. "Because she was clasped in an embrace with Mr Fernby in the Le Hameau dairy, and I could not see her face." A private hope that it was not Louise flitted through his mind. Louise's tryst, he hoped, had been in the grotto. Unless that was Alice, biding her opportunity? He grasped at this second ray of hope.

"And both ladies are married, but not to Mr Fernby?"

"Unfortunately," Auguste belatedly admitted, there is a third Marie Antoinette, clad in an identical costume. She too is missing."

There was a long silence. Then Chesnais sighed. "Begin

once more from the beginning, if you please, Monsieur Didier. Tell me everything about everyone and *in order*. You understand?"

"Yes, Monsieur l'inspecteur. You are very thorough, I know."

"*Oui*, Monsieur Didier, I am thorough. The King of England is presently in the Petit Trianon, and he tells me he was present at Le Hameau as well as at luncheon. I shall therefore have to talk to him again. He likes people to be *thorough*, I understand."

A glance of common accord passed between them, which slightly cheered Auguste.

"I have one more question for you," Chesnais had listened attentively and in silence to Auguste's detailed reconstruction, "and then you may return to the Petit Trianon. Is Madame Gaston the King's mistress?"

Auguste endeavoured to answer in the same expressionless voice as Chesnais had asked. It was not a question Egbert Rose would have dreamt of being relevant. In France, however, policemen were pragmatic diplomatists. "I doubt it very much."

"*Bon*. Then I shall arrest her."

"Didier!"

Auguste felt as if he were once more an apprentice cook in Monsieur Escoffier's kitchens, being called to account for the imperfect garnish on the *gigot*.

"Your Majesty." He bowed as he entered, summoned by the irascible voice from inside the room to which His Majesty had chosen to retire. He and his private detective Mr Sweeney were sitting there alone, a good sign that His Majesty was far from happy. However, since the chosen room was the Queen's boudoir, with its reinstalled mirrors, Bertie's presence was multiplied many times over, which did not help Auguste's confidence. There was a gleam in Sweeney's eye as though he appreciated what Auguste was about to undergo.

"What's all this about?" His Majesty demanded

"The Countess Mirabelle, sir, has been found dead." Wrong move.

"Yes, yes," Bertie said testily. "I know that. Terrible business. Murdered with her throat cut, I gather. Chesnais tells me that Robert is distraught – naturally – they've only been married a couple of weeks." He glared at Auguste as if he had a shrewd idea that the culprit had already been found. "Odd the way murder follows you around."

Auguste was well aware that Bertie was a man of deep compassion – except where Auguste Didier was concerned. "That's the last time I invite you on any of my private engagements," Bertie grumbled. "I gather Alice did it. I can't take it in. Good family, only a girl. What did she do it for?"

"Although she was found with the knife, it's not certain she committed the murder."

"You call yourself a detective?"

"No, sir. I don't. I am a chef."

He was fixed with a beady eye, and Bertie suddenly relapsed into being a human being. "Look into this, there's a good fellow. Perhaps it was suicide. You never know." There was a note of hope in his voice, which puzzled Auguste. Usually Bertie's first instinct – and Sweeney's on his behalf – was to remove His Royal Presence as far as possible from trouble, and that would include any continuing interest in what had happened.

"I doubt it, sir. It is a method few women would use, particularly those so proud of their looks as the countess.

Also her hat was covering the face and wound, and though there was some blood on it, it is difficult to see how it could have got into what looked like a carefully arranged position when it fell. It is true the blood was beginning—"

Auguste stopped, for His Majesty was as pale as bechamel sauce. "I don't need to know the details, blast you." There was no fire in the rebuke, however, another sign that Bertie was not his usual self.

Nor was he! Auguste realised he had overlooked something. *The hat!* Why had Alice cried out that the queen had been guillotined? The hat would have prevented her from seeing what had happened, unless she had committed the crime herself. Or had she lifted it to see what lay beneath? If so, why replace it so carefully? Surely the natural thing for a woman – or man come to that – would be to let it drop where it would, after such a discovery. A puzzle here which should be looked into. But not by him. He said firmly, "I regret I cannot investigate the murder for you, sir."

The royal irritability swept back in full force. "You're French, Didier. You know how these fellows think."

"Inspector Chesnais will treat me as a suspect, as is everyone here today – except of course yourself," he added hastily. "I am particularly suspect after the unfortunate events last year." It was bluff, but it might work.

A pause. "I too," His Majesty eventually replied, "appear to be a suspect from the way that inspector fellow was talking. Isn't that so, Sweeney?"

"Surely not, sir," Auguste managed to say, when he recovered his speech. "It is only protocol that he came to you first."

"I hope you're right," Bertie said darkly. "Nevertheless, I'd feel more comfortable if you were at Chesnais' side."

Coming from His Majesty, this was an appeal on mentally bended knees, and there was no point in further resistance.

"Very well, sir, provided you will personally inform Inspector Chesnais I am your representative."

"Splendid." Bertie glanced at Sweeney, who nodded slightly.
Auguste's heart sank. There was something he was not being
told, and usually when that occurred it meant trouble for
Auguste Didier. Could it be that Alice Gaston *was* or had
been Bertie's mistress? He couldn't believe it. Bertie liked
mature confident women, not girlish *ingénues* like Alice.
Auguste racked his brains, which obligingly produced another
signpost to the correct footpath through the jungle of His
Majesty's affairs.

"It seems to me, sir, that should Inspector Chesnais need to
trouble you again, he will merely be concerned with the time
you were at Le Hameau alone with Madame Danielle, since
she had most reason to wish the countess dead, and now has
disappeared."

From the glare he received he knew he was on the right
track. "No mystery, there, Didier. Louise has always had a
high regard for my advice so, when I suggested she had more
to gain by lying low and letting Robert tire of Mirabelle than
by making a fuss here, she naturally followed it and went home
after her rest."

"You know that for certain, sir?"

Bertie went red. "It's obvious, isn't it? She'd disappeared
from the Queen's cottage, and she isn't here in the château. Of
course she went home. She wouldn't have had long to wait, in
my opinion."

"For what, sir?" Auguste was bewildered.

"For the marriage to reach the point where Madame Danielle

could resume her former relations with the count." Sweeney had quickly intervened.

Bertie's was an informed opinion in Auguste's view. If anyone knew about the balancing act of marriage and mistresses it was he. There was one difference between His Majesty and the count, however: his former's ex-mistresses were sensible enough to accept friendship after intimacy had ceased. He doubted whether La Dervicheuse would ever see herself as a valued friend and confidante. However, the audience appeared to be over, and Auguste began his backward march to the door as etiquette demanded of him.

"One more thing, Didier." Bertie had been thinking.

"Yes, sir?"

"What are you planning to do about dinner this evening?"

Dinner? How could he have forgotten it? First the garnish had slipped his mind, now the whole meal. His mind raced over those delights spread out in the kitchens; the *blanquette* for the lamb cutlets; the *timbale de nouilles, oeufs à l'Aurore*; the *fanchonettes* . . . It was nearly seven. The banquet had been planned to begin at eight. He presumed that despite the tragedy Monsieur Grospied would be trying to muddle through, having had no orders to stop. But without him, the *maître*, it was an orchestra without the conductor, the meat without the sauce. Nevertheless, how could they serve dinner in the present terrible circumstances? Surely they could not.

"Perhaps the hotel, sir. The count would not wish—" Auguste caught sight of Bertie's face and quickly rearranged his thinking. "I agree sir, you are right. Despite the murder, the count's guests must eat. Could I suggest that we hold an informal dinner at which attendance is not obligatory, and from which all celebratory touches have naturally been excluded?"

His Majesty beamed. "Splendid, Auguste, splendid. You're not a bad fellow at heart."

In the adjoining drawing room, the grand *salon de compagnie*, Auguste found George and Winifred, Tatiana – who looked immensely relieved to see him – Jacob and, to Auguste's surprise, Robert. They were all under the eagle eye of a policeman.

"Is Pierre . . . ?" Auguste began tentatively.

Robert raised a haggard face. "Gone with that murderess to the Préfecture."

"It's a shocking business." George coughed to indicate he was in charge of the proceedings. "We've been trying to work out why Alice did it."

"She said nothing about murdering Mirabelle when I was playing the cottage woman with her," Winifred said anxiously.

No one commented, and Auguste seized the opportunity he had so unexpectedly been given. "I heard two women quarrelling on the lawn about half past three, but it seems odd that if the quarrel led to murder Alice should still be there at nearly five o'clock. I might have heard Louise with Mirabelle, of course, and I thought I glimpsed one Marie Antoinette in the Le Hameau dairy. Of course, with three—" He broke off to see whether Jacob would volunteer information.

Jacob spoke quite readily. "The one in the dairy may have been a ghost. It's haunted."

"I thought you were with her, Jacob," Auguste said firmly. "I saw the Chapel Man's black costume." He was puzzled. For one who had just seen the murdered body of a woman he was in love with, Jacob seemed remarkably unbothered about pinning down his own role in the afternoon's events.

"As I said, Auguste, ghosts – the mob believed Marie

Antoinette a harlot, and now you reveal her lover was the Chapel Man." Jacob dropped his mocking tone to ask sharply, "Could I enquire what right you have to ask us all these questions?"

"His Majesty, who has retired to the Queen's Boudoir, has asked me to investigate the circumstances of the tragedy."

"He could join us," George said fiercely and disloyally. "He's involved as much as we are."

"The circumstances are quite simple," Robert said curtly. "Alice has always been unbalanced, but until today when she murdered my wife, no one realised quite how much. Now, if you would excuse me, I shall return to my home, if the police will permit me."

His Majesty's dinner loomed up before Auguste's eyes. "I have suggested to His Majesty an informal meal here in place of the formal dinner this evening. His Majesty is agreeable. Would you have any objection, Robert?"

"I shall not attend, if His Majesty would excuse me, but naturally you are my guests and must be considered. The routine of life must continue."

How could dinner ever be classed as routine? Even in the depths of tragedy it provided comfort, in times of joy it was a crowning glory, and in everyday affairs it gave a never-ending variety of pleasure. Auguste hurried down to the serving kitchen, as he had named the one allotted in the château itself. It was deserted, and he ran round to the service block fearing what he might find. He found it. The paradise that seldom failed him had done so tonight. Cooks, maids and liveried footmen were rushing round in what was all too obviously complete disorder. He ran into the main kitchen to find the roasts pleading to be released from their ovens, sauces with long-formed skins on them, and the *potage du printemps* boiling. In the entrée kitchen the *boudins* were unmade and the truffle and mushroom garnish was embellishing the floor, and in the baking and patisserie kitchen dollops of cream adorned everything but the *fanchonettes* and the *bavarois*, where they were needed. One splodge adorning the chin of Monsieur Grospied was the whitest thing to be seen on him. This dinner, this precious dinner, from which he had carefully constructed twenty-one dishes from the 407 served to the Swedish king was causing more organisational problems than the original.

"*What*," Auguste asked in horror, "is *this*?" With trembling hand he pointed to the timbales.

"We ran out of noodles, so I used macaroni," Monsieur Grospied explained with obvious pride at his ingenuity.

"Macaroni?" Auguste shrieked. "His Majesty is a demanding gentleman when it comes to his food, but usually only as to its cooking. He has catholic tastes. His Majesty likes game, His Majesty likes fish, His Majesty likes vegetables, His Majesty even likes offal. In short" – his voice rose even higher – "there is only one thing he does not like, and that is *macaroni*."

"We are one footman short, *maître*," Monsieur Grospied pleaded. "It is not my fault."

"Not an insurmountable problem," Auguste said drily, as he braced himself to restore order in time to serve a reasonable dinner to His Majesty at eight o'clock. He suspected the servants had been devoting themselves to the finer details of the gory events outside rather than those of cuisine.

At five to eight, just as he was constructing a timbale of raviolis and vegetables, Tatiana suddenly appeared in the château kitchen, clad, thanks to Héloise he suspected, in a suitably dark-maroon chiffon evening toilette.

"What is it, *ma mie*? Did Bertie not like the menu? *Where*," he hailed a passing sous-chef, "is the *sauce aux tomates*?"

"No, Auguste, I'm worried about Louise."

"Not now, *please*. Inspector Chesnais is sending someone to her home to which she probably returned, as Bertie
suggested."

"It is not like her to give up and go home, Bertie or no
Bertie. And, furthermore, Inspector Chesnais has just told me
that Louise is *not* at home."

"That is Chesnais' job," Auguste pleaded. "My job at the
moment is to serve this dinner as quickly and as perfectly
as I can."

"I have been thinking about what you said."

"Very commendable, but not now." He rushed to the bain-
marie on the kitchener, where a *sauce allemande* was still in
danger of death, then back to continue his task of arranging
the dishes in order for the footmen to serve. Tatiana followed
him doggedly round the table. "You said Bertie was in the
Queen's Boudoir."

"So I did." His voice floated back as he made a dash for
the next kitchen.

"It reminded me," Tatiana rushed after him, "that in Le
Hameau there is also a Queen's Boudoir. Bertie said he'd sent
Louise to the Queen's *cottage* to rest, meaning the Queen's
House outside which we had tea. But suppose Louise took
him literally, and went to the Queen's private retreat there,
also called the Boudoir? It stands back from the path, near
the mill."

"Then why is she not awake?" Auguste asked patiently,
realising Tatiana was not going to go away. "It's a long time
for an afternoon doze."

His wife did not reply and a sudden chill ran through him.
He looked at the dishes he had laboured so lovingly over and
knew he must leave them. "You are right, Tatiana. We must

go now while there is still light." Quickly he gave crisp orders
to the harassed staff, crossed his fingers on behalf of Bertie's
dinner, and abandoned paradise for a possible hell.

"This way. Bertie's car is outside," Tatiana said, hurrying him through the ground floor of the château into the
courtyard.

"Did he say we could take it? he asked anxiously, as
he saw the familiar blue Daimler with the royal monogram
majestically awaiting its royal occupant.

"Not exactly, but his chauffeur is off duty. He won't
know."

"I hope he's taken that dog with him, *he'll* know." Bertie
seemed to have trained Caesar specially to attack on sight
when he saw Auguste, but the dog had been banished into
the chauffeur's company.

Auguste closed his eyes, as Tatiana drove smartly off,
raising a cloud of dust, the short distance along the avenue
des deux Trianons, round a sharp corner into the allée des
Matelots, then round another sharp corner until they could
barter with the *gardien* for admittance at the Le Hameau farm
entrance. Tatiana leant from the window, apparently claiming
to be His Majesty's chauffeur, while Auguste endeavoured to
look like Bertie. The *gardien* saluted respectfully and they
approached as near as possible by car. As they hurried along
the rest of the path, the dimming light of the summer evening
made ghosts all too possible, but for once Auguste felt they
would be a small price to pay for reassurance. If Louise were
still in the tiny cottage by the mill – he did not pursue the
thought, as they reached it, and raced up the curved flight of
steps to the only entrance they could see.

Auguste thrust the door open and Marie Antoinette's small
salon lay before them. A white marble chimney was visible

at the far end, oak panelling and rich tapestries covered the walls. As he stepped inside, however, he saw that the room held more than that. To one side was a daybed, upon which Louise Danielle lay sprawled. She was still dressed as Marie Antoinette, and she was dead.

Five

For the second time that day he was alone with a corpse. It would not be long before the police arrived, again summoned by Tatiana, and the whole business would begin once more. Any hopes that Louìse lay deep in a coma induced by too much laudanum taken accidentally had been dispelled by the absence of pulse or breath. Nor could this be a sudden natural death, for the contracted pupils of her eyes immediately suggested otherwise. Auguste was too tired even to begin to imagine what had happened here.

One fact seemed obvious. His Majesty had suggested that Louise retire to the Queen's cottage, and Louise had misinterpreted this as the Boudoir, Marie Antoinette's very private retreat, with just one salon, and a garde-robe. Probably a legion of staff would have been somewhere close at hand to fulfil her every whim but from outside, this cottage portrayed nothing but rustic simplicity. Like all the buildings in Le Hameau, however, that only went skin deep. The magnificent parquet floor, the furniture, the decorations, were hardly those to be found in a Norman village. Could the Queen be blamed? She had been born to the life of the Austrian royal family and come straight to marriage at an early age into the equally rich, royal Capet family.

Auguste became aware that shock was taking his mind from

where it should be. Whatever use Marie Antoinette had had for this room, La Dervicheuse had danced her last dance here. Without the vivacity of life she looked older, not younger than her years. Should he search for evidence that might help the police? Undoubtedly not. He, His Majesty's recently appointed investigator of the circumstances of Mirabelle's murder, was trapped. Half French, half English, he was neither *poisson* nor *poulet*, obligated to the British King, and viewed with suspicion by the French police. If only he could dive under the bedclothes from which he had arisen on this terrible day and wake to find its nightmares had vanished as he slept.

He supposed there was nothing to stop him from using his eyes. Louise's dark hair was splayed round her and there was no sign of the fair wig. He looked for some indication that she had taken an overdose, but there was no glass, no paper, no bottle; only a small dorothy bag. As it was within his reach, he decided it was only a small extension of his prerogative, and picked it up, hoping that Chesnais would not stride through the door to catch him at it. There was nothing of interest, only a handkerchief, no cologne, nothing, not even smelling salts, and certainly no laudanum preparation. No granny's remedy for Louise Danielle, although he suspected opium poisoning might well be the cause of her death.

He stood, as he had seen Egbert do, quite still, smelling the scene, as it were. Was it right, was it wrong, what did his instincts tell him? He had to admit they told him very little. Perhaps Mr Sherlock Holmes could deduce what had been happening from the very absence of clues but he, a mere Auguste Didier, could not.

It occurred to him that he had had no dinner, but the thought of the delights that he had sweated to prepare for the past few days, repelled rather than enticed him. Furthermore, it looked as if a long night lay ahead. Louise's husband must be summoned and questioned, and the police enquiries would begin all over again. Surely they could not believe Alice guilty of two murders? The horrors of the situation removed any remaining hope that he would ever eat again, let alone cook. His Majesty would now most certainly have to be questioned, and he tried to suppress a lingering suspicion that Bertie had not told him the whole story, and that his task as His Majesty's representative might be even more tricky than he had feared. He had cravenly suggested to Tatiana that she break the news about Louise to Bertie. She had cast him a look that implied firstly, that she understood his motives perfectly, and, secondly, that she thought him a coward for suggesting it. He was, but it didn't change his mind.

"Monsieur Didier!"

Auguste had been so preoccupied that Inspector Chesnais's arrival took him by surprise, before he had had an opportunity to prowl round the garde-robe. Chesnais's eyes went to the daybed, and Auguste was temporarily forgotten as he muttered something under his breath that might have been "*Merde*". He studied Louise silently for a few moments, felt routinely for a pulse, sighed heavily, and said, "The doctor will be here shortly. Also Monsieur le Préfect de Versailles. Alas, it is his wife's birthday; she will not be pleased."

"Nor will His Majesty," Auguste said, more pertinently.

"Nor the comte." Their eyes met, and Chesnais continued, "I assume this is Madame Danielle, your missing Marie Antoinette. *Pauvre dame.* What an end to the career of La Dervicheuse." Then like a whiplash he said, "How did you come to be here? By chance, Monsieur Didier?"

"*Non*, Monsieur l'inspecteur, my wife thought Madame

92

Danielle might have mistakenly come to this cottage and not the larger one, when the King suggested she rested." Surely Chesnais could not believe that he and Tatiana were in some dreadful conspiracy to murder the entire party, including Bertie? Wild fantasies flitted through Auguste's mind, knowing Chesnais could all too easily suspect anything if it concerned him.

"Suicide?" Chesnais murmured.

"There is no evidence that Madame Danielle took the poison herself."

"Ah, so you know how she died. Monsieur Didier, is there no end to your talents? Master chef, master detective, and now master doctor also. *Mes felicitations.*"

Auguste struggled to control himself, always as well with the French police. He had dismal memories of the French prison cell in which, like the unfortunate Queen, he had awaited his fate a year earlier. At all costs, he instructed himself, keep your head.

"It is my supposition only, monsieur. But Madame Danielle told His Majesty she was tired and her pupils are contracted; these facts suggest poison, do they not? Were the poison—"

"As always, grateful for your assistance, monsieur." Chesnais bowed as Auguste broke off. "You were about to tell me which poison, perhaps?"

Auguste had indeed, but it suddenly seemed impolitic to continue. "His Majesty will be able to tell you at what time—" He broke off once more as he and Chesnais realised simultaneously that His Majesty King Edward VII, King and Emperor who presided over a quarter of the globe, was (theoretically of course) a suspect for murder if suicide was ruled out. He had been the last person to see Louise alive. After a moment, the inspector observed casually, "When I tell His Majesty about this second death, there is no need for you to be present, Monsieur Didier."

Auguste tried not to reveal that this was one crumb of comfort in a terrible evening. His Majesty would have to be rudely interrupted in the midst of digesting his *côtelettes d'agneau garnis d'une blanquette,* to be questioned about his proximity not only to one but possibly two murders, and the further Auguste Didier was from the scene the better.

"I am sure," Chesnais said reflectively, 'that we should consider His Majesty's feelings, should we not? I recall he is – or was – a personal friend of Madame Danielle."

"He met her, I believe, during his visits to the Moulin Rouge, many years ago. Before he came to the throne," Auguste added hastily.

"Of course." Chesnais appeared dutifully shocked at any suspicion that a reigning monarch could have any interest in dancers' legs. "And I believe you commented earlier that Madame Danielle had the most motive of those present today to kill the countess."

"Yes." Auguste began uneasily.

"Yet Madame Danielle has a devoted husband who is active in politics." Chesnais sighed. "A policeman's role is not easy."

Auguste took up the point that hovered in the air. "Madame Danielle came uninvited to the count's wedding and created a disturbance. The wedding had been a surprise to everyone, since it had been assumed that the count was as devoted to Louise as she to him."

"*Pauvre femme.*" Chesnais began to look suspiciously cheerful. "You too were well acquainted with La Dervicheuse in the nineties?"

"*Non,*" Auguste replied emphatically, seeing quicksand

ahead. "I was already working in England when the Moulin Rouge opened. I met Madame Danielle once in 1894, and the other guests only recently."

"Did all the guests already know each other well?"

Auguste remembered the ominously disastrous dinner at his home two months earlier, and told Chesnais of La Dervicheuse's triumphant 'How nice to meet so many old friends.'

"Including His Majesty." Chesnais almost purred.

"Yes." Auguste could hear the sound of voices outside, and Chesnais said quickly, "I am sure, Monsieur Didier, your friend the estimable Inspector Rose will have taught you not to touch or move anything."

"He has," Auguste replied virtuously.

"Excellent. This seems to me a case where Monsieur Bertillon must yield to Sir Edward Henry."

That a French policeman could even admit to the advantages of fingerprinting (as classified by Sir Edward) over the rival system of identification by body measurements (as worked out by Monsieur Alphonse Bertillon) was another sign that Chesnais foresaw the possibility of deep waters ahead.

"Your fingerprints will in due course be taken," Chesnais continued, "together with everyone else's. But I think, once my men search this place thoroughly – you did confirm you had not gone into the garde-robe, did you not? – we will find our solution."

Auguste took the hint – he was dismissed. He walked quickly along the garden paths back to the Petit Trianon, entering the service block from the avenue entrance. He had no desire to encounter Bertie before he had to. He was in need of food, and perhaps a cup of vervain tea to calm his stomach. The kitchens appeared deserted of human life. The piles of plates and half-eaten dishes told their own story but for once he did not wish to read it. Then he realised he had been mistaken. He was not alone, for Tatiana was waiting for him.

"*Mon brave.*" She rose and went to the kitchener. "I have some soup warm for you. The *potage d'été.*"

Soup! That great soother of human stomachs. If only the leaders of warring nations would eat soup before throwing down their gauntlets the world would be a more peaceful place. Gratefully Auguste sat down as Tatiana put a bowlful of creamy green manna before him. As he at last laid down the spoon regretfully, he asked, "Where is everyone?"

"Bertie and what remain of our party are all in the *salon*, the cooks have gone home after being interrogated, and the waiters are upstairs serving brandies and coffee."

"And left you to be scullery maid?"

"No. They were ordered by the police not to touch anything as soon as they heard about Louise. I would not have minded being a scullery maid," Tatiana said almost cheerfully. "There is much to be said for washing dishes – if one does not do it too often. It must be like repairing a car, making everything clean and ready to be of use again."

Auguste let this pass. It was obvious Tatiana had never worked on the kitchen-side of a green-baize door, though interesting that from her view it had its attractions. The forbidden always held mystery. "How did Bertie take the news?" he asked warily.

"Surprisingly well. He was very quiet anyway."

"Not always a good sign."

Auguste's eye fell on the asparagus ice-cream, now resembling his soup in consistency. It had been an experiment and though from the amount that remained it had not been over-popular, he was proud of it. Food was clear cut: it was as it was, either success or failure. Unless it was poisoned.

This disagreeable thought – which had undoubtedly occurred to Chesnais – made him push away the plate before him. How and when could Louise have been poisoned? The soup had clarified his brain like arrowroot, for the dismal answer came: at his luncheon. Assuming His Majesty to be telling the truth about Louise's movements, teatime would have been too late. Assuming? His brain wasn't clarifying, it was congealing. He couldn't seriously be suggesting that Bertie had lied?

Tatiana watched him sympathetically. "We must go, *chéri.* But not like that."

Auguste glanced down to see he was still in his working clothes and hurried into the larder that doubled as a changing room to don more suitable apparel. When he had done so, he felt better equipped to face the ordeal ahead of him in the *salon* where the assembled group now included not only His Majesty but ominously, Pierre, who had returned from the Préfecture. He walked into a silence that had obviously been reigning for some time. This was a delicate social situation and Auguste fell back on etiquette, waiting for Bertie to speak. His Majesty, however, seemed sunk in deep thought as though he were debating whether to play Marie Antoinette's clavichord or make an offer for her two Austrian vases of petrified wood. Finally, perhaps because Tatiana had entered, he made an effort.

"What's all this about Louise? She was only tired. You must have made a mistake, Didier." There was an appeal in his voice.

"Alas, no, sir. She is dead. Inspector Chesnais and his men have arrived."

"But I was there. She can't have died."

"How?" Jacob asked jerkily. "Heart disease?"

"Yes, of course," Winifred chimed in eagerly. "That must

be it. She has been over-excited recently. We saw her at the wedding – and again this morning."

"Winifred is right sir." George's shocked expression changed to one of great relief, and Bertie bestowed what seemed to Auguste a look of gratitude on his friend. "The tiredness she complained of must have been the first symptom."

"I agree," Pierre suddenly spoke loudly. "It was not Alice who killed Mirabelle, it was Louise. Then the shock of what she'd done killed her." He half rose from his chair as though ready to rush out to demand Alice's release.

Jacob forestalled Auguste's objection to this theory. "Louise was capable of anything."

"Not of walking past me unobserved," Bertie snarled, and Jacob, seeing a future knighthood fast vanishing, subsided into speedy agreement.

"Unless you were asleep, Your Majesty," Tatiana observed less than tactfully, and about to relinquish her place as Bertie's favourite second cousin once or twice removed. Fortunately his attention was deflected by the reappearance of Robert, whose glance immediately fell on Pierre.

"What," he asked wearily, "are you doing here?"

"It wasn't Alice who murdered your wife. You must agree now it was that terrible woman," Pierre replied.

"This new blow, Robert, must be very hard for you," Tatiana intervened quickly.

"What new blow?"

"Haven't you heard? Louise is dead too," Jacob informed him. His voice was sombre, but Auguste detected a distinct relish in his expression.

"Louise dead?" Robert repeated blankly. "What can you mean? How can she be? Isn't she at home?"

"She died of heart disease," Winifred said importantly.

"No," Auguste corrected her, "that is not yet established."
Robert was ashen-faced. "Then how?"

"The police are investigating the cause."

"You mean she might have killed herself?" Robert's voice
was incredulous. He turned in appeal to the group. "Your
Majesty, George, Jacob, Pierre – you've all known Louise
for years. She'd *never* do that. She was too full of life to seek
such a craven death." His voice choked. "Where is she?"

"In the Queen's Boudoir in Le Hameau," Tatiana replied.
"It seems she was there all the time."

"I shall go immediately," Robert said distractedly, "if you
will excuse me, sir."

"I think you should remain here for the moment," Auguste
said quietly, "until the police return. It is possible she may
have been murdered."

"Murdered?" Robert seemed bewildered. "But that is impossible. It is Mirabelle who was murdered."

Auguste glanced at Bertie, who was looking far from happy.
It was ten o'clock. Usually he would be playing cards by this
time, and the change to routine coupled with His Majesty's
unease, which Auguste sensed whenever Louise's name was
mentioned, was taking its toll. There was only one way to
restore equilibrium.

"I could organise some supper, sir."

"Splendid, Auguste." A beam almost returned to the royal
face before it recollected that beams were not in order.

Auguste returned to the service-block kitchens, determined
to find something to soothe him out of what remained unused
from the provisions for dinner.

Unfortunately he found several policemen on guard, refusing
him entrance, and when he pointed out that the King of England
was waiting for supper, he received the reply that no doubt

His Majesty would prefer to be hungry than to be poisoned. Argument was useless. His only recourse was to send the footmen over to the Hôtel Trianon for emergency supplies, but here too he ran into resistance.

"We're short-handed, *maître*," the chief footman announced with satisfaction. "We can't do it."

"You managed this morning."

"There were seven of us then. There's only six now."

"Monsieur le comte told me he was sending six footmen – what is this nonsense?"

"There were seven of us, sir. Six of us, and the footman you brought yourself who wore our spare livery."

The world was going mad. "I brought no one," Auguste retorted.

The footman drew himself up haughtily, implying that liveried servants of the house of Tourville never made mistakes.

"He informed us, sir, that he came from your Paris home and that you had asked us to provide him with the spare livery. We did so. I have to tell you, sir, that his standards did not match ours. Very slipshod."

"I sent *no one*." The prickly feeling at the back of his neck returned in full force.

He eventually won the battle to persuade the footmen to produce a supper for His Majesty, fought out in front of the police guard who listened in amusement. Auguste did not care. His Majesty considered a little light supper of cold quails and a warm chicken dish in lieu of his beloved out-of-season grilled oysters, quite sufficient after a heavy banquet, but today his dinner had been interrupted. Supper was therefore essential in some considerable shape or form.

Unfortunately Inspector Chesnais arrived before supper could be served and the postponement did not help soothe ruffled royal feathers, judging by the testy messages relayed by the footmen.

Auguste quickly returned to the *salon* himself to explain the situation to find that Chesnais was accompanied by Alice Gaston. As Auguste entered, Alice was hurling herself across the room into her husband's arms without so much as a nod to Bertie. "I told them I didn't do it," she cried.

"What's she doing here?" asked Robert furiously.

"We are releasing Madame Gaston," Chesnais replied blandly, "with our apologies for having detained her."

"It was horrid." Alice waxed indignant. "They didn't believe me but I said I didn't do it. And I really didn't, Your Majesty. Now they do believe me."

"Is this true, Chesnais?" Bertie rumbled.

"Yes, Your Majesty. It is quite clear what has brought about today's terrible events, is it not, Monsieur Didier? Madame Danielle came here today with the express purpose of murdering the countess of whom she was jealous."

Chesnais had opted for the easier path, Auguste realised.

"*Quoi?*" Robert blanched. "This is madness."

"That is why she wore the Marie Antoinette costume, not to rival the countess, but to confuse the issue if she were seen," Chesnais continued as if he had not spoken. "Or perhaps she did not set out to kill her, but merely to threaten her. The knife used resembles those in the kitchens below. I understand the kitchen in the château itself was merely a staging post, and not always tended. Or she could have taken one at luncheon. Monsieur Didier heard the two ladies quarrelling on the lawn, and shortly afterwards Madame Danielle killed the countess. Overcome with horror at what she had done, she committed suicide."

"Louise is dead too?" Alice screamed.

"But—" Auguste objected, only to be interrupted.

"Yes, *ma petite*, I will tell you all later," Pierre said soothingly.

"How?" Alice ignored him.

"A sleeping poison, madame." Chesnais obliged.

"But that's terrible," Alice moaned.

"Suicide is terrible," Pierre agreed gravely. "It is a crime."

"Poor dear Louise," Winifred sighed, "so sensitive. And she believed in ghosts too."

"What a loss and by such a means," Jacob echoed. "You are *sure* it was suicide, Inspector?" he asked casually.

"*Mais oui*. When she saw the comte's genuine grief at his wife's death, she must have realised life held nothing more for her. She had committed a *crime passionnel* for nothing. All that was left was for her to kill herself."

"But—" Auguste began again.

"You wish to know about the timing, Monsieur Didier?" Chesnais swiftly interjected. "The poison – the doctor believes it might have been opium, possibly a laudanum preparation – would have taken about half an hour to react, and several hours to kill. But although tiredness is a symptom, Louise's sleepiness at Le Hameau was a fiction so that His Majesty would provide an alibi for her. She had not yet taken the poison. She killed the countess, *la pauvre*, just before afternoon tea. She had retired to the Boudoir – a conveniently remote cottage, as the Queen's House is not – but did not take any rest. She crept out through its garden and through the far part of the grounds, and then hurried to the lawn to perform her evil deed. Overcome with the horror of what she had done, she returned to the Queen's Boudoir, took the poison, which she had perhaps originally intended for the countess, and lay down for it to take its effect. You found her body, Monsieur Didier, just before eight o clock, I believe."

"Yes, but—"

"It wasn't me, Pierre," Alice sobbed. "I told you."

"No, madame. As you told us, you simply picked up the knife like a good mistress of the house, having seen it lying on the ground. The doctor confirms she probably died up to an hour before you arrived, perhaps as much as an hour. We shall know more shortly, but that corroborates your story."

"But—" Auguste tried once more, as Robert showed signs of agitation.

"Fingerprints you were going to say, Monsieur Didier?" Chesnais interrupted blandly once more. "The knife has now been checked. Madame Gaston gripped it very firmly and with all her fingers. She was not wearing gloves and there are now so many prints on the knife that it is impossible to get a clear picture of any. Anyway, it is not now necessary for it is clear what has happened this terrible day. My commiserations, Monsieur le comte. Monsieur and Madame Gaston, my apologies for the inconvenience. And above all, Your Majesty, my regrets for having had to trouble you with tedious questions."

"But—"

"Didier, don't keep interrupting, there's a good fellow," Bertie's stentorian voice broke in. "The Inspector is right. It's obvious what happened and that's that."

After Inspector Chesnais left, a long silence was broken by Robert's saying jerkily, "I realised Louise still loved me deeply, but how could I ever have guessed that it would come to this?"

Auguste did not comment. It had not, in his view, come to this at all, but little would be gained by saying so here as the official investigation had closed. Moreover, so had his unofficial investigation, so he was relieved of that unwelcome task.

"What can we do to help you, Robert?" Tatiana asked.

"No one can help me. My friendship with Louise has brought about this catastrophe and I have paid the bitter price."

Alice continued sobbing on Pierre's shoulder and for once sympathetic to Bertie for the trials of the day, Auguste said hastily, "Supper will be brought to the small dining room, Your Majesty, if you care to adjourn."

"Oh what a good idea," Winifred said immediately, then realised eagerness was out of place. "The poor dear countess would have wanted you to keep your strength up," she added unconvincingly to Robert.

Auguste ran down to the ground floor to notify the footmen that supper could now be served. Supper, it appeared, did not feature quails as requested. But the fates were kind: the hotel had substituted lobster salad and while it would not be *à la Didier*, it would save His Majesty from starvation with one of his favourite dishes. As he returned he found Chesnais in the entrance hall, deep in discussion with a middle-aged gentleman in evening dress.

The latter turned round at Auguste's approach. Auguste, feeling slightly sick and heartily tired of the day, had one more shock to face. Surely he knew this man? He had seen that face recently, only it was not then accompanied by evening dress. He had seen it with livery, and he had surely seen it with a greenish-grey guard's uniform this afternoon.

"May I present," Chesnais said, "*le mari de la victime*, Monsieur Bertrand Danielle."

Six

The troop of Russian lancers of the Imperial Guard riding briskly round the water-basin in their bright-red uniforms was the last straw, as Auguste leant over to attack his teeth with Floriline liquid dentifrice. In the early morning such eccentricities (the brainchild of Tatiana's father) could be endured, but tonight they would merely add to the nightmares that must even now be conspiring to ruin his sleep. At least the lancers were an improvement on the bowl of the pedestal closet which portrayed a large bottle of vodka rising majestically up at the rear and hands eagerly grasping goblets, reaching out round the curving sides towards it.

Tatiana's father, once Auguste's employer, had been unconventional, to put it politely, especially in his later years, but now he was no longer alive Tatiana would have nothing changed. Even the bath still terrified the unwary with a graphic portrayal of Napoleon's retreat from Moscow on the bottom, together with a few Russian flags round the sides in case one had missed the point. It had been hardly tactful to his employer's host country, Auguste had thought then, but time accustoms one to much. He accepted the bath as a family heirloom, and suppressed his desire to drill some tiny holes in the retreat from Moscow in the hope of condemning it to the scrap heap.

By the time he reappeared in their bedroom Tatiana had already been dismissed by her maid Héloise for the night and was brushing her hair at the dressing table. He lifted the great mass of dark locks and kissed the nape of her neck.

"And now, *chéri*, you will tell me what is troubling you so much."

"Today." Auguste had decided not to mention Monsieur Danielle until the morrow, by which time fantasy might have condescended to tear itself apart from reality.

"There is more, I'm sure. Something happened just before you joined us at the supper table. You were very silent, and you have remained so."

Auguste hesitated. If he discussed it now, it might remove the clarity of his half-formed images of recollection, yet on the other hand he longed to share it with her or with *anybody*, merely to reassure himself that he was not out of his mind. The latter consideration won and, as he explained, Tatiana swung round on the rickety stool, another family heirloom, which had a line of hearty Russian farmers' wives, arms akimbo, embroidered across it by her grandmother (which was obviously where Tatiana's father inherited his eccentricity).

"Your mind is playing tricks after what you have been through today," was her first natural reaction.

"No. I thought I recognised him this afternoon, but I could not remember from where." Even now, he reflected, he could be wrong. With someone of Monsieur Danielle's prominence, he could be carrying an unconscious memory of a picture in a magazine. There had been certain movements of his hands and face, however, that would rule those possibilities out.

"If he *was* your footman, and the second guard with Pierre, he would deny it. I remember Louise had some kind of shock while we were taking coffee. This might have been it. What reason could he have had for being here?"

She was taking him seriously, and a great load rolled from him. "He could have been involved in one or both murders, or he could have come to keep an eye on Louise."

"Then he did not succeed, *mon héro*," Tatiana observed soberly.

"Unless his plan succeeded all too well."

"Ah." Tatiana sighed. "How I wish I had seen him. Did you accuse him of being your missing footman? A difficult question to ask."

She was right. Monsieur Danielle was the kind of politician against whom one would hesitate to lay the accusation that he might be other than a man of strict probity (save perhaps where politics were concerned). To suggest he would demean himself by dressing up as a footman and then as a quasi-ghost would require a great deal of tact, especially in the terrible circumstances of today.

"I believe we have met before, monsieur," was all he had managed to say.

The calm grey eyes considered him for a moment. "I regret not, monsieur. I would surely have remembered." The subject, his voice implied, was now closed.

Nor could Pierre, the other guard, offer any help. "Monsieur Danielle?" he had cried incredulously. "He is a highly respected politician. *C'est impossible.* I can't recall the face of the guard you sent, only that the uniform was correct. He was only with me for a short time. After you had passed, he vanished—" then realising this might be misunderstood, he had swiftly corrected himself, "left immediately."

He had received similar reactions from the footmen. With the spare footman's powdered hair and livery correct, they had taken little note of the face. Even the one who had given him the livery could only concede that Monsieur Danielle's face bore some similarity, but how could they be the same? Monsieur Danielle was a *gentilhomme*. The other man was a servant.

"The police are confident they have the solution." Tatiana soothed him. "It fits the facts, or they will make the facts fit the solution. The alternative is so bizarre that it makes the police theory look logical. Could someone have enough hatred in them to kill two women or could there be two murderers within a small group of people, who decided on murder at precisely the same time? I cannot believe that."

"There is one other explanation," Auguste pointed out excitedly; his mind cleared rapidly, and he forgot that his job as Bertie's representative must now be at an end, "that Mirabelle poisoned Louise and, realising what had happened as she began to feel sleepy, Louise took her revenge and crept out to kill her."

Tatiana regarded him with astonishment. "*Mon ami*, it is past one o'clock. You have had a long day, a great deal of champagne, and your detective powers are deserting you. At least for tonight." She rose purposefully to her feet.

He remained in the boudoir chair at her side, for her words had reminded him all too vividly of Inspector Chesnais's parting words, "If you bring me cast-iron evidence that I am wrong, naturally the Paris police will consider it. Do take care, however, Monsieur Didier, for if you were right, one of the highly respectable people present here today, who include the King of England, would be responsible for two murders. And of these highly respectable people, only you, Monsieur Didier, are closely connected to murder in the eyes of the Paris police."

He had laughed, but Auguste had little doubt of his underlying seriousness. Chesnais was a politician by nature and training, King Edward VII was present and so shortly would be most of the world's newspaper journalists and photographers. One murder in the vicinity was bad enough, but public knowledge of the king's presence could be kept to a minimum. A second murder, however, whose victim was found within a stone's throw of where His Majesty had been peacefully dozing, reeked at the very least of carelessness on the part of those responsible for his security. At worst . . . Auguste decided to ignore the worst. Mr Sweeney was undoubtedly going to have something to say about French vigilance over security arrangements, and if Auguste hinted that one or two murderers might still be numbered amongst the King's friends, he could count on losing Sweeney as a friend at court. Moreover, in view of the King's annoyance at being pursued by packs of photographers at Marienbad last year, His Majesty would be supporting Sweeney in person and with great forthrightness.

Relief that he no longer had to investigate the murders battled as usual with his detective instincts which might drive him on to ferret out the truth. Relief won. "I will do nothing more. The Entente Cordiale is in danger," he announced unsteadily.

Tatiana laughed. *"Mon brave,* to bed."

Marriage was a set of miraculous kitchen scales. When troubles were piled on the one side, one's partner could sit firmly on the other. Auguste watched the fall and rise of Tatiana's breast under the lace of her nightgown, and thanked *le bon Seigneur* for his gift to his *batterie de cuisine.*

"No more of this foolishness, *mon brave?*" she asked.

"Or this?" He took her in his arms.

"Ah, *mon amour*, that is entirely different."

"There is a large motor car awaiting us outside." Tatiana peered out through the curtains at nine o'clock, considerably later than her usual time of rising.

"Have we bought it?" Auguste asked sleepily.

"This one is not for sale, and I do not think you would like it anyway."

"In that case I will go back to sleep."

"I think not, my love. It is a Daimler; it is dark-blue with claret-coloured trimmings, and it belongs to His Majesty."

"Surely not this early?" He groaned, hauling himself out of bed to join her. There was no doubt. Not only was it identical to His Majesty's car but it had the royal chauffeur standing at its side. That meant that downstairs in the morning room, Gold Stick or some equally formidable courtier would be waiting to drag him off to Bertie yet again, probably with Caesar in tow.

"*Attention, chéri*, you are not wearing clothes and while personally I admire this very much, His Majesty's chauffeur would be somewhat surprised if he glances up."

Auguste hastily removed himself, seized a robe and rushed into the bathroom which was just as well as Héloise, having heard the sounds of movement, was busy running water on to the retreat from Moscow.

Half an hour later, Auguste was downstairs to greet the day and his doom – but not his *petit déjeuner*. The presence of Gold Stick meant immediate compliance. What could have happened to require his presence so promptly? He appealed to Tatiana to accompany him, but she had plans of her own.

"At a garage, no doubt," he murmured bitterly. Bertie was her relative after all, and she bore some responsibility.

Generous host as Bertie usually was as regards food, His Majesty was not going to be interested in Auguste's lack of breakfast. He gloomily allowed himself to be frog-marched out of the front door by Gold Stick and away from his soothing croissants and *café du matin*.

His Majesty, clad in the mourning clothes that accompanied him everywhere, was working at his desk in the hotel, as was his custom. He seldom appeared before midday in public. He wasted no time in courteous preliminaries. "Where have you been? It's almost time."

"For what, sir?" Auguste panicked. What had he forgotten?

"There's a meeting at eleven in the hotel here. They're all coming to discuss the funerals, including Robert – and blasted Danielle. Poor fellow," Bertie added hastily.

"Why?" It seemed very strange. The death of a partner surely suggested conferring quietly with one's family, not a semi-public discussion.

"It's George's fault. I don't know what's wrong with the man. In the circumstances there had to be some agreement about it. Unfortunately Monsieur Danielle refuses to have Robert in his house – natural enough I suppose – nor will he go to Robert's. Without a word to me, George brightly suggested they all come here. It's not like him. If he thinks I'll be present, he's wrong. That's why I needed you – as my representative. You're in the family after all."

"Certainly sir." It sounded an awkward, but not impossible assignment, and fortunately Tatiana had insisted he wear black. "Will Your Majesty remain in Paris for the funerals?"

Bertie cleared his throat. "Unfortunately that may not be possible. I'm due at Marienbad shortly and, more importantly, I've decided to meet the Kaiser at the Castle of Friedrichshof in Kronberg in four days' time. Always look forward to seeing

Willie." His expression dared Auguste to differ. Since Bertie and his nephew were hardly on speaking terms, Bertie would have to work rather harder than that to convince anyone that they were bosom chums.

"So when are you leaving, sir?"

"Now. Important diplomatic considerations," Bertie added blandly. "I rely on you to convey my sincere regrets."

"Thank you, sir." Auguste was surprised and relieved to be dismissed so relatively lightly and once more began the backward march to freedom. Bertie's voice halted him, sounding suspiciously casual.

"Incidentally, Auguste, I gather you have some notion that Chesnais is wrong about Louise's murder, and that it wasn't Louise who" – His Majesty paused – "did this."

"I certainly do not believe Louise would have killed herself."

There was a long silence. "Nor do I," Bertie admitted. "But I don't want you prowling around. You're one of the best when it comes to food, but you go off the rails as soon as you get the sniff of murder in your nostrils."

"I understand, sir." Auguste was greatly relieved.

"Splendid." Bertie seemed relieved too, but incautiously added, "You could have done more harm than good."

"In what way, sir?" This sounded ominous, and when His Majesty did not reply, he added cautiously, "If there is anything you wish to tell me, that might have slipped your mind while Inspector Chesnais was talking to you—"

His Majesty considered this. "I daresay," he said carefully, "man to man, there are a few things in your life you'd prefer Tatiana not to know. From before you were married, of course," he added, ever the diplomatist.

Auguste had a good idea that Tatiana suspected most of

them. "It is as well to leave the past buried, sir," he answered obligingly.

"My thoughts exactly."

His Majesty's relief was evident, and instantly Auguste saw to the heart of the problem. He had fallen into a trap of his own making. He was one of His Majesty's favourite *bécassines*, ready to be skewered, grilled and devoured. He could blame no one but himself, and he could make no other answer than the one he did.

"Since we both agree, sir, that there is more to these tragedies than Inspector Chesnais's solution suggests, I believe it would be in your best interests if I continued to watch the situation as your unofficial representative. With the greatest delicacy, of course."

"Why?" Bertie's glare shot at him like a Maxim gun.

"It would be unfortunate if, for instance, Monsieur Danielle did not accept the slur on his wife, and demanded fuller investigations. Anything that Inspector Chesnais then discovered that had not been revealed to him earlier, might carry greater significance than it might otherwise have done. The past, however deeply buried, can always be accidentally disinterred."

Another silence. "Get on with it then," barked Majesty at last. "And, Didier . . ."

"Yes, sir?"

"Don't be so blasted eager to poke and pry. Stick to cooking in future."

As soon as he left the royal presence Auguste was aware how much his stomach was crying out for food. Before luncheon he had to sit through a long discussion between quarrelling people, to represent His Majesty who, in Mr

Lewis Carroll's immortal words, would 'softly and suddenly vanish away'.

"Ah, Auguste," George bellowed as he entered the private *salon* allotted by the hotel. "Delighted to see you." He didn't look delighted; his normally pleasantly vacant expression was today preoccupied, even agitated. After Mirabelle's death he had been shocked but still the unflappable Englishman. Louise's death had apparently shaken him much more severely. Curious.

"Surely there can be no problems? Monsieur Danielle and Robert are two bereaved widowers with a straightforward dilemma to discuss."

"Er – yes. They're French of course," George pointed out dubiously, then hastily added, "I know you are too, but you live in England, so you understand the way things should be done."

Auguste fought off both annoyance and laughter. "I do indeed."

"I'm glad you've arrived first. I want to ask you about the wager."

"Wager?" Auguste had by now forgotten the whole point of yesterday's gathering.

"Theoretically the wager is still on, since Robert is the challenger, and only he can call it off with honour. Awkward problem."

What had happened to drive the bet from their minds was considerably more awkward in Auguste's view. "As we never completed the ghost hunt, I presume the challenge can be declared void – even for English gentlemen," he replied gravely.

George was shocked. "No. Looks like backing off."

"Then what do you suggest?" Auguste's temper was growing shorter with each pang of his stomach.

"There's nothing for it. We'll have to restage it. We'll give it a few weeks of course."

All Englishmen were mad, but some were definitely madder than others. "I do not think His Majesty—"

"No, no. Robert and I will have to do it alone. Only proper. And you will be umpire, of course."

Auguste reeled. So much for attributing George's agitation to Louise's death. Fortunately he was not called upon to reply, as the subject was hastily changed with Winifred's entrance.

Robert was close behind her, looking drawn and grey; Auguste could hardly recognise in him the gay boulevardier of earlier times. A moment later Jacob strolled in to join them, but there was no sign of Pierre or Alice. He, George and Winifred had done their best in the matter of mourning, with dark suits and dark-purple walking dress respectively, but they were all clearly uneasy at this unorthodox gathering, which was not covered in books of etiquette.

"Is Monsieur Danielle not here?" Robert asked quietly. "I suppose I'm early. I couldn't sleep. Now this. How can I bear it? We must have a double funeral for a double tragedy as soon as possible. Would you suggest that to Bertrand, George? He won't accept it coming from me, but it is the dignified thing to do."

"Mirabelle and Louise hated each other," Jacob pointed out, with some relish.

"No longer, *mon ami*. They are with *Le Seigneur*," Robert replied.

As if on cue Bertrand Danielle now joined them. Once again Auguste mentally dressed him first in guard's uniform and then footman's livery, although his memory of those brief glimpses was already fading. The guard's small three-cornered hat would have hidden the powdered hair, so Danielle could have managed both roles.

"I trust we may discuss arrangements calmly and agree what would be best for our beloved wives, Bertrand," Robert began. "For myself I should prefer to leave the funeral for some days."

"*Monsieur le comte*, let me make myself clear," Bertrand replied, unmoved, "it is of no concern to me as to when the funeral of your wife takes place."

George coughed. "I say, don't you think with all the publicity it would be best to have a double funeral?"

"To that I will never agree," Bertrand said stiffly. "My wife's funeral will be at a place and time of my choosing. I came here merely in order not to be discourteous to His Majesty." His eye flitted round the room and found it wanting. "According to the police, Monsieur le comte, my wife murdered yours, and a double funeral hardly seems appropriate."

"His Majesty—" George began.

"His Majesty is King of England and not of France," Bertrand cut him off coolly. "My wife's funeral will be for family and friends alone, and I must unfortunately make it clear, Monsieur le comte, that you will not be welcome to attend."

"The churches of Paris are open to all, I believe," Robert replied quietly. "They are the houses of God, not of Bertrand Danielle."

"If you attempt to enter, the door will be closed in your face."

The glorious twelfth, the first day of the grouse season, was a glorious day for the grouse this year, for it fell on a Sunday. English gentlemen had, therefore, to restrain their impatience until the glorious Monday since slaughtering game on Sundays was unchristian, whereas on weekdays, apparently, the grouse had no objections. This Monday was a glorious day for Auguste too. He could eat his breakfast undisturbed. As he entered the dining room he found Tatiana already present, deep in the newspaper.

"You are early," he said briefly, delaying his passage to the warm croissants to kiss her.

"Yes, I have an appointment. What will you do?" She turned the pages of the newspaper. "Mirabelle's funeral is announced for the Day of our Lady, the fifteenth of August, at three o'clock. Oh!" Auguste jumped, spilling his *café au lait*. "So is Louise's, and at the same time."

"That's good news." A civilised decision had been taken in the end.

"At different churches, Auguste," his wife added hollowly.

"Probably Monsieur Danielle's idea." It was bad news for civilisation, but it would be interesting to see who went to which funeral.

"George and Winifred will go to Mirabelle's of course," said Tatiana, clearly thinking along the same lines. "So will Jacob. Alice and Pierre would – I presume – go to Louise's to avoid Robert. Perhaps it's for the best. That will keep the warring parties apart."

It was only after Tatiana had left that Auguste realised it presented a problem for them. Which should they attend? He saw little of Tatiana in Paris, which was hardly surprising with both Paris friends and French motor cars to occupy her time, and so it was that evening before he could speak to her. By then he had three things to discuss.

Firstly, in her absence he had cooked a delightful *soufflé de volaille*. Her chefs would never permit him to cook while she was present, which had infuriated him, until she pointed out that his presence was a challenge to their own capabilities. Secondly, he thought they should attend Louise's funeral, and thirdly, "I shall keep more than the close watch I suggested to Bertie. I shall discover who really killed Mirabelle and Louise." Auguste waited for her objections, but all Tatiana said was, "Then I will go to Mirabelle's funeral, *ma mie*."

Louise's funeral was to be held at the Eglise Nôtre Dame des Victoires in the place des Petits Pères behind the jardin du Palais Royal, a fitting venue for the Day of Our Lady. The burial would be in Montmartre, where Louise had come to fame. The church was small enough to be intimate, grand enough for the dignity of the occasion, full of rich sculptures and wood carvings. As Auguste entered the small square in which the church stood he saw, to his great surprise, George and Winifred arrive, followed by Jacob. Jacob had loved Mirabelle, hadn't he? Had Robert forbidden him to attend?

Behind him as Auguste entered the church, the funeral coach and horses had drawn up, and Monsieur Danielle was about to enter. The familiar smell of incense hit his nostrils as Auguste went through the outer door. Inside the usher was handing out service leaflets, and another was obviously in charge of a book of condolence for Monsieur Danielle, a charming and unusual touch.

"Thank you, sir," the usher said in English, as Auguste wrote his name and address, lit his candle and walked up the aisle to find an empty pew, his mind on whether Pierre and Alice were here. He could see no sign of them – which meant the opposite of what Tatiana and he had predicted for the funerals had occurred.

Auguste was in the midst of praying for the soul of Louise

Danielle when a sudden thought struck him. Didn't he recognise that usher's voice? In fact he knew that face, surely, although in an entirely different context and costume. Or was he having more illusions? For a moment – how ridiculous – as he settled down once more to commend La Dervicheuse to God, he had thought the usher was Chief Inspector Egbert Rose.

Seven

"I'm here on holiday," Egbert explained with a straight face. "Edith fancied seeing a bit of the world. Your cooking must have set her off, Auguste. When Tatiana telephoned us, we decided we'd come over to try a little high living."

"We were going to Ramsgate again." There seemed to be a wistfulness in Edith's voice. "The tea doesn't taste like it does in England – although it's very nice of course," she added hastily. "It's a little like that funny tea you made when I made a little mistake over Mrs Marshall's lovely recipe for chicken purée in aspic à la Victoria, and added three tablespoonfuls of coralline pepper instead of three pinches."

"Try it with lemon, Edith," Auguste suggested. In his opinion, *every* recipe of Mrs Marshall's required the healing qualities of vervain tea.

"And how will you be spending your holiday, Egbert?" Auguste enquired politely.

"Funny thing, but I bumped into Inspector Chesnais earlier on. We had a chat, as one does. After what Tatiana had told me when she met us at the railway station, I told him it would be as well to be forearmed. If there's anything to sniff out, it's better to sniff it out now. He saw my point; with a bit of luck, he may even relent so far as to let me see the medical reports in exchange for the list of mourners at the funeral."

"You will not miss Ramsgate, Edith," Tatiana said consolingly. "I will take you to the Louvre, and while Egbert and Auguste walk round the Petit Trianon, I will take you to the château of Versailles. And perhaps we will all go to Montmartre – even to the Moulin Rouge."

"From what I've heard," Edith pointed out, "the can-can wasn't a very nice dance. But if you approve of it, Tatiana, I daresay I'll enjoy it."

Once Egbert was comfortably established in Auguste's study later that evening, Auguste demanded a full explanation of his presence. It was simple. Tatiana had summoned him by telephone.

"She told me you weren't happy with Chesnais' diplomatic solution and you wanted to know what really happened." Egbert glanced round the study which bore even more signs of Tatiana's father's eccentricity than the bathroom, since this had been his private domain. Instead of a bird, the cuckoo clock sported a head of Ivan the Terrible, which shot out regularly to terrify the masses; Catherine the Great stared down from her portrait bearing a golf club and a samovar for imperial regalia, and a large print of Napoleon was pasted on to cork for use as a noticeboard.

"Then she, too, was being diplomatic," Auguste replied. "His Majesty also wishes to know what really happened, although he pretends to accept Chesnais' solution."

"He's usually all too anxious to get away from the scene of the crime."

Even to Egbert, Auguste could not speak entirely freely as regards Bertie. He decided on part truth. "I believe he considers he could be a suspect for the murder of Louise Danielle."

A long silence. "You're accusing the King of England of murder, Auguste?" Egbert asked at last.

"No!" Auguste was appalled. "Assuming – and it seems probable – that it was someone in our party who killed Mirabelle and Louise, I believe that the roots of the crime must lie in the past, for most of them knew each other from many years ago. Robert met Louise in her days of fame at the Moulin Rouge and so, I'm sure, did some of the others, including the King. It's just possible he thinks he could be seen as having had a motive to kill her."

Egbert sighed. "Tell me *everything*, right from the beginning."

"Three Marie Antoinettes, and impossible to tell the difference between any of them?" Egbert asked some considerable time later.

"At close quarters, obviously yes, but at a distance, no." Auguste had grown so used to the bizarre proceedings at the Petit Trianon that he had underestimated the effect on Egbert. "Two were fair and Louise was dark, but wore a blonde wig."

"Ah yes. Chesnais told me they'd found that at the Queen's House. The gentry have some strange goings-on, and that's a fact. That's the lot, is it? I know everything?"

"Yes, Egbert." It was not absolutely true. He had not mentioned his fears at the grotto, but now he realised that this could hardly have been Louise, they were not relevant – save to him. "I have not been able to question the party on their movements during the afternoon, however, and so I don't know where they would each claim to be."

"There I can help you. Chesnais was only too happy to give me copies of their statements. I've got them here." Egbert frowned. "I've an idea there was something he wasn't telling me, though. Whatever it was, it was amusing."

"Amusing?"

"Perhaps I'm wrong, but he could hardly hold back the smirk as he wished me good luck."

Chesnais was arrogant enough to consider no Scotland Yard detective a match for him, in Auguste's opinion. That was the reason he was smirking, but it was not something he would say to Egbert.

"What about motives?" Egbert continued.

"Robert is the central figure. He was thought to be devoted to Louise, his mistress, yet he married Mirabelle only ten days ago. Louise was not taking the insult lightly, and so he had a motive for killing her, to rid himself of trouble. Not for killing Mirabelle, however."

Egbert consulted his notes. "According to him, after his chat with you as the Running Man, he thought he glimpsed Louise, and thought she was going to cause more trouble for Mirabelle. He had a word with Mirabelle, about twenty past three, and then went in search of Louise. He didn't see her in the grounds, so he went into the Trianon to see whether she was causing any problems there, bearing in mind that tea and dinner still had to be served. Not finding her there either, he relaxed, realising she must be at Le Hameau, and decided to drive there himself. There was a hullabaloo in the house, and on investigating he found something had been left behind when the footmen had taken the picnic hampers to Le Hameau. He offered to take it, and arrived about ten past four, and stayed there."

"Yes, I saw him arrive with the swan." How could any chef forget to send such a masterpiece? Auguste smarted with fury all over again. "Did anyone see him in the Trianon?"

"The cook and the footmen apparently. The cook confirms it; none of the footmen can recall him. Who else would have a reason to want the count's wife dead?"

123

Amy Myers

"Jacob Fernby, the artist, expected to marry her."

"From what you tell me, he was consoling himself with one of the other Marie Antoinettes in the dairy. That's not what he says, however. He claims," Egbert studied his notes, "that after he'd seen you, he decided to stroll to Le Hameau, but met Mrs Gaston, who was very distressed because she'd had an argument with Mirabelle."

"So it was Alice I heard quarrelling with Mirabelle on the lawn."

"According to Mr Fernby, she was by the Temple d'Amour ahead of him when he met her, on the route to Le Hameau, and he had just passed Mirabelle alive and well. He claims he naturally thought it was Louise he could see, since she was wearing Marie Antoinette costume, and was surprised to find it was Alice. They parted about four fifteen. Since Pierre is a jealous man, he walked straight to Le Hameau, and Alice went the longer way to it. Or so he had assumed."

"Does Alice's statement confirm that?" Auguste asked eagerly. If so, that meant it could not have been Louise whom he glimpsed in the grotto, but it *could* have been Alice, before she went to talk – and quarrel – with Mirabelle.

"More or less. She's equally vague about the place where they talked, however. She claims she left Jacob somewhat earlier, about five past four, and went to the grotto to see if Marie Antoinette's ghost was there. Escargot Hill. Does that make sense?

"Yes." Snail Hill. What a name for an artificial mound. Snails should be covered in a sauce *d'ail*, not in ruins of old grottos. His hopes plummeted once again. If Alice believed Snail Hill was the grotto, what of his own experience which had definitely not been at Snail Hill and therefore could not have been Alice?

124

"Anyone else hate Mirabelle enough to murder her?"

"I can think of nobody, unless someone mistook her for Louise wearing a blonde wig."

"Impossible at close quarters, you said. All right, anyone want to kill Louise? Apart from Robert or presumably the husband, and it remains to be seen whether he was at home as he claims or prancing around as a ghost, as you claim."

Auguste ignored this. "I was surprised that Alice and Pierre attended Mirabelle's funeral. At first I assumed it was to emphasise that Alice was innocent of any reason to want to kill Mirabelle, but it could have been because they, or at least Pierre, preferred to honour Mirabelle, not Louise. I shall look into it. Everyone in this party seems to have known each other for some while, and there could be much that we don't yet know, including other motives."

"You've given me your movements and Tatiana's. Let's look at the others then." Egbert studied the notes once more. "Pierre Gaston claims he chatted to Winifred for a short while after you passed them, then went in search of Alice. He couldn't find her, so he wandered round the grounds until it was time to go to Le Hameau. He says he passed Mirabelle not long after three thirty, and she was alive. He got lost in the grounds and didn't arrive at Le Hameau until quarter past four."

"That's right."

"George Ladyboys claims much the same. He wandered round the grounds in search of Winifred, but failed to find her. Couldn't remember whether he passed Mirabelle, and arrived at Le Hameau just after four."

"It is odd he could not find Winifred if she was talking to Pierre Gaston nearby," Auguste pointed out.

"Right."

"Winifred claims she chatted to Pierre," Auguste continued, "then went to hunt for the Queen's Theatre by the French Gardens and, after finding it closed, she 'retired' for a few moments to the Petit Trianon. Mirabelle was alive when she left – about twenty to four, and she made her way slowly to Le Hameau."

Egbert grunted. "Sounds like that Shakespeare play – *Midsummer Night's Dream*, is it, where they all get lost in the wood?"

"And about as believable," Auguste commented. "I am quite sure the answer must lie in their pasts."

"I can't agree with you this time," Egbert said. "It's well over ten years since Louise's heyday at the Moulin Rouge. No one waits that time for revenge, save in Mr Sherlock Holmes' casebook. It's my guess something happened at that dinner at your house in June, and it's something to do with the husbands. *Cherchez l'homme*, Edith always says, and here we've got two of them."

"And Jacob," Auguste admitted. "He threatened to kill Robert for marrying Mirabelle."

"There you are then. Murder springs from present passions, not old embers."

"But you must have eggs before you can create a soufflé."

"Tell you what, Auguste. I'll tackle this my way from the present situation. You sniff at the truffles of the past, eh? We'll see who's right."

"Very well."

Egbert grinned. "When I'm proved right, you can cook me one of your banquets fit for a king."

"And if I am proved right?" Auguste asked politely.

"I'll cook you one."

"It seems to me this is not an entirely fair basis."

"I'm the challenger."

Auguste remembered Egbert's efforts to subdue a mutton chop into submission at the Old King Cole music hall, and heartily hoped this would be a wager he would lose.

The famous red sails still crowned the Moulin Rouge in lower Montmartre, but since the years of its greatest fame under its founder Zidler in the early nineties, the old building had vanished, as well as some of its glory. How different a place can look by day and by night. Pigalle, in lower Montmartre, had little allure on a working day, crowded with shoppers and traffic, and the hill of Montmartre from which Auguste had just come had looked a sorry place uninvested with the mystery of night. Despite the dramatic whiteness of Sacré Coeur at its summit, it was impossible to ignore the narrow streets lined with the cottages of the poor, in which their residents scraped a meagre living. The market stalls in the square would have resembled any other Paris *quartier*, had it not been for a few would-be artists, anxious to prove their expertise by sketching the same views as their illustrious predecessors. Even the windmills for which Montmartre was famous were fast disappearing; only three now remained, and merciless daylight revealed them to be dilapidated and blackened with age and weather. Even the popular dancing hall, the Moulin de la Galette, needed Renoir's brush to invest it with magic.

By night, however, both Montmartre and Pigalle sprang to life. The old toll barriers barring entry to the city of Paris had led to the proliferation of cheap wine cafés and shops, and then to places of entertainment, where local people came to enjoy themselves; they were followed by those seeking adventure from the city of Paris. Society had then followed them after the opening of the Moulin Rouge, and the lights shone all night as singing cabarets and drinking places of far less respectability found ever increasing markets.

Paris society still rubbed shoulders with the local people out to enjoy themselves at dancing halls; after they closed for the night, the cafés and cabarets flourished. Nevertheless, it seemed to Auguste that Montmartre now feasted on its own carcase. The Moulin Rouge, the Elysée Montmartre, the Chat Noir *café-concert* and its successor Le Mirliton under Aristide Bruant – Auguste remembered them all, from the time he worked in Paris or from later visits. In particular he recalled the visit he had paid to the Moulin Rouge in 1894, just before Zidler had left. He had brought his dear Maisie on a visit from London. She had been a chorus girl at the Galaxy, and it had amused her greatly to see the famous can-can. As the girls rushed into the dancing hall with the customers, legs whirling up in the *chahut*, he had tried to restrain her from hurling herself into the fray with them. He'd failed, and even Maisie had admitted when at last she had returned, sweating but happy, that the splits at the end had been beyond her.

"We'd be closed down if we did that at the Galaxy," she'd declared wistfully. "We have the Lord Chamberlain round if we show a blooming ankle." A slight exaggeration, as Auguste knew full well.

Shortly after that visit, Zidler had left, and within a year La Goulue and La Dervicheuse had also departed. And Hélène Mai.

Hadn't she been Robert's first wife? A strange feeling of excitement seized him, as he racked his memory. Hélène Mai had been to La Dervicheuse as Jane Avril to La Goulue, the artistic side of dancing to the brazenly erotic. Whereas the whole aim of La Goulue and La Dervicheuse had been to display the few inches of bare flesh between their stocking-tops and their drawers, Hélène Mai never lifted her skirts above knee level. She did not need to. Where La Dervicheuse was earthy, Hélène was ethereal. In the *grand écart*, the splits, she sank down like Pavlova's dying swan; she danced the *chahut* dreamily, like a ballet dancer herself, and yet she had as much – perhaps more – appeal than La Dervicheuse. She had the sensuousness that Louise had lacked. After leaving the Moulin Rouge she had gone to the Jardin de Paris in the Champs Elysées district, where vulgarity was frowned upon, and then she had disappeared from public consciousness. Auguste racked his brains. He was almost certain she had married Robert. If so, when did she die, he wondered, and of what?

Louise, Mirabelle – and Hélène. There were not two women in Robert's life, but *three*. Had Mirabelle been in Robert's life then? He knew nothing of *her* early life. What had been her background, he wondered. Had she known Louise and Hélène in their working lives, or had she come from higher up in society? He could not imagine the stately blonde beauty doing the *chahut* at the Moulin Rouge, nor even singing in *café-concert*. Or was he just influenced because she had married an English milord? Many such had taken their brides from the entertainment world, in London at least.

He walked in to the Moulin Rouge, which was not the building he remembered. Under Zidler, the clientele had entered through the garden, which had been an entertainment in itself, with the plaster elephant and other attractions. The dance hall had lain beyond, and its floor had been cleared for the finale of the can-can. In his imagination, he could still hear the roars of the audience, the girls' shrieks, and sense the heavy air, full of the smell of sweat and the scent of excitement.

By day, the frou-frou dresses, the exotic performers and

gaudily dressed audience vanished to leave a humdrum emptiness. Only a harassed manager was to be found. No doubt by night he would be elegantly dressed, twirling his Aristide Bruant type moustache, but now the moustache drooped, the shoulders sank in sympathy with it, and lines of anxiety crawled down his face.

"There," the manager pointed impatiently to the stage. "Show me what you can do and then go."

"I am not an artiste."

"You're not?" He looked surprised. "Then what are you?"

"I am a chef but—"

"We've got a cook. We do need an apprentice to turn out the sausages and potatoes, however. And I had been thinking of branching out into *rillettes*. What do you think?"

With some difficulty Auguste managed to explain that he wished to talk to any of the girls who had danced here in the Zidler days."

The manager looked resigned. "I've met your type before."

And I yours. Auguste tried again. "I was a friend of La Dervicheuse, whose funeral took place yesterday."

This aroused even more suspicion. "The whole of Montmartre came to watch that funeral. Let her rest in peace."

"I am a reporter for *Le Matin*. I wish to write her obituary." Auguste abandoned integrity. "Also, *mon pauvre*, I see you seldom have time to eat a good lunch." He produced sufficient francs for several and was rewarded by cautious interest.

"I cannot help all that much, monsieur. There is no one performing or working here who knew the Zidler days – everything has changed. *Ça ne fait rien*. Times move on." His face brightened as he took the francs. "Now I come to think of it, there is Françoise, Madame Cerigny. A cleaner.

130

Very shortly she will come through. Her work is finished until this evening."

Auguste observed, when at last Madame Cerigny arrived, that her print blouse, black skirt and heavy pinafore had obviously done sterling service for many a year and her gloveless hands revealed her years of labour. She looked sixty, but was probably only about forty.

"You work hard, madame."

She shrugged. "All work is hard. But one has to live." She showed no signs of wishing to linger in the Moulin Rouge and, uninvited, Auguste walked beside her on her trek home. It was a hard climb to the rue de la Bonne, but he was gasping for breath sooner than she. As they reached the door of the crumbling stone cottage, it shot open and he had to leap aside as a terrifying sight met his eyes. A large packing case on wheels was being propelled furiously through the door by the gorilla-like arms of its inmate, a wild-eyed crippled man with long unkempt dark hair. He shouted an obscenity to his wife, sized up Auguste's clothes, and stopped.

"Money," he demanded.

Obediently Auguste put some francs in his hand, appalled at Madame Cerigny's plight and at what he could see and smell of the cottage within. The packing case moved grudgingly on, disappearing down the steep slope with practised ease.

"It is as well as you paid him, monsieur." Madame Cerigny sighed. "He does not like being crossed. If they refuse to give, he will chase after them, and cause a public disturbance. One day he will be caught by the gendarmes – you will not tell the gendarmes, monsieur? Yesterday, you see, being the Day of our Lady, he was allowed to beg by law, and that makes him worse. He feels he has the right to ask for alms every day."

Auguste remembered that in Paris it was forbidden to beg

in the streets save on the first of January, the fourteenth of July, and one or two other days. He had always thought it hypocritical, if convenient for attracting visitors to the fair face of Paris. Poverty and disfigurement must be shovelled up and kept from sight, so that those that strolled along the grand boulevards should not be disturbed.

"Let me take you to a café, madame," he said firmly.

Madame was overwhelmed, and when an absinthe was placed before her on the table, she grasped the glass immediately, in case anyone should attempt to remove it.

"Ah, that is better," she pronounced, after drinking it greedily. "Now what did you wish to ask me, monsieur?"

"I am interested in the early career of La Dervicheuse. Did you know her?"

"The whole of Paris knew her. Also La Goulue. Ah, those were the days."

"Did you also know Hélène Mai, and the Comte de Tourville? I believe Hélène danced briefly at the Moulin before she went to the Jardin de Paris."

Madame Cerigny grinned, showing blackened stumps of teeth. "I wouldn't know. I am a cleaner. I have always been a cleaner, not one of Madame Foot-in-the-Air's pupils."

"Who is she?"

"Everyone knew Nini. Another absinthe, monsieur, *s'il vous plaît.*"

"Not till you tell me about Nini," Auguste said amiably.

"She knew all of them. She taught them all the *chahut*, the can-can. It was not a new dance, monsieur, but it was not respectable. Nini gave it discipline and control, and she taught all the new girls. Ah, I remember Nini and the *pont d'armes*, her foot at her shoulders, as straight a leg as a marionette on wire."

"Is she still alive?"

"To me she is dead, those days are past." She drew her sleeve over her face. "I do not know whether she is alive to others."

"Tell me of La Dervicheuse then."

"One did not cross La Dervicheuse. Only La Goulue dared do that. They were enemies, but when they worked, they worked together. La Dervicheuse was cleverer than La Goulue, not quite so noisy, so blatant in her dancing. When La Goulue kicked high, or when she turned her back and lifted her skirts, she stayed there too long. La Dervicheuse timed it better."

"Did you know any of her lovers?"

"*Mais non*, monsieur." She looked shocked, and Auguste hurriedly bought her another absinthe, a large one.

"*Merci*, monsieur." This was payment beyond expectations and in reward for such generosity beyond the limits of service rendered, service paid, she tried hard to please.

"La Dervicheuse did not begin her career at the Moulin, monsieur, but at the old Elysée-Montmartre which closed down after the Moulin Rouge opened and took all its leading performers. It has re-opened but, as at the Moulin, there are few there now who remember the old days. I do know someone who may remember her in her early days."

Early days? Louise could only have been twenty or so at the height of her fame at the Moulin Rouge.

"This gentlemen I know," she continued, "gives me an absinthe from time to time. He played the accordion with the band at the Elysée-Montmartre."

He thanked her. "One last question, madame. Do you remember the King of England coming to the Moulin?"

"Many gentlemen came, monsieur, but they did not always come under their own name. It was whispered that he came; La

Goulue called out to him once. Monsieur Zidler was annoyed. I do not know if he came again."

An accordionist who played at the Elysée-Montmartre dance hall in the eighties would hardly move in Plâce Vendôme society; but to Madame Cerigny he was a gentleman because he gave her an absinthe. Social position was a strange thing, Auguste reflected as he walked down the hill again towards his new quarry.

Henri Martineau lived alone in two rooms in the rue Ganneron overlooking the Cimétière Montmartre, and the offer of a good lunch at a nearby brasserie won his immediate co-operation.

"I like to see the cemetery," he told Auguste mournfully. "I think of them all as my friends, Berlioz, Stendhal, Zola, Prince Ernest of Saxe-Coburg. Where else could someone like me have such neighbours? Dear Hector, dear Emile. Ah well, I daresay I'll soon be joining them."

He certainly would if he put away as much duck, wine and *pommes de terre* as that at every meal, Auguste thought irreverently.

"In my young day," his guest continued heavily, wiping his mouth delicately with his handkerchief before clutching his wine like a drowning man, "we ate but one meal a day. True, it was very large and it was sufficient. *Eh bien*, times change, monsieur. And not always for the worse. May I trouble you for some more of that excellent *blanquette de veau* I really must try it at home."

In his mind's eye, Auguste saw him bending over the small oven in his rooms, struggling ineffectually with a *blanquette*, but reminded himself that good things could come from simple pots, a lesson for all chefs. *Faites simple*, was his former *maître* Escoffier's guiding rule, and it was all too easy—

"La Dervicheuse," Henri said reflectively, bringing Auguste abruptly back to the present. "Let me think. She came to the Elysée-Montmartre a year after La Goulue, when she was barely sixteen. When Monsieur Zidler opened the Moulin Rouge, he stole them both away, and many others – myself included," he added somewhat shamefacedly. "Now I play once more at the Elysée, but it is too late to atone. It is Ichabod, monsieur, as the Bible says. The old days have passed, the days of glory are gone forever."

From what Auguste had heard, the glory of the Elysée-Montmartre was retrospective only. The dancing hall in the Boulevard Rochechouart not far from the Moulin Rouge had been Zidler's model. Its garden, embellished with mock palms, had resounded to dance music from its brass band and Monsieur Martineau's accordion. When the can-can was reintroduced, waltzes were forgotten in the excitement of *les filles*. Those were the days before the Parisians had discovered the pleasures of slumming it outside the city limits, and Nini's skills of control were not necessary here.

"The young ladies," Henry whispered, lasciviously, "would arrange their undergarments, so that *flesh* might be seen. Even remove them on occasion. But mystery is more appealing," he added hastily. "Monsieur Zidler and Nini knew that."

"Did La Dervicheuse perform like that?"

"That I cannot say, Monsieur. I could not always watch, I was working," he explained with dignity. "I think not. La Goulue perhaps, but La Dervicheuse was different, she was from a better class, a farmer's daughter. I bought her a baguette when she arrived, for she had no money until she was paid. But she was clever, that one. She saved up money and when they went to the Moulin Rouge she saved much more. Not like La Goulue. Poor woman."

Auguste remembered La Goulue. Where Louise had been darkly sensuous, she had been animated, vulgar and boisterous. Blonde in contrast to Louise's dramatic black hair; they made a good couple. Her arrogance and supreme confidence had been her undoing. She had left the Moulin Rouge, and a few years later she was appearing in a circus, and since then little had been heard of her. It was said she was dead of drink.

"Did the King of England ever come to the Elysée-Montmartre?"

"Perhaps, I do not know."

Auguste doubted it. Even as Prince of Wales, Bertie's consciousness of his position prevented him from overstepping the boundaries. Unlike La Goulue.

"Did you know Hélène Mai, or anyone called Mirabelle?"

"That I do not recall. I know of Hélène Mai, who does not? She enchanted all Paris. There was a young artist came often to the Moulin Rouge. He was English, I recall, and a student in Paris. Ah, how he admired her, he and all the others. Just as Monsieur Toulouse-Lautrec drew Jane Avril, he drew Hélène incessantly. He had a delicate touch, suited to her."

"Do you remember the student's name?"

Henri contemplated this for a moment. "His Christian name, yes, for I heard he told her she was his Rachel, he would serve fourteen years for her. His name was Jacob. Also from the Bible, monsieur," he added knowledgeably. "La Dervicheuse was jealous, and so she set out to capture his heart."

"Did she succeed?" Surely this must be Jacob Fernby? If so, he had struck gold, a link between Hélène, Louise and Jacob.

"I know nothing of hearts. But she did, it was said," he added primly, "capture his body. And then when she had had enough, she discarded him."

Auguste glowed. This evening he could tell Egbert that he would soon be cooking him that meal.

"La Goulue might be able to tell you more," Henri added casually.

"She is still alive?" He was unable to believe his luck.

"Her shell is, monsieur. But some days her memory still clings to life. You will find her on the hill in the rue Lamarck."

"Here in Montmartre?" Auguste rose eagerly to his feet, calling for the bill. It was well worth climbing the hill once more for such good fortune.

"Where are you going, monsieur. I have not had my *tarte aux fraises.*" Henri was querulous.

"I will leave you the money. I am going to find La Goulue."

The old man's shoulders shook, tears rolled down his face, and he slapped his worn trouser legs,

"What amuses you?"

"It is *trois heures moins quart*, monsieur. La Goulue can talk only in the mornings, if then. After noon, she is drunk. I will have a *petit café* and a *marc* also, if you please."

Auguste did so please. He returned home cock-a-hoop with his own good fortune and impatient to talk to Egbert whom he found deep in discussion with Tatiana over the merits of French versus English cars. There was no sign of Edith, and it emerged that she had got lost in the Louvre, and once found by a frantic Tatiana had declared she would go round again and make her own way back by that delightful omnibus. She was now upstairs resting, having admitted the second tour had been just a little tiring.

The highly technical explanation of the merits of the Royce seemed to be endless, and Auguste grew fidgety. "I have made great progress, Egbert," he burst out at last.

"So have I. I never knew Royces were so interesting."

Tatiana laughed, seeing Auguste's impatience. "Do not despise the subject of cars, *mon brave*. Egbert told me for instance that Robert's landaulette was seen drawn up at the rear of the Queen's House at not long after four o'clock."

"I know, *ma mie*." Auguste replied patiently. "He brought the *pièce montée*. In a washing tub," he added bitterly.

"*Oui*, but Robert does not strike me as the sort of man who would go out of his way to help his servants, and I believe he gave Louise the opium earlier, and wanted to see if she were dead before he joined the company."

"*Why* should he kill her? He had been devoted to her, and even if he no longer was, it's a large step from that to murder."

"It's preferable to your theory that the King killed her," Egbert pointed out with a straight face.

"I did not have—" Auguste broke off. "You are joking, Egbert," he said resignedly.

"Perhaps. Chesnais told me that Louise appears to have died not long before you found her, which would mean she was given the opium before you all departed to play ghosts, either at luncheon or in the coffee. If she had killed Mirabelle and then taken the stuff herself, she would have died much later. I had to work that out myself, for he's not committing himself. It seems to me as though you're right to think Louise was murdered, and Mirabelle most certainly was."

"Perhaps one in mistake for the other," Tatiana suggested.

"By jingo, you may well be right, Tatiana," Egbert replied. "It seems to me you can start preparing your menu for my banquet, Auguste. I'm going to see Bertrand Danielle tomorrow and I think he could provide me with a lot of answers. What will you be doing, Auguste?" he asked, as an afterthought.

His moment for boasting had come. "I am going to see La Goulue."

"Who?"

Deflated, Auguste explained, then asked, "Did Inspector Chesnais find anything in the garde-robe to suggest Louise had taken the poison herself?"

"No. That's the reason I think he's secretly pleased to help us. In fact," Egbert added, "what's more interesting is what was found elsewhere."

"What was that?"

"He discovered not only the wig but a woman's undergarment in the Queen's House at La Hameau."

"What does that have to do with Louise?"

"Plenty. When they undressed her body at the lab, they made an interesting discovery. She wasn't wearing any drawers."

Auguste's face must have reflected his immediate horrific thought.

Egbert nodded. *"That*'s why Chesnais was smirking."

Eight

Thwarted, Auguste wandered onto the terrace of Montmartre's rue Lamarck, while he decided what to do next. There had been no answer at the address he had been given for La Goulue, and he had been pondering whether eleven o'clock were already too late in the day to rouse the inmate's interest in life, or whether she was installed at a neighbouring bar. Then a laundress, judging by her burdens, had hurried from a nearby cottage. She grinned knowingly and settled the matter for him. *"Elle n'est pas là."* She had disappeared upon her own business and if she had any clue as to where La Goulue might be, she took it with her. There was nothing he could do but admire the view over Paris, tour the nearest bars, or reflect on the implications of Louise's state of undress. He chose the first, since the last instantly raised the spectre of His Majesty King Edward VII's unfortunate – and, Auguste devoutly hoped, coincidental – proximity to her at the time.

There was no one to disturb his enjoyment of the view, save an old woman stomping towards him, basket on her arm. In England, the old and the poor were swept into workhouses, but was that preferable to a miserable life and slow death in these damp primitive cottages? Who could say? It was scarcely surprising that with fame and looks vanished, La Goulue had taken the only apparent path of escape open to her.

140

Turning his back on poverty, he could see spread before him the magnificent view of the fair face of Paris, an elegant mass of grey buildings, with the occasional patch of green; he could just pick out the Seine winding its way through the city, and here and there a church tower. He could see Les Invalides and Saint Sulpice, but always the eye was drawn to the dominating and ugly Tour Eiffel. It had been built to last for a few years only, but seventeen years later it still remained, vulgarly proclaiming the advent of the twentieth century.

There was a hoarse cackle at his side and, startled, he saw that the old woman, who at close sight looked like a walking bundle of rags, was at his side. The smell of drink and dirt hit his nostrils.

"All Paris once lay at my feet, monsieur. So I came to live here – and, see, it does so still."

A terrible thought came to him. Surely she could not be La Goulue? This woman must be sixty at least; she was lined and wrinkled, completely toothless, with matted hair, a worn workman's cap, and straggly, black rags like a heap of mussel shells.

"Madame." Auguste swept off his hat politely. "Could you tell me where I can find Madame Louise Weber, La Goulue, please?"

"Who wants her?"

"Auguste Didier, master chef."

"A chef." She spat delicately on the ground, narrowly missing his boots. "I have my food already." She indicated the basket, which had a bottle of what looked like pure alcohol in it, and a large stoppered jug which probably held the roughest wine sold off cheaply. "Absinthe and wine from the good Montmartre vineyard, is all La Goulue needs now."

"Would you permit me the honour of talking about old

times with you, madame, the days of your greatest glory?"

"*La gloire?*" A spark of interest came back to her eyes. Carefully she placed the basket on the ground and hobbled round in a circle, saluting, and shouting, "*La France, mesdames et messieurs, la gloire, la patrie!*" The hobble turned into a brief hop, rags flying. "*Houp-la!*" A foot rose up revealing a grimy torn petticoat and a bare leg, gnarled with veins and flabby with lack of use.

As though reading his thoughts, she yelled at him, "I can still do the *port d'armes*, monsieur. Those days are not so far past." The foot remained where it was but that was nowhere near the shoulder height required in the can-can. Auguste averted his eyes, and she cackled again. "You would not have turned away once, monsieur." The foot waggled, and at last descended with a heavy sigh from its owner. "*Entrez dans mon palais, Monsieur le chef.*"

Reluctantly Auguste followed her into the cottage. There was only one room downstairs and another upstairs. There seemed to be no kitchen, and probably only a tap outside, if that, to wash with. Not that washing seemed a high priority, either of her person or of such household utensils as he could see.

"Pray sit, monsieur." She waved her hand grandly. "I had a chair once." Now there were only wooden boxes, although sitting oddly in such a place there was a low table – covered with a red plush cloth displaying photographs in cheap frames. One of them displayed her stocky figure in the lions' cage during her circus years. It was a far cry from the days at the Moulin Rouge.

"Did you regret leaving the Moulin, madame?"

She shrugged. "*Ca ne fait rien.* Zidler left. He understood us. He knew it was not the money or the gentlemen that made us dance. It was life, monsieur, it was art. Still," she looked round hopelessly, "life is not so bad here. In the afternoons."

That life would not last much longer, if her appearance and diet were anything to judge by. Once a lady in Tatiana's motoring club, one of the new militant 'suffragettes' as they were being called, had asked him fiercely if he were not ashamed of being a chef when so many lived in need. He had thought carefully about this, then answered no, for the task of a *maître* chef was to create art out of materials provided to him, as an artist from his palette. He knew he could create a masterpiece from bread and rough wine, with the help of the herbs *le bon Seigneur* provided. Moreover he did so. Just as Soyer had set up his soup kitchens for the poor to relieve the effects of the Irish famine he, with the help of Mrs Jolly, had organised cheap pie stalls in the East End, near where he had worked at the Old King Cole music hall.

"An art indeed," he now said to La Goulue. "Would you tell me of your time at the Moulin Rouge and the Elysée-Montmartre?"

"*And the* Moulin de la Galette. I was only sixteen then. There you danced for the people of Paris alone. You see, my memory is still good, although I am" – she counted – "thirty-two. Or three. Or one. I don't look it, do I?"

"No," answered Auguste truthfully.

"Inside, monsieur, like everyone, I am still sixteen," she said matter-of-factly. "Ah, those were the days, *mon ami*. Old Zidler's Moulin Rouge. When the lights went on in the trees of the garden, and Le Petomane farted his tunes in the plaster elephant, and *mon cher* Valentin, the 'boneless one', in his top hat took me in his arms and we waltzed. No one drank then. They were watching us. Those who say

I was a *sale*, dirty, dancer, they never saw me waltz with Valentin. Even the Prince of Wales came to see us, and he's King now."

"And yet you insulted him, it is said."

"He," replied La Goulue with dignity, "insulted *me*. When a gentleman puts his hand on your bum, why should he mind if you yell, "You're buying the champagne, Wales!""

"Because you did it in public."

"So what? He wanted me, I could tell. I could see him up there in the gallery, leering down, *and* he came to the private shows. Oh yes, I could have been another Madame de Pompadour – whore to a blooming prince, if it hadn't been for *her*."

"Who?" Auguste held his breath.

"La Dervicheuse. That *petite salaude* Louise. Fancy her having the same name as me. She stole him from me. Always she was jealous. Not just of me, of everyone. Jealous of their fame, jealous of their lovers. She didn't always want them herself, but she wasn't going to let anyone have what they wanted if she could help it. Especially me, when Wales took a fancy to me. It was a threat to her. I was always the best dancer, you see, the main draw. At the Moulin de Galette and the Elysée-Montmartre – that's where I first met her – you could pull your knickers up to show a nice bit of flesh, down too if you liked. But at the Moulin Rouge Zidler went more respectable, and she began to think she was as good as me. I was the first in the line, the first to do the *pont d'armes* kick and the first to do *le grand écart*, the splits, too. She didn't like that, oh no. She introduced her own little whirls and jigs, that's how she got her name. Know how I got mine? From the gutter, I swallows everything in my mouth." She guffawed, and at the spectacle of that open mouth now, Auguste felt like rushing straight out into the fresh August air.

"So Louise became friendly with His Majesty?"

"Very friendly," she mimicked. "Oh yes. Course, I couldn't say exactly *how* friendly, but Louise didn't keep herself to herself, and nor did Wales from what I heard. She boasted they'd done it. Maybe she lied."

"Did you know her husband?"

La Goulue shook her head. "*Non*. She married later. Off madame went to the Jardin de Paris, after Zidler left. I wasn't smart enough for them. Well, I know what the people want, and that's more important than stroking the *boulevardiers* at the old Jardin. *C'est vrai ou non?*" Belligerently she stuck out her considerable jaw at Auguste.

"*C'est vrai*, madame. You were an artist true to your calling. Do you remember the Comte de Tourville? He was a *boulevardier*, and came to the Moulin Rouge with the Prince of Wales."

"*Mais oui*. He too came to the private parties. I did not fancy him myself, but Louise couldn't resist a comte, no matter what he'd got inside his trousers or his pocket. She'd made the money, she told me, and he was going to put a tiara on her head."

"Yet he married Hélène Mai. She was one of the can-can girls too?"

"One of *us*? Miss Hoity-Toity? She danced with us, I grant you that, sir, but she was wrapped up in herself, ambitious. All that funny dancing of hers was just to get Zidler to accept her as a solo dancer, so she could sing with it. Louise got jealous of her when that artist fellow—"

"Jacob Fernby?" he interrupted eagerly.

"I don't remember his name. You expect a lot, don't you?

Not old Toulouse-Lautrec, anyway. He was a regular, legs or no legs. He even took lodgings on the boulevard Clichy to be near us."

No packing case on wheels for Toulouse-Lautrec, for he was the son of a count. Auguste's mind flashed back to Madame Cerigny's husband, and he had to force himself back to what La Goulue was saying.

"This artist fellow painted Hélène night and day at the Moulin. Louise tried to put a stop to that. She made a play for him, *le pauvre*, and he fell for it. His body did, that is, but he went on painting Hélène just the same. *Elle est une merde*, pretending to be a lady, with her don't touch me approach. That's how Hélène caught the count, Louise reckoned. It would be a feather in his cap to have Hélène Mai as one of his conquests, but marriage was her price. Marriage," she repeated bitterly. "Funny word, isn't it. Doesn't mean much round here. Finding money is what counts. You'll join me in a drink, monsieur?"

The last thing Auguste wanted was to drink out of one of the filthy glasses she produced with a flourish, but consoled himself that the strength of the alcohol would kill the germs. Gingerly he picked it up.

La Goulue regarded him sardonically. "It won't kill you, chef. You poison yourself far worse day by day with all that rich stuff you cook."

"Take a little wine for your digestion's sake, St Paul advised." Auguste managed to laugh as he valiantly sipped it. He spluttered. This rough red wine must be 16 percent at least.

"This Paul go to your restaurant, does he?"

"Not recently," Auguste muttered.

"Ah, I remember. He's one of them saints. I went to church

once, not on purpose, I was taking in laundry, and I saw a fellow who never paid his bill, so I went and stood by him, and when everyone was kneeling quiet, I yelled out, "What about the twenty sous you owe me, *salaud*?" They threw *me* out, not him. Doesn't seem fair, does it?"

"Life isn't. Could you tell me more about Hélène Mai?"

"Not much to tell. She was only at the Moulin for six months or so, before Zidler left, and she was off like a pimp for his francs to the Jardin. La Grieve they called her there. She said it was because of her voice, she sang like a song thrush. But I reckon it was because men found her cheap to eat." She sniggered. "The count did anyway."

"She died some years ago, didn't she?"

"I heard so."

"What of?"

She shrugged. "*Je ne sais pas.* Countesses don't often come to the circus, so I never saw her after she married. La Dervicheuse could tell you – she'd know. She never lets go till she wants to. There was a man – can't recall his name – a photographer of sorts, if you get my meaning – committed suicide over her. She couldn't wait to get him into bed for he'd spend plenty of money on her, but she got bored quicker than a flea on a waxwork when he became infatuated with her. Nor did she take kindly to the count going off with someone else, once he'd had the privilege of Madame Louise's body. She'll have kept her hooks in him, that's my bet. You ask her."

"She was murdered last week."

"Murdered?" Even La Goulue drew breath for a moment at that. "On the streets, was she? I always said she'd come to a bad end, God rest her soul."

"No, she was killed at Versailles, during a party where the King of England, the Comte de Tourville, and his new wife Mirabelle were present. La Dervicheuse married a politician."

La Goulue chortled. "Politics? Don't sound like the Louise I knew. *Alors*, it proves what I said. She never takes her claws out. All the old gang. Was George there too? He was one of Louise's *petits amis* – only not so *petit* in Big George's case."

"George Ladyboys?" Auguste asked faintly.

"*Alors, mon ami*, I can't remember all their names. Not even the ones I slept with, let alone all Louise's cocks. Georgie is what she called him. If Wales wasn't around, he would do. He was drowning out of his depth, a real old plodder. When Madame Salaude saw Wales fancied me, she set out to get him, and having got her talons on the real meat, she waved goodbye to Georgie."

This raised several unappealing thoughts to His Majesty's unofficial investigator, but there were other avenues to pursue before he need face them. "Did you know George's wife, Winifred?"

"Wives?" She snorted. "You're joking, of course. At the Moulin?"

"Or the count's new wife Mirabelle? She was murdered at the same time as La Dervicheuse."

La Goulue clapped her hands and cackled. "*Merde*, you see some high life, don't you? Better than swells' night at a *maison de tolerance*. Did them both in, did he?"

"As yet, we don't know."

"I didn't think he had it in him. Less spunk than a plate of jelly. La Dervicheuse must have flickered her beady eyes when he married again. *Madame l'elephant* has a long memory. Perhaps she did her in. Thought of that?"

"I have, so have the police. She died too, however, and it's not likely to have been by her own hand."

"It's that husband of hers then. Politicians would do anything."

"He's unlikely to have killed the count's wife too."

She shrugged. "Nothing to do with me, anyway." A sudden thought occurred to her. "They said someone was getting buried here yesterday. Was that her?"

"Yes. She lies in the Cimetière Montmartre."

"That's down Clichy way. I might stroll down to pay my respects for old times' sake. Funny thing, but I remember her as clear as anything with her black hair. The way she'd stare at you sometimes, you felt more snakes crawling up your spine than after a couple of bottles of absinthe. I didn't like her being behind me in the line, I can tell you. Rayon d'Or, or Cri-Cri, or Nini Foot-in-the-Air – they were all right – or – what's her name?" She groped around in the vast memory bank of time, and Auguste seized his opportunity to show her a photograph of Mirabelle which Egbert had obtained from the police.

"Do you remember this face, madame?"

"Don't keep calling me that. Makes me sound like a brothel," she snapped. Her grimy hands pawed it, as she gave it back, the thumb over Mirabelle's face. "No. Dolled up like that, I wouldn't recognise my old mother. She's a familiar look about her, but then everyone has after a glass or two." She helped herself to another. "So La Dervicheuse is gone, eh? *Alors*, the Devil's will be the last pair of arms to enfold her." She looked at her wine. "But then, perhaps she repented; it's never too late, they say."

"No, madame!"

The head shot up proudly. "I told you. Just call me La Goulue."

"Then let me pay my tribute to my memories of a great

149

dancer." He put a considerable number of francs on the table, as she stared in astonishment.

"Memories, mister? *Merde*, for that amount of money you deserve a show *now*."

"No," cried Auguste tactlessly, but he was ignored. She pulled the packing cases out of the way, and let out something between a howl and a screech which made him jump and to his relief spill the wine he was politely finishing. Her heavy body remained immobile for a moment, as she closed her eyes and began to slowly hum Offenbach's famous can-can melody. Then her body began to sway, her hands to creep out towards him, enveloping her audience in her own erotic imagination. The humming increased in tempo, her body jerked, the hips swayed and twisted, and the feet began to dance, then her abdomen, then her waist, then back again. He found himself almost mesmerised, the music inside her own head must be reaching crescendo after crescendo. She was shouting now, the legs higher and higher, ugly bare flesh seemed to have vanished, and the grey rags of her petticoats were irrelevant as he watched spellbound. The creases on her face were ironed out as she concentrated, and some of the earthiness and youth of the girl he dimly remembered from twelve years ago returned.

"*Le port d'armes*," she shouted in glee, as the leg came up almost to waist level.

"Bravo!" he called, genuinely impressed.

"*Le grand écart*." The hum became a feverish unintelligible moaning.

"No," he called out sharply, but was too late. She jumped perhaps an inch from the ground and began the splits, but her legs no longer supported her and she toppled heavily sideways into a heap of rags.

He rushed to help her up. "You have hurt yourself?" he asked anxiously.

She groaned. "Nothing that a glass of absinthe won't cure," she said, heaving herself up with his help. "Out of practice, aren't I?"

"The artiste in one never dies."

"You're a good sort, sir. Wish I'd known you then. Do you want to see my backside?" she added hopefully. The performance had always ended with her bending over backwards, and flinging back her petticoats to reveal her not unsizeable charms.

"No, La Goulue," he said gently. "Who could forget that?"

She cackled. "Not Wales for one. Give him my love."

Politicians were difficult suspects, Egbert was thinking, even when they spoke English like Bertrand Danielle. It was like talking to a actor always playing a part. As the old Queen had once complained, he felt as if he was being addressed like a public meeting. He did his best, but it took some time to be rewarded. Danielle had been as stiff as a post to begin with.

"I am a recently bereaved husband, monsieur. I see no reason to answer your questions, even if, as you maintain, the French police have no objection to your putting them."

"I understand, Monsieur Danielle." What was the fellow thinking behind that bland exterior? Egbert wondered. He did himself in style, in an apartment in the place Vendôme that even His Majesty wouldn't find unbecoming to his status. "You'll appreciate, however, that the King, being an old friend of your wife's, is naturally anxious to know exactly what happened."

"You do not consider the Sûreté competent then?" was the cool reply.

If what Auguste had told him about La Dervicheuse was true, no wonder she needed a lover, after this cold fish.

"Oh, perfectly competent, sir. But it's an odd situation, isn't it? I'm sure you wouldn't want your wife to go down, even in secret Sûreté files, as a murderess if she wasn't. It wouldn't do your name much good at all."

The fishy eye glared at him. "My wife committed suicide."

"After murdering her lover's new wife – according to the police records. Naturally," Egbert swept smoothly on, "I've no means of knowing whether that's true or not, but it's a nasty accusation to have on file – particularly if it's wrong, and someone did murder your wife."

There was a pause. "I see your role more clearly, now, Chief Inspector Rose," Bertrand said at last, handing a glass of port to Egbert, who eyed it cautiously. He didn't like port, and he most certainly didn't like it before luncheon. When in France, however . . . "Obviously I would wish to co-operate if my poor wife could be exonerated from this dreadful charge," Bertrand continued, "even though it would imply that someone had wished to do her harm. That I cannot believe. She was beloved by everyone." His smooth voice challenged Egbert to deny it.

"Odd the way the nicest people can get misunderstood, sir. Even yourself."

Bertrand stiffened. "I believe my reputation to be unsullied. There have been no scandals attached to my name."

"There are rumours everywhere, sir, particularly about a prominent politician such as yourself. Goodness knows how they get around. They're often groundless, but they have to be squashed or they grow. Take the crazy events of last week that ended in such tragedy. There's a rumour spreading that one of the two gentlemen dressed up as Marie Antoinette's guards looked remarkably like yourself, not to mention one of the liveried servants. I've no doubt that in fact you were with a dozen people all afternoon, probably in the Palais du Luxembourg, or the Elysée palace."

"Do these rumours suggest why I should condescend to such a foolish masquerade?"

"Without proof, rumours grow, as I said. I'm sure we can discount murder in the case of a politician such as yourself. There'd be no reason for you to kill the Countess of Tourville, and most certainly not your own wife. It was a very happy marriage, I've no doubt."

"If there was any truth in these rumours at all, you may take it that I had no reason to murder my beloved Louise, or Mirabelle whom I scarcely knew."

"Naturally not, sir." Egbert appeared shocked. "I would have thought your motive for being there would have been more on the lines of the need for protection."

"Of my wife?"

"Perhaps. Or if you had heard those rumours about your wife threatening publicly to murder both the count and the countess, you might have wished to be present to ensure these were idle threats."

He smiled. "You suggest I would descend to such lengths in order to protect Robert? *Non*, monsieur. There your hypothesis is widely astray. Robert, it is claimed by Paris society generally, was a former lover of my wife's, and by some that he continued to be so up to his recent marriage. I myself know these rumours to be false."

"Of course."

"Nevertheless, I would not exert myself one millimetre to protect either Robert or his wife from Louise, even had there been any need of it However, my wife's threat was merely idle words.

"Then perhaps you might have wanted to keep an eye on your wife to ensure she did not endanger your reputation in front of the King of England. A very nasty situation that could be."

"You are not drinking your port, Chief Inspector Rose. Your sense of appreciation, so sharply developed in one direction, fails to extend to this noble drink."

Nine

Robert's house near La Madeleine was furnished with exquisite taste, and with little sign of his rumoured impoverishment. It was, in this elegant salon, easy to see that Louise, even had she been free, would have been an unlikely candidate for becoming the new Countess of Tourville. Mirabelle, on the other hand, whatever her background, had had a superficial charm of manner which would blend into this understated elegance. The pale greys and greens, the white paint, would have made Louise's boisterous vitality seem ostentatious at the very least. The paintings on the walls, to Auguste's slight surprise, were modern rather than obviously inherited heirlooms. Several were in the Impressionist style, perhaps Monet – he thought he recognised the garden at Giverny; only one painting stood out, demanding instant attention, a portrait of a woman in a blue dress, posed as if swaying to music, eyes half closed, arms raised above her head, hips curved to one side, lost in a dream of her own.

"My first wife." Robert had entered the *salon* unnoticed, as he was studying the painting. "An early painting by Jacob Fernby."

Auguste had seen several portraits by Fernby, and none had shown the depth of feeling displayed in this one. "May I present my friend, Chief Inspector Egbert Rose, from Scotland Yard?"

Robert's face, already drawn with grief, looked as if this were yet one more blow delivered by fate. "Scotland Yard? Will this horror never end?"

Auguste hastily stretched the truth. "As a personal matter, of course, His Majesty has asked us to investigate the full background of the terrible events last week. As he was the last to see Louise alive, he naturally feels involved. He finds it hard to believe she killed Mirabelle."

"Of course not," Robert said bitterly. "Alice Gaston murdered my wife."

"The medical evidence suggests otherwise," Egbert said mildly. "She died nearer to four o'clock than five."

"Alice Gaston did not appear at Le Hameau. She obviously killed Mirabelle, and was so horrified at what she'd done that she remained there to confess as soon as someone arrived. She has *some* human feelings, no doubt."

"Possibly, monsieur, but why should she kill Mirabelle?" Auguste asked.

"How should I know? You heard Mirabelle quarrelling with someone. Alice wanted to play Marie Antoinette, and she lost her temper when Mirabelle refused. *Mon dieu*, of all the stupid reasons."

"She'd hardly have gone armed with a knife, sir," Egbert pointed out. "She would have had to have taken it from the luncheon room or kitchen. I gather, however, that Madame Danielle *did* have a motive for killing your wife, and could very well have planned it beforehand."

"Louise was a difficult woman," Robert replied slowly. "She was, in my view, capable of murder, and I agree she had reason to hate Mirabelle. She had been my mistress for many years. I met her long before I married my first wife and when Hélène died, I was drawn to her again. She was bewitching, exhausting and demanding, both sexually and in her personality, and one cannot drive one's motor car of life continuously at twenty miles an hour. One must take rest. Hélène gave me rest. Mirabelle gave me rest. Louise did not. Does that answer the question you have not asked, Inspector?".

"Did you love her?"

Robert laughed. "What is love, Auguste? Can *you* answer that? You are happily married, yet in the past I hear Kallinkova, the Russian ballet dancer, was your mistress. Do you still love her? Do you still love Emma Pryde? Do you still love your Galaxy chorus girl?"

Auguste longed to plant a large custard pie in Robert's face, followed speedily by his fist, but Egbert forestalled him by saying firmly, "I'm grateful to you for explaining about Madame Danielle. Can't have been easy. You'll be glad to know since you were fond of the lady that she is very unlikely to have killed your wife, since she took or was given the poison earlier on in the afternoon."

"Perhaps you might have mentioned that earlier, Inspector."

"Must have slipped my mind, sir. Now let's suppose Louise *was* murdered. Take Monsieur Danielle. The husband is always the natural suspect."

"Not in my case," Robert pointed out coldly. "Nor can I tell you about Louise's relations with her husband. I understood from Louise he knew about our relationship and did not object. I may have been misinformed."

Egbert ignored him. "Always hard to tell what goes on between man and wife, although crimes of passion don't usually take place in public. And especially not in front of the King of England."

"He was an intimate friend of Louise at one time." Robert studied his immaculate fingernails.

Amy Myers

"I think we'll assume that the King of England isn't likely to go around committing crimes of passion, especially after one of Auguste's meals."

Auguste still seething, was grateful to Egbert for deflecting this line of enquiry. His earlier assumption that Bertie had never been sufficiently thwarted in his desires to feel the urge to commit a crime of passion had been shaken by Chesnais' discovery in the Queen's House. There was no evidence, according to Chesnais, that Louise had had sexual intercourse that day, but in the light of La Goulue's revelation that Louise had at least claimed to have ensnared Bertie when Prince of Wales, now supported by Robert, there must be at least a question mark over whether Bertie had revealed the whole truth about what had happened at Le Hameau that afternoon.

"Unlike Inspector Rose," Auguste managed to say calmly to Robert, "I believe the answer to at least one, if not both of these crimes, lies in the past. Yesterday I heard a rumour that Louise had many lovers beside yourself in her days at the Moulin Rouge and the Elysée-Montmartre."

Robert laughed. "You must be thinking of our upright family man, George Ladyboys. If one night constitutes a love affair, then yes, they were lovers. Poor George. Louise was the passion of his youth. He badgered her till the poor girl surrendered, and then he wouldn't let her alone. He followed her round Paris, wrote atrocious verse to her, deluged her with flowers, demanded more of her attentions, and became extremely peeved when she wouldn't grant them. Why do you think he dislikes me? Because Louise gave me the task of getting rid of him, and so he still views me as the evil genie who lost him Louise. That's why he challenged me to this wager and is so eager to win it."

"Since it is easier to prove the non-existence of ghosts than their existence, he would seem to have chosen the subject for his wager unwisely," Auguste pointed out.

"Unless he fakes some evidence. You wait, he'll come up with some plan to renew the wager. If *he* murdered Louise, I could understand it. George has a nasty temper when roused."

"He seems to control it well," Egbert commented. "Twelve years is a long time to plan revenge."

Robert shrugged. "George probably hadn't seen Louise in all those years. Seeing her in June might have rekindled the flame. He is stupid enough to have persuaded himself he still had a chance of repeating his grand night of passion, and hoped to arrange it at the Petit Trianon."

"He would have to have planned the murder in advance," Auguste said shortly. The mocking smile on Robert's face was for them, not George.

"There was Jacob too, of course," Robert said helpfully. "He also had reasons for killing Louise. As with George, it was *revenge*," he announced in sepulchral tones.

"A very serious passion. Not," Egbert said, "to be taken lightly."

"You must forgive me. It is my manner. One must preserve a mask."

Need it be such an unpleasant one? Auguste wondered cynically.

"Jacob was in love with Louise as a young art student," Robert continued, "and I regret to say Louise spurned his advances."

"Having first encouraged them?" Auguste could not resist asking.

"Louise, I am sorry to admit, found love a game."

"If he loved Louise, why paint that portrait of your first wife with such dedication?"

For a moment the mask – if it were one – slipped. "Jacob was drawn to Hélène as a model, since he was fascinated by her dancing and singing. His baser passions he reserved for Louise."

"I heard that another of Louise's suitors was a photographer who committed suicide when she tired of him as she did of Jacob."

Robert glanced at him with sudden interest. "I had almost forgotten. That's how I first met Pierre. It was his brother, Michel. They were in the photography business together, and by the time the Moulin Rouge opened, the craze for postcards of popular favourites had begun. Louise saw its value and probably," he shrugged, "encouraged Michel. The postcards were provocative enough to sell in their thousands, but insufficiently so to put her – shall we say – on the wrong side of the *salon* door. Louise, unlike La Goulue of whom you may have heard, used her intelligence where her career was concerned."

"So Pierre might well have borne Louise a grudge for his brother's death?"

"Indeed. It hit his pocket too." Robert laughed. "Somewhat easier to reach in Pierre's case than his heart. Their photography business was ruined, since it was Michel who had the flair for taking photographs. It took some years for him to re-establish himself with the partner he now has, and with whom he has so successfully launched himself into society. Paris society is remarkably undiscerning when money blurs its eyes. Photographers, cooks – my dear Auguste, my apologies. Of course I do not include you among these *parvenus*. After all, you are related to the King of England, if only by marriage."

"You are too kind," Auguste said through gritted teeth. The thought of the pleasure of having Robert arrested for murder was as exquisite as the first oyster on a rainy Sunday. "Pierre, *parvenu* or not, has been your friend for many years."

"Friend?" Robert considered the word with distaste. "Useful acquaintances are not always friends. However, you may be right in believing the answer to these crimes may lie in the past. Perhaps your excellent dinner in June rekindled more passions than those of love."

"In that case sir," Egbert said easily, "perhaps you could tell us a little of your wife's past."

"My wife?" Robert looked startled. "Ah, Mirabelle. She was the widow of Lord Harper, one of those splendid gentlemen who sit in your House of Lords and quietly fade away. They lived in Tunbridge Wells, and he died two years ago."

"The Lords are sometimes tortoises to the hares of the Commons." Auguste wondered what it was about Robert that made him so eager to defend England.

"Lord Harper rarely emerged from his shell," was Robert's retort.

"And what of your wife's life before her first marriage?"

"She rarely talked about it. She told me we had often met in Paris before her marriage when she was a singer, but I could not recall that, only that I came to know both her and her husband after their marriage. She came from Clermont-Ferrand, but no family members came to our wedding, only friends from her days in England. Perhaps she had no family left. She was a lady born, however, unlike Louise." His face twisted in pain. Another mask probably, Auguste thought. "I loved Mirabelle," Robert continued, "and someone has taken my wife from me. It may have been Louise, but you say not. So who else but Alice could have murdered my wife? As for Louise, if she did not take the poison herself, it must have been her husband. I would not be at all surprised to learn he came to the Petit Trianon that day. Louise was endangering his career by making scenes in public."

All Egbert replied was: "We'll look into it, sir." He seemed to be ready to leave, but Auguste was determined to have his own revenge.

"One last question, if you please, Robert. We have spoken of the past – of all but one person."

Robert laughed. "*Chère* Winifred? Ah, what skeletons lie in her cupboard, with her sturdy Englishness and oh, so respectable disapproving air of our gay Paris?"

"Not Winifred. Your wife, Hélène."

"Hélène has nothing to do with this. She is dead," he replied shortly.

"Would you mind talking of her?"

"I would – but if you insist, I will try. Hélène – you know of her great reputation as a singer and dancer, I presume? – did me the honour of accepting my hand, and we were happily married for five years."

"Forgive me, but how did she die?"

"Of consumption. She was not strong; she was a farmer's daughter, but had been delicate since birth. The hard work on the farm made her run away to Paris. The long hours necessary to establish herself on the stage – *without*, gentlemen, resorting to the means to which so many are forced – added to an already weak chest and brought about her death, despite all I could do. I was unimaginably stricken with grief, and I still do not care to talk about her."

"And then Louise returned to comfort you." Auguste tried hard not to sound sarcastic.

"Louise was very different to Hélène, and therefore she was indeed a comfort. Unfortunately she did her job only too well, and I married again for love. It was unfair to Louise not to warn her, but it was inevitable. Had we announced the wedding sooner, Louise would have found some way to prevent it."

"How?" Egbert asked baldly.

"There speaks one who did not know Louise."

"He did it, you mark my words." Egbert stirred his coffee vigorously as Auguste enthusiastically agreed. "I wonder what Edith makes of these cups? They're half the size of the ones my sister-in-law gave her children to put out for the fairies. Order me a tea next time."

The trees were already beginning to show the first signs of yellow, as they sat at a table outside the Flottille café in the gardens of Versailles, but the holidaying crowds were oblivious to these indications of approaching autumn. Parasols, sailor suits and muslin dresses made the spectacle a bright one, and difficult to reconcile with the horrors of 10 August. When they arrived at the Petit Trianon that too was crowded, for with the end of the police investigation it had been opened to the public once again to whom the recent murder on the lawn was apparently the chief attraction.

In the grand dining room, Auguste tried to recreate the scene for Egbert. "Robert was sitting at this end of the table, with His Majesty at the other. Mirabelle was on the King's left, and Winifred to his right. Robert had Alice on his left and Louise to his right, and the table had to be replanned to accommodate her. Pierre and Jacob faced one another in the middle."

"Then it would have been easy enough for Robert to drop something into Louise's food or drink."

"If he happened by chance to be carrying four grains of opium or several drachms of laudanum with him. But no one knew Louise was coming, except Bertrand Danielle."

"Who was, we can now assume, one of the footmen. He had opportunity enough."

"But even if he had reason enough to wish his wife out of the way, he had no reason to kill Mirabelle, and certainly not in that terrible way. If he had used poison for Louise, then he could have used the same, less risky, means for Mirabelle. I *still* believe it was Robert," Auguste said firmly, almost falling over a small sailor-suited child whose interest in pre-Revolutionary history had long since vanished, and who was sitting on the floor with a book of flicking pictures.

"If so, and she died around four o'clock, how did he rid himself of the blood? He was late arriving at Le Hameau, but not as late as some of the others."

"I have considered that," Auguste replied eagerly. "If it was done from behind, there might not have been a lot of blood on the clothes, certainly not on the lower garments. Robert was wearing dark clothes covered by a *cloak*. If he took that off before he carried out the murder, he had only to put it on again to disguise what blood there was. *And* he had a room available to him alone in the Petit Trianon – the Queen's bedchamber."

"Where Chesnais found nothing, when he searched. It's possible, though, especially as this must have been a pre-meditated crime if the same person killed both Louise and Mirabelle."

"*Eh bien*, we return to my earlier point. Why not poison both?"

"I reckon the poison was given to the wrong Marie Antoinette, and he had to act quickly."

"But no one could mistake the two women at close quarters, wig or no wig, even in the crowded boudoir where the coffee was served. Look, I will show you." Auguste led

Egbert through the drawing room and into the small boudoir. Auguste had a sudden inspiration, and continued, "Perhaps it *was* possible to confuse the two. The mirrors have been taken away now, but they were at right angles here. Suppose, looking at the mirror reflection in the crowded room, the murderer chose the wrong cup. Louise was on the left *here*, I believe, and Mirabelle on the right, with Jacob between them. Suppose, seeing only their reflections, Robert made a mistake?"

Egbert roared with laughter. "There you go again, Auguste. I thought your old boss Escoffier told you always to keep things simple. The minute you put your Sherlock Holmes hat on, you can't resist complicating things. In any case, even if he approached from behind and was looking at the reflection, he would realise the image was wrong, even if he couldn't see the faces. Mind you," Egbert added cheeringly, seeing Auguste's downcast expression, "this setting for the murder makes Bertrand Danielle a strong candidate. Not to mention most of the rest of the party, including Mirabelle herself."

By the time they arrived at Le Hameau, having walked round the entire route, Auguste was hot, tired and confused. He was also trying to convince himself that his failure to find the grotto was irrelevant to their present task. It had not been Mirabelle he had glimpsed there, nor Louise, nor Alice – it had been his imagination. He had come round to the back of the huge rock by the Rocher Bridge by mistake, and seen some movement that in his tense state he had misinterpreted.

Egbert by contrast was still keenly interested in everything around him, especially the dairy, the Queen's House and the Boudoir. Finally he said, "Didn't you mention some suggestion from George Ladyboys that the wager should be replayed?"

Auguste stared at him in horror. "Yes, but surely he could not have been serious?"

Egbert ruminated. "Why not? Let's have a word with him, shall we?"

"George." Robert's elegant eyebrows arched. "What can I say, save that I'm honoured to receive a visit?"

"You can say what you blasted well like, Robert," was the curt reply. "Winifred and I are off to London by the night train, and I want to settle a few outstanding matters first."

"Such as?"

"The wager."

"Do you know, George, I guessed you were going to ask me about that."

"I am aware," George continued stiffly, "that what happened last week makes the wager unimportant, but it's the form of the thing. It doesn't look good, it looks as if I'm backing out."

"Then what do you suggest? That I summon Auguste to demand whether he saw any ghosts?"

"I thought – you may not agree – that we should replay the whole afternoon at the Petit Trianon. No need to trouble His Majesty to attend, of course." George neatly removed the one objection Robert might raise, that His Majesty would not have the time to spare. It would help obscure his own movements that afternoon, to which there was no witness save himself. And, by Jove, a good thing too.

"You are quite mad, George," Robert replied icily. "Replay it, when my wife and my—"

"Mistress," George supplied as he stopped abruptly. "I know. The thing is – why not?"

"Because two deaths are quite sufficient."

"I'm not proposing to murder you, much as I'd like to," George assured him. "I merely want to get this damned bet settled to clear it off His Majesty's books."

"The plan is ridiculous."

"If you've got nothing to hide," George returned belligerently, "what is there against it?"

A short silence. "The pain to me, George. Had you considered that?"

"No. I think we both know the truth."

"Do we?" Robert asked drily. "I doubt that. Just suppose I were to agree to this charade, what reason do I give for appearing in public so soon after my wife's terrible death, and in the same place?"

"It's a private party," George pointed out.

"After that last time, the authorities are hardly likely to agree to exclude the public."

"I can arrange it," George said firmly. "I suggest Friday, the fifth of October."

"Well, well, could it be that you are still hoping to win this ridiculous wager, and believe ghosts are likely to appear because it's the anniversary of the last day in 1789 that Marie Antoinette spent at the Petit Trianon?"

"No, it could not. It has to do with the fact I'd like to know who murdered Louise, that's all," George said gruffly. "I was – er – fond of her. Suicide is one thing, but we both know she would never have killed herself. If you didn't and I didn't, who did? Or did you? Look on it as another wager, Robert, this time just between us. If you didn't do it, you've nothing to hide, and it could bring out the truth. If you did, you can't afford to raise everyone's suspicions by refusing to come. And everyone knows what I plan to do. I've told them."

Robert stared at him. "Maybe you're not so stupid as you look, George."

"I'm not," George said shortly.

*   *   *

"Is something worrying you, Pierre?" Alice had put on her pretty pink spotted voile gown with white satin ribbons and matching parasol. It was unlike Pierre not to notice. "It's not still that awful business of the murder?" she continued piteously. "You don't still suspect me, do you? I know I was silly, but I couldn't help it. I was so shocked. I just picked up the knife – I still have nightmares about it, Pierre. Think what the poor Queen must have suffered."

Pierre made a customary mental leap to follow her train of thought. "Forgive me, *mon petit chou*, I heard something disturbing from George."

"What?" Alice was instantly alarmed.

"He and Robert are going to re-stage that ghost business at the Petit Trianon in October to settle the wager."

Alice clasped her hands in glee. "But that's wonderful, darling."

Pierre stared at her in astonishment. "What's so wonderful about it?"

"We can all dress up again – I can play the Queen after all," his wife informed him happily.

"You don't think that's a little disrespectful to the victims?"

"Of course not. The Queen is my ancestress, she won't mind."

"I meant Mirabelle and Louise."

"Oh." Her face fell.

Pierre sighed. "I suppose we'll have to replay it just as last time or it won't be a fair wager." He had just begun to relax, with both Mirabelle and Louise out of his life for ever. True, they would not be there, but their absence might speak louder than their presence.

"So everything's all right, then." She pirouetted round, and the pink spotted voile floated delightfully around her ankles. "Pierre?" she asked uncertainly, when he did not reply.

"Not quite. George told me something else. Auguste has an inspector from Scotland Yard staying with him. He thinks it too much of a coincidence; they're still sniffing around. If they are there in October—"

He broke off, but Alice knew exactly what he was going to say.

"Darling, you're afraid they'll make me a scapegoat for their silly theories to prove that nice Inspector Chesnais wrong. That's what you were going to say, wasn't it?"

Pierre remained silent.

"Isn't it glorious to be travelling home to England?" Winifred snuggled beneath the travelling rug on the open deck of the Channel steamer. George was still groaning down below in their sleeping cabin, but Winifred could not wait to greet her home shores, and came on deck in the fresh morning air, where she found Jacob leaning pensively over the stern rail, staring into the water, as though contemplating whether to leap in and swim back to France.

"I like France," he replied shortly, then added, "usually, of course. I feel that I am a Frenchman born in the wrong place." This was a platitude that had once been the truth, born of his youthful student days. It was the place that had inspired his greatest art, and Hélène's death had immortalised Paris in his mind. He had even managed to romanticise Louise's rejection of him. A broken heart, after all, was all part of *la vie bohème*. It had all changed, however, when Mirabelle had told him she was to marry Robert, and he had suddenly recalled the mission that Hélène had laid upon him and which he had dutifully carried out.

"How nice." Winifred was at a loss as to how to answer Jacob's statement. It was not a sentiment with which she could sympathise. The mere mention of France resurrected that terrible feeling of sickness in her stomach which had nothing to do with *mal de mer* and everything to do with the news George had broken to her yesterday. "It won't be long before we're all back in France, will it?" she said valiantly. "Only a few weeks."

He stared at her. "What do you mean?"

"We're all meeting again, aren't we, at the Petit Trianon on the fifth of October?" Too late she remembered that George had been fretting because the letter he had written to Jacob had gone unacknowledged. George was set on this stupid second visit to the Petit Trianon, and seemed ridiculously determined that nothing should prevent it.

Jacob was ashen-faced. "What for?" he yelped.

"George and Robert have to settle the wager. George suspects they're still investigating the murders. Auguste has someone from Scotland Yard staying with him. So if they both come, we'll know that's so. George wrote to you to tell you." She paused. "You knew Louise when you were an art student, didn't you?"

"Yes," he replied shortly. "I knew them all. La Goulue, Louise, Mirabelle and Hélène."

"George said Louise treated you badly."

"George can take a running jump into that," Jacob said savagely, jerking his head towards the foaming water.

"She treated everyone badly," Winifred said hastily, distressed at her tactlessness. "George never knew her, but he knew of her, and told me about Pierre's poor brother Michel."

"I remember him." Jacob said with sudden interest. "He

was a photographer, a good one. You must have seen his work in Paris."

"I wasn't there."

"Oh. I thought George said he met you in France."

"Not in Paris," Winifred said reluctantly, wishing she had not spoken. "My parents lived in France, when they were going through difficult times; we left England because it was much cheaper to live abroad. I met George there; we married very quickly, and he brought me back to England." She must change the subject in case he demanded more details. Fortunately the ship began to turn, and England, dear England, was before her. "Oh look, Jacob, there are the white cliffs. Don't they look splendid? So *safe*."

Ten

Auguste walked through the green swing doors of the Domino Room of the Café Royal in London's Regent Street, pleased that Jacob had suggested it as a rendezvous. He had come here only once in the nineties, when Oscar Wilde, Toulouse-Lautrec, Beardsley and all the other flamboyant individualists of the artistic world had made it their home. In those days he had been on the 'wrong' side of society's green-baize door; he had been chef at Stockbery Towers in Kent, and then at the Galaxy Theatre in the Strand. Even when he had progressed to chef at Plum's Club for Gentlemen, his status was still classified as 'cook', for cuisine was not seen as an art form. In France it was viewed differently.

The Oscar Wilde set had faded away, and new faces were now forming a new coterie of whom Jacob was apparently one. It all looked much the same, however. Its gaudy gilded and heavily ornamented walls spoke of the Frenchman who had founded the Café Royal rather than traditional Victorian England, and the atmosphere round the bare tables set close together was of a French brasserie, rather than an English coffee house.

He saw Jacob sitting alone at a table. He had not yet noticed Auguste's arrival, and with his face relaxed he looked uncertain of himself as though he wobbled precariously between the roles of society gentleman and bohemian artist. Sometimes these were the same, often they were not, and Piccadilly, to which the Café Royal was close, catered for all ranks of society, from the ladies of the night who frequented Jimmy's for their custom to the crowned heads who entered the Ritz.

The Piccadilly Auguste loved was the circus itself, a rendez-vous for the world, where flower girls found a ready market to provide for lover's meetings and gentlemen's buttonholes, and where, if you stood watching, all London's daily life would parade past you, workers, leisured society, but also those on whom life weighed heavily. Unlike Paris, there were no rules here as to which days beggars could ply their trade.

As Auguste arrived at the table, Jacob glanced up, saw him, and his head resumed its usual cocksure confidence, as he snapped his fingers at the *garçon*.

"What can I tell you, Auguste? I must hurry – the President is expecting me at the Academy." He laughed self-consciously. "Completely falsely, I'm sure, it is said that a knighthood might be in the offing."

Auguste, who was always only too anxious to escape from court, could see little reason for anyone to wish to enter the establishment. That was life, however, sheep fought to get through the gate as another flock fought to get out.

"I hear," Jacob said, as coffee arrived, "we are all expected to meet again in October. Does this mean you are investigating the terrible deaths at the Petit Trianon further? I understand you had an inspector from Scotland Yard staying with you."

"The October gathering is to settle the wager," Auguste answered truthfully, if incompletely. In fact, Egbert was still in Paris, with other matters on his mind than His Majesty's interest in winning bets.

"To find some ghosts," Jacob said disgustedly. "If they've any sense they'll stay away. You saw none, did you?"

Auguste seized his chance. "I am not sure, because what followed confused the issue. As I told you, I thought I saw you embracing a Marie Antoinette. It could not have been Louise or Mirabelle. So was it Alice, or was it a ghost in which you claim you do not believe? And if Alice, what happened to her after you parted?"

"A gentleman," Jacob said loftily, "does not discuss such matters. Moreover, there is only your word that you saw anything at all, and you were expecting to see ghosts, were you not?"

"I was not *expecting* – I was an independent witness." Was there something in what Jacob said, Auguste wondered. Had the scare at the grotto clouded his reason? No, he rejected this. He *had* seen a Marie Antoinette there. "Was it Alice?" he asked eagerly.

Jacob made great play of drinking his coffee. "If you were to reconstruct everyone's precise movements in October, it could be embarrassing for one lady."

"It will be even more embarrassing for you, Jacob, if you do not tell me the whole story."

For Jacob self-survival was obviously good reason to speak out. "The lady is a little childish. She has a worthy husband, but not, shall we say, a romantic one. Moreover, he is considerably older than she. She was carried away with the excitement of the afternoon, she had dressed up as Marie Antoinette, but could not find her husband to preen her fine feathers. She needed someone to appreciate her undoubted charms, and an artist is always romantic." He leant back, so that his carefully arranged curls could assume their full quota of romanticism.

174

Auguste thought of the aged Rembrandt and of Toulouse-Lautrec, and begged to differ. "Where and when did you meet Alice that afternoon?"

"I found a *lady* crying, just after half past three I believe. Not long before you saw us. I – er – cheered her up, and said I would accompany her to Le Hameau. The *lady* is very pretty, and I decided the best way to console her properly was to embrace her. Also," he laughed self-consciously, "her husband is very rich and might commission her portrait should she ask him. One must be practical. Never be disrespectful of money. Only those who cannot obtain it are that."

Auguste tried to look duly impressed at this worldly wisdom, though it spoke too much of the shades of Oscar Wilde to convince him of Jacob's authorship. "And what happened after this embrace, Jacob? The *lady* was not at tea." Auguste obligingly joined in the charade.

"No. We felt we should not arrive together. The husband is apt to be possessive. She left just about four o'clock and I just after her. I expected to see her at tea, but she was not there."

"So she *could* have hurried back and killed Mirabelle during the tea period."

"It is possible," Jacob said doubtfully, "but it seems unlikely she would commit murder after embracing me."

"Why did you not tell the police about Alice?"

"I assumed the *lady* would do so if necessary." Jacob looked surprised. "Alice was not found with the body until an hour or so later. How could my kiss be relevant? Besides, I thought it was agreed that she did not commit the crime?"

Auguste ignored this. "And you yourself would have no alibi for the time between Alice's departure and your arrival at tea. I did not see you until nearly four thirty."

He flushed. "That is quite ridiculous. Why should I have murdered my beloved Mirabelle?"

"You wanted to marry her, and you threatened Robert to a duel," Auguste reminded him gently.

"If I loved her enough to want to marry her, then I would hardly cut her throat." Jacob raised his voice to the great interest of adjoining tables, and promptly lowered it again. "How about Louise? Do you think I killed her too? I am sure you have discovered that we were once lovers. That she pursued me and flattered me, and presented her body to me – and then when I was hooked, she laughed and cast me adrift. Not a pretty story."

"Louise was poisoned in the afternoon."

"Then His Majesty—"

"His Majesty has nothing to do with it," Auguste interrupted hastily. "She was probably poisoned at luncheon or afterwords at coffee, when she was sitting at your side."

Unexpectedly Jacob laughed. "A busy afternoon, I poisoned one lady, cut the throat of a second, and seduced – oh God." He broke off, and put his head in his hands. "I loved them *both*," he said vehemently. "I feel nothing for Alice, and everything for them."

"So will you help me find their murderer by telling me about Mirabelle's past life?"

"Mirabelle?" His head jerked up warily. "I only met her when she was a singer at the Jardin with Hélène, and again at Hélène's funeral. By that time she was married and had changed her name to Mirabelle. Then I lost touch with her until I was commissioned to paint her by Lord Harper. I was drawn to her for she had something of Hélène Mai's quality, though she was tougher, not so refined as Hélène. Hélène was all spirit, all selflessness, all fragility. Mirabelle was – as you observed – more worldly minded. But there was something about the way she moved and looked that reminded me of Hélène, and it was a good portrait. Mirabelle was pleased, and when Lord Harper died I called upon her to offer my condolences. Within the limits of mourning, I accompanied her to events in London, and visited her in Tunbridge Wells. I grew to admire her greatly, and then to love her. It was agreed that after her mourning was over, we should marry."

It was no tale of passion, but it had the ring of truth, though that, as Auguste knew full well, did not mean it was *all* the truth, and he noticed that Jacob's nervousness had returned despite his smooth recital of facts.

"You knew Robert in your student days too, then."

"Yes," Jacob said shortly. "Mirabelle resented it when he married Hélène and not her. Once again she was second-best, and that she did not like."

"Robert said he could not recall meeting her before her marriage."

"Dear Robert cannot always be relied upon," Jacob said wryly. His eyes shifted as he added suddenly, "I regret that the same was true of Mirabelle. She had some odd ways, Auguste. I disregarded them, as lovers will, but after she announced she was to marry Robert, I began to recall them. I regretted—" he broke off.

"Regretted—?" Auguste prompted him.

"Painting her so much," Jacob finished, but Auguste had the impression that that was not what he had intended to say. "And there was the matter of her maid. She was French, and had been with Mirabelle many years. When Mirabelle decided to marry Robert she was dismissed without a pension and without notice. She was informed she was getting too old for her job, and that the count did not want her to accompany Mirabelle to France."

"Why should he be concerned? That's very strange."

"I thought it so. As I could see no reason for Robert having a view on Suzanne one way or the other, it might have been Mirabelle's sole decision."

"What has happened to Suzanne? Did she return to France?"

"She is still in England. Although Mirabelle had declared her intentions of marrying Robert in June, I still did not believe her. Seeing the announcement of Mirabelle's sudden marriage in *The Times*, I – er – found myself in Tunbridge Wells and naturally went to enquire what her plans were. I found Suzanne there, all too pleased to pour out her story."

"And is she still at the house now?"

"She had been told in June to leave within the month, but someone may know. Enquire at High Lea Court."

"Thank you." This was an unexpected path through the jungle, and he would go tomorrow.

Jacob rose to leave, and recalled the grandeur of being an artist. "Until October then, Auguste. I trust by then you will have discovered the truth about these murders, and that I am innocent of your deep suspicions. Artists are observers, not precipitators of man's behaviour."

Auguste watched him retreat, as he finished his own coffee. There were exceptions to every lofty statement. Christopher Marlowe came to mind, J. Wilkes Booth, Vincent van Gogh. Not all creative artists confined their passions to their art.

I shall drive you to Tunbridge Wells," Tatiana graciously offered. "And you may drive back." This was a concession on her part, since her enthusiasm for driving was much greater than her wish to be a passenger. Auguste had learnt to drive the Leon Bollée, but had had little chance of practising his skill. Nevertheless, Tatiana was convinced that the greatest honour she could accord him was to allow him his turn at the steering wheel.

Tunbridge Wells was a sufficient distance from London to make the prospect of the journey exciting. Fortunately, Auguste reminded himself, there was an excellent rail service there, and if the engine overheated, or the dust blew into a desert sandstorm, or punctures were unduly numerous, there would be rescue at hand.

Ladies' fashions in motoring attire were becoming less extreme, and all-enveloping armour against dust was no longer considered essential before stepping into a motor car. Tatiana had compromised with a light summer hat and tied veil, he and Mrs Jolly had packed a superb picnic, and the sun was shining. Auguste was no great enthusiast of eating on the grass when restaurants were available, but Tatiana, deprived of such opportunities during her childhood, was addicted to it. The picnic was designed to be of maximum attraction to Auguste and a minimum magnet to wasps, and Mrs Jolly's pies were ideal for the task.

It did not prove difficult to find Suzanne. She was living in a cottage in the village of Frant having, with the practicality of the French, preferred marriage to starvation. The once scorned attentions of a local milkman had been hastily re-sought and accepted, and she had been married within the month.

"It is better than the workhouse," Suzanne said, shrugging, when they found the small red-brick cottage. "And marriage is not so bad, if it is all that is open to you. I asked him if this place was rented, for he will not work for ever, and it is owned by him. A roof over one's head is better than one underground in the grave."

Perhaps she had been listening to Oscar Wilde too, Auguste thought, as he glanced round the cottage's one living room, with its familiar ovens each side of the fire, the old iron saucepans and the clutter of everyday life.

"You were treated badly by your former mistress, weren't you, madame?"

"Like *merde*, monsieur." All pretensions to being the newly wedded mistress of her own household suddenly vanished. "I had been with Madame Mirabelle for sixteen years."

Auguste's hopes rose. "You worked for her family in Clermont Ferrand?"

"*Non*. I met her in Paris when she was a slip of a girl at nineteen."

"Her family was in Paris?"

"She had no family. She had lodgings – smaller than this rabbit hutch," she said disparagingly of her new home. "She sang at a *café-concert*. By the time she arrived they were becoming more respectable, and because she looked like a lady she was taken on at the Jardin de Paris. She was a singer, not in the first rank, but she sang well enough with her looks."

"She came from a good family?"

"What is good?" Suzanne shrugged again. "She had enough when she came to pay her rent, and she was educated. I felt sorry for her. She was an orphan, she told me, but later she let slip something that made me think she was lying. I told her so, and she confessed she had quarrelled with her family and come to Paris to make her own way, and not by the streets. She was very determined. I worried over her as if she were my own child, and she treats me like this. She is hard, monsieur."

"I am afraid she is dead, madame." Obviously Suzanne did not bother with English newspapers.

"Dead?" She gave a heart-rending cry. "She was ill? That was what made her treat me thus? She said she was going to be married."

"She did marry, and a week later someone killed her."

"Killed?" she shrieked. "Monsieur, this must be wrong. Who would want to kill her? Her husband, it must be the husband. He wanted Madame Mirabelle's money, no doubt."

"She was rich?"

"I assume so, monsieur. Lord Harper married twice. There is a son who would inherit his property, but my lady always spoke of his lordship as a rich man. He was a kind gentleman and would have made provision for her, I am sure."

"She had no money of her own?"

"At first no, but she gradually became more generous to me, and more extravagant in her gowns and habits. Lord Harper liked to live simply. Madame did not, and after he died she lived well. Tell me whom she married. Mr Jacob?" she asked hopefully.

"No. It was the Comte de Tourville."

"I knew it," she cried. "I warned her. She even told me herself there were rumours that he killed his first wife."

"Was he a friend of long standing?" Auguste's excitement grew. His half-formed suspicions had some basis. When he told Egbert about this . . .

"Of course," Suzanne snapped impatiently. "Even in the old days when she was a singer. I was not her maid then, but her landlady. I went with her to the Jardin to look after her, for Paris is not a good city for *jeunes filles* on their own. When the count began to come to the Jardin, she set her cap at him. She was determined to marry him, and he was attracted, one could see that. Roses, chocolates, dinners – and she behaved like a lady, for she wanted to marry him. Then it all stopped.

Hélène Mai was singing at the Jardin by then. When the count told her he was getting married, madame thought it was to someone of his own station – and that she could have borne. When she discovered it was Hélène, she was beside herself with anger. Hélène was a talented singer and dancer, much better than madame, and madame knew it. To have the count marry her was more than she could bear.

"She was clever, however, she made herself Hélène's friend so that she could continue to see Robert, even after madame decided to marry Lord Harper and come to England. I came with her and I have looked after her ever since."

"The count says he only recalls Mirabelle after her marriage to Lord Harper."

"Then he has a poor memory When Lord Harper died, I thought she might marry the count, since he had not married again after Madame Hélène's death. But my poor mistress was thwarted once more, for he had a mistress, La Dervicheuse – you may have heard of her? – and he was devoted to her. We continued to visit France and she would see the count from time to time, but there was no talk of marriage. So I am surprised – and yet not surprised – to hear she married him."

"La Dervicheuse was murdered at the same time as your mistress."

"Both?" She slapped her knees in triumph. "Then you may be sure, monsieur, that the count is responsible. Madame doubtless had some hold over him; she enjoyed that. It was not malicious, but if she discovered someone's hidden secret, she would make it her business when she met them in society to let them know she was aware of their failings."

"A blackmailer?" Auguste asked. If so, many avenues would suddenly open before him.

"Not for money. For power only, to make herself important.

Although I did think that could have been the source of her extra money, before Lord Harper died. Were she alive, I would not say so. But now . . ."

"Could she have obtained money from the count that way?" Auguste held his breath.

"He would not have married her, had that been so."

"If his money had run out and marriage was her price?"

"It may have been so. Poor madame. And now she is dead."

"Do you believe she is right that the count murdered Mirabelle, Tatiana?" Auguste asked some time later in the middle of their picnic by the gigantic stones of High Rocks, which reminded him of the forest of Barbizon at Fontainebleau.

"Probably."

"Why?"

"Because, my dear Sherlock, you are paying no attention to Mrs Jolly's rabbit pie which has a most interesting flavour of tarragon. I therefore deduce that you are seriously considering the theory, and therefore that Suzanne is probably right."

Auguste hastily took another slice of pie. "I will give my full attention to my job of master chef."

"I have allowed you to visit me again, Inspector Rose," said Bertrand Danielle, fingertips pressed neatly together, "having considered the matter very carefully. Justice must be done."

Egbert waited. In his experience, when witnesses invoked justice, they had an axe to grind. Whatever the reason, the chance to talk to Danielle again was to be seized, but treated with caution. He had been surprised at Danielle's readiness to see him. There wasn't much more he could do in Paris. Edith was fretting for the certainties of home, for she was not enjoying staying in Tatiana's house without her and Auguste. Footmen glided in and out, treating them like royalty, but it wasn't the same. For a start, none of the servants spoke much English which meant they were on their own when wondering what they were eating. Edith had landed up eating calves' brains yesterday, all because the footmen knew the English for *veau* but not *cervelles*. Egbart had looked it up in the dictionary this morning and decided not to tell her. Mr Pinpole, their Highbury butcher, never sold *cervelles*, or not to Edith, anyway.

"I am told by Monsieur Ladyboys," Danielle said carefully. "that there is to be a gathering in October to settle the wager in which my poor Louise was involved."

"That's correct."

"I also understand that it is possible you may be present."

"That's correct also. It depends how far we've got by then."

"In fact, if everyone is forced to dress up once again, it may prove to be what one might call a reconstruction of the events of the tenth of August. It would thus assist you in your investigation of the crimes, as well as encouraging the ghosts, to settle the wager for Monsieur Ladyboys and the Comte de Tourville."

"Right again, sir. It may stir up memories."

"Will His Majesty be present?"

"He'll be informed, naturally, but I doubt if he'll attend. He'll be home from his annual cure by then, and up at Balmoral."

"That I know. Biarritz no longer has attractions for the King of England. Marienbad is the preferred location. And doubtless not only for its waters. It is convenient for a visit to Kronberg, is it not?"

"That I can't say, sir."

"That's what the French parliament does say."

Egbert decided to avoid politics. "Why were you so willing to see me, sir?"

"I am determined that my wife's killer shall be found. I presume you have definitely decided that she is innocent – as I always believed – of the murder of the comtesse, and I would like any news you have of your findings. I have therefore decided to explain my role at the Petit Trianon more fully, in the interests of your investigation. I have also decided to repeat that role on the fifth of October."

"Really, sir?" This was better than he could have hoped for, but he'd tread cautiously.

"When I learned of Louise's plans to cause trouble at the Petit Trianon, after Robert's wedding, I decided, as you so astutely deduced, that with His Majesty present, my reputation could be at stake. She was in a strange mood; it had been made clear she was not welcome, for obvious reasons, yet she insisted on going. I therefore quickly devised a plan of my own. She had told me what the roles in the ghost hunt were, and we laughed together over the costumes George had specified for them. Details of these arrived before Louise's invitation had been withdrawn, and I saw it would be easy to play one of the guards. That would allow me freedom in the grounds and, as for the house – I have observed the duties of servants myself, and thought them easy enough to copy for an hour or two."

Egbert was glad of Auguste's absence.

"I made careful enquiries," Danielle continued, "from our own servants as to how such dinners would be served, and learned it was customary for there to be a spare livery available in case of food or wine being spilled on one of the footmen. It was simple to persuade Robert's servants that I had been

185

sent by Monsieur Didier to assist, and to persuade Pierre and Madame Didier that Auguste had sent me to play the second guard."

"I'm interested in what you saw and what you did after Auguste had passed by you in the gardens, sir."

"At luncheon" – Bertrand continued at his own pace as though Egbert had not spoken – "I merely observed what was going on. Fortunately nothing. Nor did I notice anything being added to Louise's wine. However, I would not necessarily have done so, for the life of a footman serving at table is not, I discovered, an entirely stationary one. As soon as coffee was served, I retired to one of the unused rooms on the upper floor, and changed into the guard's costume. As for the afternoon, once Monsieur Didier had passed me, I decided to find Louise as quickly as possible. I had learnt of her decision not to fight with Mirabelle over the role of Marie Antoinette from Pierre, and was horrified to be told that she had gone alone to Le Hameau with His Majesty. What harm, I asked myself, might she be doing to my reputation in his eyes? It had to be thought of. A word from him to the President or the Prime Minister and my future might be jeopardised."

Privately Egbert reflected that if he knew the King, Danielle's future prospects would be enhanced by Louise's intimate attentions, but no doubt her husband viewed the matter differently.

"I rushed back to the house by the lane and the avenue des Deux Trianons," Bertrand continued, "then into the house by the main door in order to change back into livery. I then hurried down to the kitchens to resume my role. I regret my colleagues were not impressed by the standard of service from Mr Didier's footman." It was the nearest thing to a smile, Egbert had seen on his face. "I went to Le Hameau in the horse wagon with the other footmen, ready to serve tea, and had just begun to do so, when I realised that Louise was missing. Where was she? Surely, I even wondered, she could not be challenging Mirabelle after all? I ran back to the English Garden to seek her, but there was no sign of Louise. Mirabelle was, however, alive. I ran into the house by the north front steps, up to the first floor, entirely forgetting my servile role, and then made my way down the main staircase to go to the kitchens in search of a pretext for returning to Le Hameau, where I would need to explain my absence. When I still could not find Louise, I assumed she must have returned to our home and later, after I had finished my work at Le Hameau, about a quarter to five, I did the same. My chauffeur and motor car were waiting outside Versailles."

"So what can you add to our knowledge of the murders, sir? Can you tell me who did them?"

"No, Inspector, but I can tell you who did not." His mouth twisted wryly. "I am not a great admirer of his, but I respect the truth. I had left Mirabelle alive in the garden, and I reached the kitchen of the Petit Trianon at about four o'clock, where I met someone coming out carrying a large washing tub with a cake inside. He told me to take it to his motor car in the Petit Trianon courtyard. I did so. He cranked the motor car and drove off at great speed to Le Hameau. I watched him turn the corner. Naturally he did not recognise a mere footman but I knew him, of course. It was Robert."

"Egbert!"

Auguste's voice came over the crackling telephone line as an excited squawk. "I have great news for you. We are right about Robert. I'm sure these murders are something to do with his first wife."

"Auguste—"

"Mirabelle was a blackmailer."

"Auguste—" Egbert barked again but was disregarded.

"There were rumours he killed Hélène. I was sure the answer lay in the past. Suppose Mirabelle had proof—"

"Auguste!" Egbert shouted in desperation, and this time was heeded.

"Yes, Egbert?"

"You'd better starting thinking hard about that banquet you'll be cooking me. The answer doesn't lie in the past – not so far as Robert is concerned, anyway. His arch enemy Danielle has given him an alibi. He's in the clear, more's the pity."

Eleven

"*Non*, Mrs Jolly, there I do not agree," Auguste said happily. "The best omelette deserves the finest garnish. There is nothing to beat Monsieur Escoffier's Omelette Maxim, with crayfish tails and truffles, surrounded by frogs' legs dipped in flour and sautéed in butter."

"To my mind, sir, there's nothing to beat a nice plain omelette with one or two marrow flowers added." Mrs Jolly, while never quite entering into the full spirit of the game, was quite willing to enter into such debates if it pleased the master. It never changed her mind, but sometimes it did his.

"Ah." Auguste looked anxious. "It is true that the *maître* preferred simplicity to complication. I wonder whether you could be right? Were an omelette a pie, I would most certainly not disagree with you, for your gifts reign supreme in pastry." It cost him a lot to admit this. "Save perhaps," he added, "in a raised rabbit pie. So over this omelette let us compromise. I concede that were you to add a delicate tomato sauce—" He broke off, astonished to see Tatiana hurrying into the kitchen. "Ah, my love. Come and give us your opinion on the question of omelettes."

Tatiana sounded – and looked – very annoyed he belatedly realised. "Isn't there something you've forgotten?" she asked crossly.

"I don't think so." Auguste was worried. "The argument seems quite clear. Marrow-flower omelette and simplicity versus—"

"How about a very angry chef waiting at the club for a non-appearing *maître*?"

Auguste was appalled. "But Thursday is not one of my days to attend." He usually supervised the kitchen of Tatiana's Ladies Motoring Club in Petty France on Wednesdays and Saturdays.

"This is Wednesday."

An anguished yelp from Auguste. "I was misled by the meat delivery, which arrived early. My love, I will go immediately. Mrs Jolly, I leave it to you to serve whichever omelette you like."

"Yes, sir." Mrs Jolly had no intention of doing anything else. Marrow flowers were no longer in season, but potatoes were, and an *omelette parmentier* fitted the menu nicely.

Auguste was already halfway through the tradesmen's door when Tatiana stopped him. "I've a message for you, Auguste. From the palace."

The dreaded word – palace. "I saw Her Majesty this afternoon." That, Auguste *had* remembered, especially since it posed no problems for him. What he was anxious to avoid at all costs was a meeting with Bertie. He had calculated the King would have only a day or two between his return from Marienbad today, his visit to the Doncaster races, and his leaving for Scotland, and was unlikely to have the time to devote them to Auguste. It was now the tenth of September and frustratingly little progress had been made in the Trianon affair. There was much dough of interesting background information but little in the way of golden-brown pastry, and the longer Auguste could delay imparting this to His Majesty the better.

Preferably after his return from Balmoral in mid-October, by which time the Trianon reconstruction might have baked a few pies for Bertie's consumption.

"There was a message from Bertie." Tatiana delivered the death knell.

"Did he have a pleasant stay in Marienbad?"

"Not very. The cure behaved well but the press photographers didn't. It wasn't the best of holidays. Before he went, the Kaiser marched him round a Roman fort he'd recently restored, and insisted on dressing up in the uniform of the Posen Mounted Jäger. The Kaiser then told Bertie he took a dim view of his not staying for the christening of his son, whereupon Caesar promptly bit him. And finally, when he reached Marienbad, Lady Campbell-Bannerman, the Prime Minister's wife, died and there had to be a memorial service. He's not happy."

Auguste's heart sank even further when Tatiana added, "He wants you to dine with him at the Carlton tomorrow night."

The worst of all possible worlds, but even Voltaire's *Candide* could not have envisaged anything so terrible as this.

Normally a dinner at the Carlton Hotel, where his old master Auguste Escoffier reigned supreme, was something to be savoured, relished and enjoyed. Not tonight. A private room with John Sweeney outside the door, and Bertie inside it, did not bode well for peaceful gastronomy. True, Bertie would not sully his own digestion by discussing controversial matters with Escoffier's food before him, but it did mean that Auguste's *filets de soles marinette, selle de veau à la Tosca*, and *pêches Melba* could not be enjoyed to the full, with a sword of Damocles about to fall at Bertie's pleasure.

Bertie's preference was always champagne to red wine,

but Auguste was under few illusions that the Veuve Clicquot signified that he had been summoned for a celebration of His Majesty's release from his annual cure. The appearance of Bertie's usual choice of excellent brandy after dinner was the signal for ordeal by Bertie to begin. His Majesty cleared his throat, and sat back in his chair – a somewhat easier matter after his recent slimming diet.

"I expect you're wondering why I invited you here?"

"Yes, sir." There must be a thousand people Bertie could have chosen in preference to himself, to indulge in Escoffier's finest cuisine.

"I've been thinking about that dreadful business at the Trianon. I gather from George that the wager is to be settled after a repeat performance of your ghost-hunting walk in October, and that you'll be there. Correct?"

"Yes, sir."

"I won't be," Bertie declared. "Not because I wouldn't see it as my duty," he added hastily, "to stand by old friends, but I'll still be in Scotland. It's not fair to Her Majesty to abandon her there."

This was an unusual argument for Bertie, Auguste reflected, as he murmured agreement.

"So I rely on you to spot a few ghosts. I've got fifty pounds resting on it."

So far so good, Auguste thought, though there might be a few problems if the phantoms failed to oblige the monarch's request.

"Now it seems to me, knowing you and that Scotland Yard fellow, that you may well have other ideas in mind, such as settling once and for all who carried out the murder. Or murders. I hear you've a *Hamlet* gambit in mind, hoping that re-enacting it will make the murderer confess." After this unusual burst of cultural knowledge, Bertie sipped his brandy complacently and waited for Auguste, who took a deep breath, a sip of his own brandy, and plunged in.

"Yes, sir. If, for example, on the walk through the gardens, I meet someone whom I did not see before, that could well be significant. And we have made progress in confirming that Robert could have had nothing to do with the crime, for his movements are corroborated by Monsieur Danielle."

"Louise's husband? What the devil do you mean? How could he know what went on?" Bertie's face went white.

"He has admitted he was there in disguise as a footman."

"Sure you haven't had too much champagne, Auguste? Better have more brandy – might clear your head."

Auguste doubted this very much, but fear was performing the same function as he explained Bertrand Danielle's role and motive.

Bertie listened attentively. "Do you think he did it? It sounds a damned queer thing to do otherwise."

"It is possible, sir, but his willingness to clear Robert seems equally strange if so."

"Then I'm glad I decided to see you, Auguste. For a man to man discussion. I've recalled a little more about that afternoon." His expression dared Auguste to display any disbelief in this unlikely statement. "Not that it has anything to do with the murder, but it's best to have it in the open. *Strictly* between us."

Wild fantasies began to race through Auguste's mind of Bertie stealing round to the lawns to murder Mirabelle at Louise's request, and he hastily disciplined himself to listen.

"I told you Louise was tired that afternoon and I suggested she lay down in the Queen's cottage. That was more or less true," Bertie said airily. "Now, none of this is to go further than these four walls, not even to your Scotland Yard fellow. It had to be you, unfortunately," he added ingenuously. "I couldn't very well tell Tati.

"Now, as an old friend, Louise naturally wanted to chat about the old days. She explained she hadn't really wanted to cause trouble by coming along in that Marie Antoinette costume, and that she had agreed to Robert's suggestion that having made her point, she should keep out of the way and not spoil Mirabelle's day." This was sounding very unlike the Louise Auguste had met, but he kept silent. "I – er – told Sweeney to wait in the Daimler, because I wanted a private – um – talk with Louise. She was still a damned attractive woman, even if troublesome. She came with me in the motor car to Le Hameau, but once there, she fell into a funny mood, and couldn't stop talking about Mirabelle, and how although everyone thought she, Louise, was beyond the pale, she would never stoop to the depths that woman did. She was still furious about her having married Robert, and announced that given half a chance she'd murder the bitch. Naturally, I didn't take her seriously. Anyway, as I said, she was an attractive woman, and she recalled a certain – er – night many years ago, and suggested we – er – relive it. Now," Bertie glared as Auguste sat appalled at such a direct confession, "this is even more strictly between us or I'll have your head off on Tower Green."

"I understand, sir." Was he going to be escorted into His Majesty's very bedroom?

"I'm not the man I was in that regard. It's like food – sometimes you gobble up everything that's there, but as the years go on you get more discriminating and stick to familiar dishes. Do you follow me?"

"I do, sir."

"Besides, after a heavy lunch isn't the best time. A siesta is better for the digestion. As you know, however, I don't like to offend ladies, so I suggested we took our siesta together and – shall we say – take it from there, but not very far. You understand?"

"Yes, sir." Auguste's reply was almost a bleat.

"Louise said she was tired herself and that was a good idea, so we went into the Queen's cottage – the large house, not the small Boudoir where she was eventually found. I decided the salon was best. I didn't want to get caught in a bedroom if the servants arrived early. I left my bowler and stick outside the door as usual to signify I wasn't to be disturbed, and in we went. Well, Louise suddenly became a different woman. You've never seen anything like it. Reliving her youth, I suppose. She whipped off her drawers and started doing the can-can for me, kicking her legs up and shouting out the old tune. I was glad Sweeney was out of earshot, he'd have been in like a flash. I don't mind telling you I've never been so embarrassed in my life. After all, we weren't twenty any more. Then she announced she was going to strip off all her clothes, ripped off her skirt, and started on the petticoats. I could see she meant it, and I could find myself in a fine pickle. I'd had in mind a little light dalliance, not a full-blooded orgy."

"What did you do, sir?" Auguste was agog.

"I ordered her to put her clothes back on, rushed back for my bowler and stick, and hurried out into the open air. I needed it."

"And what happened to Louise?"

"Before I could reach Sweeney and the car, Louise came out after me, respectably dressed – on the outside at least," he added, "but still dancing away to some music inside her head, la-la-la-ing, and doing the can-can round some of the

---

cottages. I stayed where I was, in case she followed me and Sweeney saw what was going on. She'd dance into the mill or a cottage, then rush out shouting 'Boo to you, Wales!' I was waiting for a chance to make a dash for it, but suddenly she tired again. I told her to go and have a nap in the Queen's cottage and, as soon as she agreed and started to walk back there, I hurried out to find Sweeney to return post haste to the château. Then I could see the first signs of tea arriving by wagon, so I – um – came back for it. Even Louise wouldn't take her clothes off before the servants. When I returned, there was no sign of Louise, and I assumed she was in the cottage asleep. You can see why it was embarrassing to tell anyone, can't you?"

"Of course, sire, the symptoms you describe are the early signs of opium poisoning, but if the euphoria returned, it is still possible she could have carried out her threat to murder Mirabelle. We think she was given the opium at or just after luncheon."

There was a silence. "I meant embarrassing to me personally," Bertie muttered, "but I see your point."

"I understand, sir," Auguste said hastily. "Did you tell Louise you were going to leave?" he enquired. "It's possible she saw her chance to take her revenge."

Bertie frowned. "I may have done. In fact I think I did. I thought it might keep her calmed down. Odd. You mean Louise could have murdered Mirabelle not knowing that Mirabelle had already murdered her?"

Auguste regarded His Majesty with great respect. That thought had never occurred to him. "I think, sir, that you would be quicker than I in solving this murder."

"No, thank you," rumbled His Majesty. "Balmoral is quite enough excitement for me." It was almost a joke, and Auguste took advantage of the relaxation of tension to remember his own message for Bertie.

"I saw La Goulue while I was in Paris. You remember her? She asked me to give you her good wishes."

Gone was the sudden benevolence. "Remember her? I could hardly forget. Damned presumption. She yelled out to me as though I were some stage-door johnnie. In *public*. At least Louise had the sense never to do that."

"She is paying for her lack of wisdom. She is very poor and near, I would say, to death with drink."

Bertie stared at the last few sips of brandy in his glass. "I'll see something's done."

"Thank you, sir."

"One has a duty to one's past."

"But you, sir, bring compassion too."

"How was the evening?" Tatiana asked at breakfast next morning.

Auguste had returned late, and had barely managed to reach their bed before falling asleep. "Bertie's not so bad, after all." He began to open his post.

Tatiana laughed. "I shall remember those words. What did he have to say?"

She never received a reply. Auguste was too busy staring at the contents of an envelope with a French stamp and a typewritten address. It was a postcard; on one side it was blank, on the other side was the photograph of a lady — though that word might be disputed given the pose and lack of dress. Moreover, it was a lady whom he thought he recognised.

The Whitehall Café, close to Scotland Yard, did not provide

the same ambience as the Carlton, nor the same cuisine, but it was convenient and Egbert was in a hurry.

Auguste was battling with a pie that Mrs Jolly would have used as a doorstop and Egbert fared little better with his steak and kidney pudding. He had blushed when Auguste's accusing eye fell on him as he ordered 'the usual'. Fortunately Egbert did not obey the same rules as Bertie about not talking shop during a meal, but their circumstances were somewhat different.

"I wanted to see you because I've had some information from Chesnais, Auguste. It's a line you suggested the Sûreté should follow up. I know that the count has an alibi, but it's interesting all the same. You told me there were rumours about Hélène Mai's death, and I made a few enquiries. If that's so, there was no public or police suspicion of it. The death certificate gave consumption as the cause of death as the countess had undeniably been ill and had, rightly or wrongly, spent some weeks in a sanatorium. No eyebrows were raised when she died. Chesnais is thorough though, and it turns out that Hélène Mai was a very wealthy lady, not a poor little singer marrying for position and money. In fact, the count was on his beam ends when they married."

"Hélène must have saved the money from her singing?"

"No. It was inherited money. She came from a Breton farm, yes, but apparently it's a famous one. You may have heard of it. The Ferme de la Paix in Deauville."

"*Quoi?*"

The abysmal pie was forgotten. *Everyone* must have heard of the Ferme de la Paix. It was not a farm, but a hotel which had been in the same family for a hundred years. The building had started life as a farmhouse, but now bore little resemblance to it. The outside had been restored to resemble a rustic farm, but the inside was furnished luxuriously, and the cuisine all but faultless. To anyone other than an Auguste Didier, it *was* faultless.

"It seems that Hélène Mai was actually Hélène Juillet, the heiress to the entire place. She wanted to sing, the family disapproved, so she went off to prove herself. She wanted to earn her own money, so she ran away to Paris, where I gather she made quite a name for herself. Not long before the count married her, Monsieur Juillet died and Hélène inherited the lot – apart from provision for her mother. She put the hotel into the management of her cousin Philippe and when Hélène died, Robert sold the place to him for a fortune."

"But that's strange," Auguste said, attention momentarily diverted by the arrival of a chocolate pudding. "Robert was in financial difficulties, so it was said, when he married Mirabelle."

"Hardly surprising, if he spent money all the time as he did at the Trianon. It's interesting information though, and might well confirm that Mirabelle was a blackmailer, as you were told. She could well have tried her skills on Robert, but I wonder who else she practised on?"

"This chocolate pudding is not at all bad." Auguste was momentarily deflected. "There is an interesting flavour to the sauce."

"I'll get Edith to make you a chocolate pudding if you're so keen on them."

Visions of the heavy dark lump that might emerge from her hand, despite her loving anxiety to please, rose before Auguste's eyes. "How kind," he managed to say, before passing hastily on. "I brought this to show you." He handed the postcard that had arrived that morning to Egbert, who nearly choked as he glanced at it.

"Does Tatiana know you go in for this sort of stuff?"

"It is not *mine*," August retorted firmly. "It came to me by post and anonymously, and it bore a French stamp. Who does she remind you of?"

Egbert looked at it closely. "You'll get me arrested for pornography if I'm seen with this. I don't know the faces of our chums as well as you do, but with that figure – not that I've had the pleasure of seeing her with only a flash of gauze for clothes, and she's put on even more weight, I'd say from memory it's—"

"Winifred," Auguste finished for him.

Egbert looked at it again. "She's a lady, Auguste. It can't be her."

"Then why was it sent to me?"

"Perhaps you told someone you were starting a collection."

"There was a craze for these postcards in the middle to late nineties, and films too. Especially in France. I wonder if Winifred was there then?"

"How do you know so much about it?" Egbert joked.

"I was working at Plum's Club for Gentlemen," Auguste replied with dignity. "Gentlemen sometimes use the privacy of their club to regale each other with tales of naughty Paris, and to display their trophies."

"I wouldn't know," Egbert grunted.

"If this is Winifred, she'd most certainly be vulnerable when she married so respectably."

"Perhaps George Ladyboys has reason to worry too. He indulged in the life of Gay Paree too, after all. Anyway, if this hasn't come from one of your lady friends to get you in trouble with Tatiana, what is it for?"

"To show that others had something to hide. I suspect Robert or Bertrand Danielle sent it."

"Or the photographer. Has that occurred to you? Pierre

Gaston, for example. Perhaps his early career needs looking into."

"If it does, *mon ami*," Auguste pointed out, "he would be
the last person to send this postcard."

"Back to the past again, are you?"

"Yes. I'm going to win that wager, Egbert."

"I wouldn't be too sure of that, Auguste. I've a great fancy
for one of your meals."

Winifred watched George anxiously as he sat in his favourite
armchair placidly reading *The Times*. Tomorrow they would
be leaving for France again. She had congratulated herself on a
narrow escape from the last visit there, and now that the second
loomed so close her fears redoubled. If it was only to settle the
wager, she could bear that, but there were the two murders and
that Scotland Yard Inspector and that nice Auguste poking and
prying into the past. George had been in a very odd mood since
they returned from Paris, and this worried her greatly.

"George, we are happy, aren't we?"

George stopped in the middle of the Court Circular and
wondered what the deuce had made Winifred ask such a
question. He hadn't really thought about their marriage in
those terms. Now he did consider it, embarrassing though it
was, since she was looking very anxious.

"Yes, old girl. We are."

Winifred breathed a huge sigh of relief. It was worth
fighting on. So far she had escaped exposure, and she might
yet continue to do so.

"I suppose," she asked tentatively, "we couldn't say that the
wager's off and stay here? After all, we don't really need the
money and—"

"You feeling quite well, are you, Winnie? I've already

explained I can't, and what's more, Bertie has asked Auguste to find out what really happened that day. We have a duty to go."

"Have we, George?" It came out almost as a moan.

"Of course we have. We're British, aren't we? Don't worry, old girl. You'll enjoy it when we get there."

Winifred moaned outright this time, rose hastily from the luncheon table and fled to the sanctuary of the bathroom. George stared after her in disquiet, reflecting that it must be true that a woman went crazy in her middle years.

Alice danced with happiness. Only two more days to wait and then she could play Marie Antoinette. It was a pity His Majesty wouldn't be there to see her, but Jacob would and so would all those nasty policemen who had been so rude to her. She would say a special prayer this evening for the late Queen's soul, not that its whereabouts could be in any doubt. She was in heaven. Pierre had told her there would be another splendid luncheon again, even if not on such a grand scale as before. She wondered why not. After all, the descendant of Marie Antoinette was almost as important as a King of England. She supposed, however, that poor Robert could hardly be expected to pay for all that again.

She couldn't understand why Pierre was not more enthusiastic. After all, apart from a few fancy-dress balls she had never publicly worn a Marie Antoinette outfit, and this was a different one to the usual formal court dress. Pierre should be proud of her. She'd ask him to take some photographs of her, though he didn't take many nowadays. She had a sneaking hope that now that she was playing Marie Antoinette, the ghost of the dead Queen would really appear, knowing she would be in the company of her family descendants. True, this meant Pierre would lose his bet, but Pierre had been rude, saying he didn't want to dress up again, and go through the charade. She had had to point out that if he could take the first photograph ever of a ghost he would win a lot of public acclaim, and perhaps lots of money too. Rich as they were, it would be nice to have some more.

An artist should not have to suffer this way, Jacob fumed in his hotel room. He disliked being forced to recall the unpleasant sights of the Petit Trianon. He preferred to remember the Louise and Mirabelle he knew, both captivating, both lovely, both young. Not as lovely as Hélène of course, who was forever young. Auguste had said he had seen Jacob's portrait of her in Robert's home. That surprised him, since he'd never believed that Robert was as attached to Hélène as he pretended to be, just as he didn't believe Robert loved Mirabelle either. If he didn't, why had he married her? One possible reason came uncomfortably to mind, as he recalled Mirabelle's less than attractive side. Hélène had believed Mirabelle was her closest friend, and at her funeral he had had a mission to discharge, which now – if he put two and two together – bore sinister implications. On the whole, he decided to avoid doing the arithmetic.

The idea of walking through the pantomime again in order, he suspected, to reveal who could or could not have murdered the two women, was a most uncomfortable one. Perhaps it would appear that no one could have murdered Mirabelle but Louise herself. It was much better to ignore the past now. He had made appointments with galleries in Paris, in the hope he could avoid going to the Petit Trianon, but then cancelled them. It would look as though he had something to hide.

*   *   *

Bertrand Danielle too was thinking about the morrow. It would be a difficult day, and he had a difficult role to play. He must ensure his deportment was correct, or he would look ridiculous, for he was well aware that his impersonation of the footman would make him look like a jealous cuckold to most people. On the other hand, in the context of what else might be revealed, that now seemed of trifling significance.

In the service block of the Petit Trianon, Auguste rushed from table to table, from kitchen to kitchen. Although Robert's servants, including his chef and kitchen staff, were all returning for the purpose of recreating the events of 10 August, Robert had not unnaturally refused to pay for anything. Auguste had therefore volunteered to pay for the luncheon and tea, and Chesnais had arranged for the Petit Trianon to be at their disposal, intending to come himself.

Because there were three gaps in their cast list, Auguste had cheated slightly by bringing Tatiana's staff from their Paris home. They had come without complaint for Tatiana's sake. He was merely tolerated as her husband, save by two who could recall Auguste from his employment as chef here in the 1880s. The scullery maid of the eighties was now their housekeeper, the lampboy the butler. To them at least he was *le maître*.

He looked at his menu, a much abbreviated version of its predecessor, and at the deliveries already made, and prepared to work for the morrow. When all was said and done, food was a great comfort. No wonder they served a meal of his own choice to a condemned man. He was beginning to feel like one himself. Unless this case was solved, the conversation with Bertie could not be expunged from the record, and if, by any terrible chance, it had relevance to the murders, then his position was as enviable as that of the steward to the mad Earl Ferrers. Only instead of the strangulation by which the Earl had murdered his servant, Bertie had promised to despatch him (metaphorically, he hoped) to Tower Green for immediate beheading. Like Marie Antoinette.

Twelve

At least today there was no need for fried blancmange, and other atrocities to his art. Auguste's eye ran automatically round the serving kitchen, as he tried to concentrate on the food about to be served for luncheon. There was too much lying ahead of him for the afternoon, however, and he was not in any condition to face it. Sleep had refused to bless him last night, as his brain jumped between the entire court of Marie Antoinette deciding to revisit the Petit Trianon in phantom form and his precious dishes being hurtled from service block to serving kitchen like eggs in an egg and spoon race.

When he had arrived, bleary-eyed and foggy minded, he had fully expected to find chaos but instead everything was remarkably in order. Save in one respect. The English have a proverb that 'Too many cooks spoil the broth', and here was most certainly a case of too many cooks. It was essential that all the kitchen staff and footmen present on the earlier occasion should once again be here, but with the much simpler menu deliberately chosen by Auguste, there were double the amount of bodies necessary to serve them.

Auguste braced himself, hoping that the sharp autumn air would clarify the butter of his mind.

"*Maitre*, what shall we do about the noodles?"

"*Comment?*" There were no noodles in his menu today; it was a simple luncheon. "What do you need noodles for?"

Monsieur Grospied looked smug. "You told us, *maître*, we were to do exactly as we did last time, so far as we could remember. I remember we ran out of noodles and you were displeased that I used macaroni instead."

"Excellent, monsieur," Auguste snarled. "However, we also have a luncheon to serve *today*, and there is little point in burning the *anchoide* while we talk of noodles." *Les nouilles* were unlikely to have played a major part in the murders.

He was also aware that Bertrand Danielle was being ostracised by his fellow servants, who disapproved of his whole escapade.

"I do not like gentry in my kitchens," Monsieur Grospied, chef, had announced earlier.

"Today they are *my* kitchens," Auguste gently reminded him. "Monsieur le comte is not paying for this luncheon, although he has kindly agreed to your attending."

"Monsieur le comte has no idea of the correctness of things." Grospied banged down a jelly. "He *himself* appeared in this kitchen in August, and insisted on taking the *pièce montée*. Employers are not what they used to be."

Nor were kitchen staff in Auguste's view, but in the interests of luncheon he did not voice it.

The table in the Grand Dining Room looked less imposing without His Majesty at the head of the table. Egbert Rose, sitting in his place, lacked the same grandeur, and, moreover, served to remind the diners that the event was not entirely social. Robert and Bertrand were of course in mourning and the entire party had done its best to veer towards sombreness, despite their eighteenth-century costumes. Nor did the presence of Inspector Chesnais in Louise's place help towards conviviality, and for once even Auguste was not disappointed over the attention paid to his food, both to its disposal and in general discussion of its merits. Everything, everyone agreed, was delightful. Meals of yesteryear were recalled, and relived, as a non-controversial topic of conversation.

Tatiana, attired once again as half peasant woman and half guard, recalled a luncheon with the Grand Duke Igor in Cannes, to which he insisted on bringing his own cow for milk, whereupon Auguste, who had been there as chef, had insisted on using it for 'syllabub straight from the cow' in the old-fashioned way. George, stolidly sitting next to her in his black suit, remembered his first snails tasted in the 1890s. Having been ordered by Auguste to change into her cottage-girl dress, Alice sullenly spoke of the meals at the Austrian court partaken of by her ancestress. Pierre and Jacob confined themselves to eating, but Winifred made a valiant effort to diversify the conversation by discussing whether Monsieur Santos Dumont's flying machine experiment in August could or could not be considered to rival the Wright Brothers since it had been yoked to a donkey.

Behind them, Bertrand Danielle was serving wine and his forays round the table to peer at the glasses of the guests were so artificial that Auguste wondered no one had noticed this inept footman earlier. The wine, while not helping to clarify Auguste's mind, was certainly relaxing him. Indeed it seemed somewhat stronger than he had ordered, and it briefly crossed his mind that this was one matter to which he had not given his personal attention. Even Chesnais, he noticed, was beginning to look sleepy, but Egbert, who had refused all wine, was as alert as ever.

"I can't see," Jacob announced querulously and unexpectedly, "that this afternoon is going to reveal anything new. After all, the murderer is not going to replay his own movements exactly, is he?"

"Or she," Alice contributed brightly.

"It's the wager you're here to settle," Egbert replied blandly. "Inspector Chesnais and I are just here to wander round and get the feel of what everyone was doing in August. This sole's excellent, Auguste."

George coughed. "Quite right, Rose. I'd like to emphasise that the purpose of the afternoon for *us* is not to reopen memories of the – er – happenings in August, but to spot ghosts."

"Perhaps those of Louise and Mirabelle will have joined them by now." Pierre laughed loudly.

"Do behave like a gentleman, Pierre," Alice pleaded sweetly, and her husband subsided, abashed.

"That's difficult for him," Robert murmured.

"We're here to see *ghosts*," George repeated, even more loudly.

"Or not, as the case may be," Robert said. "I fear the odds are on my side."

Auguste hoped very much that Robert was proved right. Dismally, he remembered that he and he alone would have to play umpire, and however truthful his verdict he was going to antagonise one side or the other. He wondered whether he could claim sudden illness. Certainly his head felt as clouded as if he were succumbing to *la grippe*. Perhaps he *was*, he thought hopefully. However, he couldn't let Egbert down, and that meant that cloudy brain or not, ghosts or not, he must retrace his steps of 10 August. Including those that found their way to the grotto.

"After I've played my part as Marion," Alice announced crossly in the middle of dessert, "I shall run down to the lawn

to play Marie Antoinette. You must have one, and now poor
dear Mirabelle is dead, who else is there?"

"There's me," said Egbert. "*I'm* playing Marie Antoinette."

Auguste tried to keep a straight face but all he could think
of was that Egbert and Chesnais looked remarkably funny.
For coffee in the boudoir with of course *croquignoles*, they
had donned the large white flower hats of Marie Antoinette,
playing their roles as Mirabelle and Louise, Egbert abandoning
the role of His Majesty. They had stopped short of the
full-skirted gowns, but the juxtaposition of flower hats and
dark lounge suits was unusual, to say the least.

Between them sat Jacob, and circulating round the room
were Tatiana, George, Winifred, Pierre, Alice, Robert and first
two, then three footmen. *Three?* Auguste realised Danielle had
joined them after a few minutes. A Sûreté detective was sitting
in a solitary chair in one corner with a respectful distance
around him as befitted his royal role. Auguste looked at
the reflections of the white hats in the mirror. If only his
mind was not so confused he ought to be able to deduce
whether Louise's cup could have had opium added to it in
mistake for Mirabelle's. It seemed likely, for no one would
have known, save Bertrand Danielle, that Louise was coming,
and it followed the poison could not have been meant for her.
Yet no one could have mistaken which was which, seeing
the two women at the table, because even if the hats hid
their hair from a distance, the faces were very different at
close quarters. Jacob would obviously have known which
cup was whose, but those moving around could not have
poisoned the cup before it was handed to the victim with any
certainty of whom it would reach. Unless the server was the
murderer.

"What's wrong?" he heard Pierre ask his wife. "You're not still upset over not playing the Queen, are you?"

"It's not *fair*," she pouted.

"You'll have your chance when you pick up the knife," he pointed out consolingly.

"Yes, but—" she glanced at Jacob. Alice had obviously recognised other dangers in too close a reconstruction of the events of 10 August, no matter how pleasant they had been.

Jacob, perhaps conscious of her gaze, turned round, and from the other side of the room Auguste's attention was caught. He blinked. He wasn't seeing things right, was he? For a moment – he forced his mind to work it out, and came up with the answer. The imperfect *croquignole* was on the wrong side of the plate for a mirror image. *Now* he saw how the murderer could have put the opium in the wrong cup.

"Aren't you well, Auguste?" Tatiana slipped her arm through Auguste's as they walked up the allée des deux Trianons towards the Musée des Voitures.

"Just lack of sleep."

"And no lack of wine."

Wives could be cruel, even Tatiana. He had drunk two cups of strong coffee and felt better, though his head felt like a stuffed snipe. He could be served up as a *bécassine à la Souvaroff* without His Majesty noting the difference. The day was grey, the heat of summer had vanished, and the full glories of autumn had not yet arrived. They walked over fallen leaves and the crunch of their footsteps were drumbeats to his private scaffold. Tatiana disappeared inside the museum with a cheerful wave, and shortly afterwards waved her white cloth from the window. He took a deep breath, and walked up the lane on his solitary march.

He turned into the lane that would take him into the Petit

Trianon grounds, and to his relief the heaviness and fears of August did not revisit him. There were the *real* Alice and Winifred, and here were Pierre and Bertrand Danielle. "La Maison lies that way," he was told, and his confidence returned. No ghosts, no confusion.

On down the footpath to where George should be waiting by the kiosk. There was to his slight alarm no sign of the kiosk itself. This was natural enough, for Robert would not have paid for its re-erection for today. George was by the side of the lane, wrapped up in his cloak. Then he heard Robert's running footsteps behind him. Robert was playing his part correctly today. "*Cherchez La Maison,*" he growled, pointing to the right.

It was but a path, the sky was grey but offered no threat as last time, and Auguste walked along it with confidence. Just ahead must be the point where he clambered down over the rocks; he felt so confident that he would do the same again, and find the grotto and stone staircase in the huge rock. Why not? There would be no one there today. A moment's uncertainty would be instantly dispelled.

This was the point where he had left the path – but there were no rocks. He hurried over the green mound, but there was no trickling water, no huge rock, and no grotto. Sweat broke out on his forehead and not from *la grippe*. He had lost his way, he must have mistaken the path. Last time he had gone by mistake to the Rocher bridge, to which the huge rock had been moved since Marie Antoinette's day. Although Miss Moberly and Miss Jourdain were quite clear that they were *not* at the Rocher bridge, he must have been and on this occasion he had simply come down a different path. Hadn't he? In any case, he could truthfully say he had seen no ghosts *this* time. If it had been Alice he saw here in the summer, there was no trace of her today. Alice must still be changing her dress, and would shortly be following him as he approached the château. He was sorry for George, and even more sorry that he would have to face Bertie with the news he had lost the wager, but his relief that there were no ghosts here predominated.

He continued happily to the lawn in front of the château, where he saw Egbert sitting on a stool on the gravel path under his white flowery hat, sketchbook in hand. Auguste resisted the opportunity to call out to him, and hurried by, conscious of Egbert's eyes on him. He ran round to the west terrace steps, and Jacob came running to meet him. So far everything had happened as before – apart from the grotto. He was shown the way to the main courtyard, where he saw Robert's landaulette, as in August.

Bertrand was just leaving with the other footmen in the wagon. Auguste had agreed with Egbert to diverge from the script to check what was going on in the kitchens, and so he now continued into the house to the service kitchen where he found the missing swan duly awaiting discovery. So far nothing odd. He would visit the service block and then return to the French Garden by the quickest way, behind the chapel, and pick up his original route. Monsieur Grospied still presided over chaos in the kitchens, but there was no sign of anything unusual and with inexplicable relief he hurried along the passage behind the chapel courtyard. It was even darker here than it was outside and *no wonder*. He suddenly realised that this passageway was once more a roofed corridor; indeed there was even a reheating room in it again. Perhaps this was a recent inspiration on Monsieur Grospied's part for he could not recall it before. Or perhaps there was some restoration work being carred out on the chapel. He remembered some talk of it.

The geraniums still flowered in the French Garden, though their lazy sprawl had become a leggy untrimmed mess now. Something else seemed to have changed, however. The Trianon looked different – the steps had altered. What nonsense! He looked ahead to the French Pavilion, so gracefully set at the centre of the garden, and past it to the fine lime trees beyond. He couldn't remember noticing the archways made by the branches before.

To his surprise he saw Tatiana walking towards him down the garden towards the Pavilion and he hurried to meet her, happy to have company. He had reached the centre, when his eyes suddenly picked up a flash of colour to his right – not in the gardens but against the grey stone of the French Pavilion. He turned his head towards it and just for an instant before she disappeared into the building he saw a middle-aged woman of voluptuous build and sensuous face, dressed obviously for a costume ball. Her hair was hidden under a tall powdered wig, dressed *à la Pompadour* with ringlets falling on either side of her head, adorned by several purple plumes. Her dress was also purple, ornately draped, ruched and frilled and clinging round her waist. What had caught his eye, however, were her jewels, diamonds, pearls and emeralds, catching the light as she moved, so many that she seemed weighed down by them.

Costume ball? At three thirty in the afternoon? Auguste rushed to meet Tatiana to escape from his own fears. She was here, solid, alive, and *real*.

"Are you ill, Auguste?" she asked in alarm.

"*Oui.* I thought I saw" – he gulped – "a ghost."

"It's easy here. There's such an atmosphere," Tatiana consoled him. "I was thinking about the Comtesse Du Barry just now, poor woman. How she loved this place, and how she hated the thought that her arch rival Marie Antoinette was its owner after Louis XV died."

"What did she look like?" Auguste tried to sound casual.

"I've no idea. I know she was once a woman of the streets, and loved jewels, and – Auguste, what *is* the matter?"

"I don't like this place," he announced firmly. "I'm going into the main gardens *now*.

"Did the quarrel take place on the lawn just as before?"

Auguste groaned. "I forgot that bit. I'm sure I didn't hear quarrelling though."

"Let's go back that way."

"*No.*"

"Very well," Tatiana replied peaceably, giving him an anxious look. "I'll go this way, and you continue on. We'll meet at Le Hameau. It's not what I did before, but that hardly matters now."

"Where *did* you go before?" Auguste tried to drag his mind back to the real quest of the afternoon, and realised that for all his careful tabling of everyone's movements on 10 August, he had not included his own wife.

"After Monsieur Danielle had turned me away from being a guard, I went to sit nearby for a while to wait for you. I must have missed you though, so I sat thinking about Marie Antoinette, and what a terrible end she had—"

"You weren't wearing a pink dress, were you?" he yelped.

"No, of course not. I was wearing trousers and a cloak as you know – Auguste, what *is* wrong?"

Tatiana's words had come back to him in full force, 'I'm afraid, Auguste, that I too, am probably a medium.'

"Where are you going, Pierre?" Winifred had called nervously after Auguste had passed them about ten past three, heading towards Le Hameau from the guards' position.

Pierre stopped. "Winnie, I'm aware we should be following our former movements, but I'm sure I'm the last person you would choose to converse with unnecessarily."

"You are," Winifred said simply. "But as we *were* talking last time, I think we should do it again." She felt doubtful about this, for they were in a lonely place, and Pierre, as she knew full well, was unpredictable.

"We needn't bother with all of it," Pierre said jovially. "After all, we were together, so we both know we could not have killed Mirabelle."

"We did part though, just after we met Auguste," Winifred said hesitantly, "so that we arrived at Le Hameau separately."

"And that was the *only* reason." Pierre's reply was curt. "What possible reason could either of us have had for murder?" He smiled, hoping to convey to Winifred that it was in her best interests to see his point.

Subtleties were lost on Winifred. "She said she'd inform everyone if she felt like it. You haven't told anyone, have you, Pierre?"

He deliberately looked her up and down from peasant hat to kerchiefed ample bosom, down to the large shabby country boots. "Hard to think of you mother naked in that film wriggling about trying to find a flea."

"*Oh!*" Winifred burst into tears. "That was the *past*. I had to do it, you know that. I had no money at all."

"That's what they all say, but you all love it really. Remember the one when you ended up naked on that couch, and I adjusted your position?" He roared with laughter.

"That's enough." Winifred strove in vain for dignity. "You

216

were *very* persuasive, and after all, it was just posing. You were just teasing me on that couch. We never actually—"

"No, you weren't my sort," he interrupted. "I'm not one for our plump game. Mind you, those 'for gentlemen only' films are becoming period pieces now. I've got them all tucked away somewhere."

"You said you wouldn't," Winifred cried. "How could you? Are you a blackmailer too?" Misery engulfed her completely.

Pierre laughed, not unkindly for once. "You can believe what I told you in August, Winnie. I'm not going to say a word about it. After all, I've left my past behind me too. Your terrible secret's safe with me, and I'm not still selling the postcards or films."

"Thank you," she babbled, unable to believe her good fortune.

He eyed her, curious now. "That's not to say I won't dig them out and give myself a private show one day."

Winifred almost didn't care, now that the main threat seemed to be lifted. The other threat had been banished in August, after Pierre had insisted they went to tell Mirabelle just what they thought of her.

At least Winifred wouldn't say anything, Pierre reflected. He'd earned her gratitude cheaply, for he was terrified that Alice might find out how their fortune had been made. Like Winifred, he'd had no choice after Michel's death. Artistic photography wasn't necessary for the saucy postcards circulating in the late nineties, nor even for the early cinematograph films. It had given him not only his fortune but a breathing space to become proficient as a photographer. Gentle persuasion on one or two of his models who, like Winnie, had

married well, had given him his first entrée into society, and
he'd never looked back. It had its disadvantages, since he
rather liked saucy films, but he couldn't have everything.
He had Alice, after all, and with all her irritating ways, he
was going to keep her. Now that Mirabelle was no longer a
threat, Alice would never know what lay in his past.

He decided he would go straight to Le Hameau. He was
earlier than he had been last time, but he couldn't retrace
his steps exactly and surely there was no harm in arriving
early. It was *late* arrival that would have aroused interest.
He was coming round Snail Hill when Auguste caught him
up, having just passed George once more.

"We'll walk to Le Hameau together, Pierre," Auguste
said thankfully. No ghosts would dare to materialise if
down-to-earth Pierre was around.

"Ah. Last time you passed me when I was talking to
Winifred," Pierre said heartily. "I must have mistimed it."

It was only then that Auguste realised they would be walking
together straight in front of the dairy where Jacob and Alice
should be embracing inside. Fortunately, when they arrived,
Jacob and Alice were standing outside the dairy.

Even so, Pierre was not pleased. "What are you doing here,
Alice?" He scowled at Jacob. "You weren't here last time."

Alice opened wide innocent eyes. "I was, Pierre. Jacob and
I walked over here after Mirabelle upset me so much. He was
consoling me for not being able to play Marie Antoinette."

"Was he indeed? Why didn't you come to tea then?"

"I couldn't face it. Not when I was so miserable."

"Then where the hell were you?" demanded Pierre. "You
didn't go back to the lawn straightaway, did you? You told
me you felt ill after your quarrel with Mirabelle and retired
to the Trianon."

"Oh, you're asking me if I did the murder? No, Pierre. If I had, do you think I would still have been standing there an hour later? How could you think I could cut a throat like that? I can't even eat a little chicken without thinking of its cruel death."

"In your statement to the police you made no mention of retiring to the house, madame," said Auguste.

Pierre's face darkened. "Where were you? With that artist all the time?"

"I . . ." Alice faltered and began again. "You'll think this silly, *chérie*, but I actually went to the grotto to enjoy playing Marie Antoinette on my own. I thought," she continued piteously, "that if I was very quiet in one of her grottoes, she might materialise to me. I talked to her and did a little dance, but she didn't come."

"You told me you don't believe in ghosts," Pierre pointed out grimly. "Remember which side we are on in this wager."

"But Marie Antoinette isn't a *ghost*." Alice was indignant. "She's real. I talk to her every day at ten o'clock, either at home in my little chapel or at her tomb."

"You go too far, Alice." Pierre was surprisingly gentle.

"So you have no alibi for that hour, madame?" Auguste asked.

"Of course I do. I was with the Queen. She suggested if I went back to the lawn, I could sit there as Marie Antoinette because Mirabelle would have gone for tea. That was just about the time you'd all be returning from tea, so I hurried there and . . . and . . ." She burst into tears, and Pierre hastened to comfort her.

"Does that satisfy you, Auguste?" he asked angrily.

Auguste ignored him. "Did you touch anything?"

"Only the knife. Pierre—"

219

"Then how did you know how Mirabelle had died?"

"It was clear enough," Pierre answered for her.

"Not until the hat was removed."

Pierre looked at his wife, waiting for her answer.

"I forgot," she said. "The hat had come off. I picked it up and threw it over the nasty sight."

The answer had taken a long time to come.

It was a curious sensation to return to the Petit Trianon lawn with the group from Le Hameau. With this afternoon still in his mind, Auguste had an irrational fear that Mirabelle's indignant ghost might be there, and he was relieved to see Egbert still sitting on the gravel path, very much alive, with Alice at his side holding a knife, this time unbloodied. On this occasion there was one other person in the group of spectators: Inspector Chesnais.

"*Mesdames et messieurs*, you may now return to the Petit Trianon, provided Monsieur Didier has seen sufficient to decide the wager."

Had he? Auguste was still reeling from the events of the afternoon, his head ached, and he longed for the coolness and order of the kitchens, where logic reigned hand in hand with its consort, art. Out here logic was lost. He nodded, however, and only Alice burst out eagerly before the party returned to the château: "Did you see Her Majesty, Auguste?"

"For someone who put her money on there being no such things as ghosts," Jacob said lightly, "that's a strange question."

Alice ignored him, her attention on Auguste.

"I shall present my report *later*," he told her firmly, and Pierre took her arm to lead her away.

"You have a smile on your face, Inspector Rose," Chesnais

observed when only the three of them remained. "It has gone well, this little comedy?"

"The countess, it seems to me, sat here like a queen bee that day, and queen bees have reason to grin."

"The bees came to visit her as you expected?" Chesnais asked.

"No." Egbert's eyes flicked to Auguste. "That's what was interesting. How about your returning to the château too, Auguste? You'll be wanting to keep an eye on my *sole au chablis*, no doubt."

With mixed feelings of rejection and relief, Auguste took the heavy hint. It suited him, for there were a few questions he needed to ask, and for that even the *sole au chablis* could be left to Monsieur Grospied.

He managed to catch up with Winifred before she entered the salon, having obviously just emerged from the ladies' retiring room.

"If I might have a word." He drew her into the small dining room, and she looked very ill at ease at this privacy. "Nothing of this will reach your husband, Winifred, but I must ask you, was Mirabelle blackmailing you?"

"What nonsense." It was almost a squawk.

"I have seen one of your postcards."

"Pierre promised he'd never tell!" she wailed.

"Perhaps he hasn't. I don't know who sent it to me. However, it's Mirabelle who concerns me."

Winifred eyed him doubtfully. "It wasn't blackmail really. She just hinted she knew, and that day she even said that since I was English and Pierre French perhaps taking our clothes off was part of the spirit of the Amis de l'Entente Cordiale. It was terrible, but then she died," Winifred added ingenuously.

"When on that day did she say this, madame?"

Winifred swallowed, and then said bravely: "Pierre and I went to see her just after you saw us talking. He wanted to scare her into not saying anything. She laughed at us – but she was alive when we left. She really was."

"And were you both together until you reached Le Hameau?"

There was a pause. "No," she said dolefully.

Auguste finally tracked Jacob down on the terrace, and persuaded him that a walk in the grounds was exactly what he needed before dinner. Jacob accepted this invitation warily.

"I believe these murders centre on the death of Hélène Mai."

"That was six years ago," Jacob pointed out, his eyes on the Temple of Love on the small island in the ornamental river.

"Nevertheless you loved her, and Robert took her from you. When he did the same not only with Louise but with Mirabelle, you said: *"Ca suffit!"* Was that the reason you challenged Robert to a duel, or because Mirabelle had told you that Robert had murdered Hélène and you wanted revenge?"

"How would Mirabelle know what had happened between Robert and Hélène?"

"I don't know, but I believe she blackmailed Robert into marrying her on the threat of making the story public."

"You don't understand."

"Then make me."

"You have to understand Mirabelle first. What both fascinated and worried me was that I couldn't *paint* her. Heaven knows I paint enough society masks covering different faces, and can usually choose to exclude one or the other if I wish. Mirabelle always eluded me, however, and its only recently I've realised why. She was beautiful and talented

222

to a degree, but that degree was not enough for her. She had to be as good as Hélène. That's why she hated her so much, especially when Hélène married Robert. By the time Hélène died, Mirabelle was married to Lord Harper, but as soon as *he* died, she determined to marry Robert in order to be equal to Hélène at last. Lord Harper was pleased with my portrait of her, but I felt I'd painted an empty shell." Jacob grinned. "You may think I'm too fashionable an artist to be worried about integrity, but I am. I tried to paint her again, not long before she married Robert, but this time the brush kept producing something I didn't recognise. I suppose it was this that fascinated me. Did I love her, and want to marry her? By the end, yes, because I think Mirabelle needed to prove that *anyone* who had loved Hélène could love her too. I would have done as a husband, until suddenly she saw the chance of marrying Robert."

"By blackmail?"

"You still don't understand. Mirabelle wasn't a blackmailer in the usual sense of the word. Taking money from Robert, as I suspect she did, was her retaliation for his continued pursuit of Louise. Louise was married, as she was, and yet Robert sought consolation from Louise and not her. I think she decided he had to pay for the insult, and when he finally ran out of money she saw the way to do it."

"Unless she suddenly came across certain proof of Hélène's murder, and could demand marriage."

"No," Jacob said slowly, "she'd had that for some time."

"She told you?"

"There was no need. It was I who gave it to her."

"George!" Auguste called after him as he spotted his quarry ambling round the French Garden, close, he was glad to see, to where the Comtesse Du Barry had materialised that afternoon. No ghost would linger long in George's stalwart presence.

George stopped unwillingly.

"I saw you this afternoon," Auguste said.

"What of it?"

"I didn't on the tenth of August."

"You must have timed it wrong."

"No. You said you were strolling round the grounds, and I would most surely have run into you somewhere. If you had been there."

George heaved a sigh. "Look, you're a gentleman, Auguste."

"I am honoured," Auguste said.

"And you're related to Bertie."

Auguste admitted he was.

"So you wouldn't want to embarrass him?"

"You were at Le Hameau then."

"I don't mind telling you it was a shock. I went to find Louise, hoping I might have a word with her about old times. Always admired her," George explained gruffly.

"And what happened?"

"I blasted well nearly walked into a highly embarrassing situation. There was Louise prancing around half-naked, dancing and shouting and His Majesty trying to get away from her. I've no idea what had been going on, and it isn't something I'd care to raise with him. I couldn't say a word to the police, could I? I mean, there's the honour of England and all that." George's face was red.

"I understand," Auguste said.

"Do you?" George brightened. "Women are odd creatures, you know. For years I remembered Louise, she was a candle in the darkness if you know what I mean. She drew you to her. And now this shattered everything for me. Winifred may be on the staid side, but you'd never catch her flaunting herself like that."

Thirteen

D inner – any meal come to that – should provide a source of comfort as well as excitement, a diversion from the problems of the day. Yet tonight that was impossible, for everyone was only too well aware that though they might discuss ghosts and wagers, their thoughts would be on murder and the presence of two police inspectors. As Auguste had foreseen this, he had chosen a menu that would principally console, irrespective of any relationship with Marie Antoinette. In fact, he suspected that everyone, save Alice, was thoroughly bored with Marie Antoinette and though even the food of Auguste Didier could be no compensation for what might happen this evening, it could at least provide comfort, even if this were a subconscious reaction. The idea of his creations going unappreciated while the guests pondered their own or other's fates was agonising but inevitable. He had therefore prepared fish dishes, omelettes and chicken dishes, and – and unwittingly – *Crème Dubarry* soup. The cream of cauliflower might provide comfort, its name did not, at least for Auguste. He only hoped that the lady did not materialise again in his kitchen to taste her favourite soup. He would instruct Tatiana to remain well away from the kitchen. If the apparition took her place at the dining table instead, soup spoon in hand, he would at least have company round him, which would settle the wager once and for all.

Or would it? He grasped gratefully at the sudden idea that occurred to him. One of his problems at least might be solved without difficulty. Nevertheless, he sighed for the glories of what might have been. In England the pheasant season would have started, and the larders would be full of game. He imagined it now, the golden light of the dying sun, the smell of the earth, the tramp of the boots returning from the field, and the kitchen overflowing with the fruits of autumn.

Only His Majesty was missing from the table as they entered from the antechamber. Auguste could hardly see Bertie in the role of murder suspect, however. He would have had to have come prepared with murder in mind, and the King of England never carried money in his pocket, let alone opium.

For a few moments Auguste entertained this fantasy, then hurriedly reminded himself that a meal was being served whose supervision had been left to Monsieur Grospied. He supposed that Monsieur Grospied was in reality a most competent chef, and it briefly occurred to him that his own presence might have something to do with this not always appearing the case. He dismissed the thought. All he ever offered was help, advice and general supervision. He was the most tactful of *maître* chefs, save perhaps for Monsieur Escoffier himself. It is true that he had occasionally shown some ire when the soup was over-salted, or the salamander burnt the gratin, but that was only to be expected.

Apart from the presence of Egbert and Chesnais and the absence of Bertie, there was another difference to the earlier occasion. Bertrand Danielle now took his place as a guest, not as a liveried servant.

An hour later, during which conversation had ranged over everything but murder and wagers, conversely having the effect of heightening the tension, the ladies withdrew at a sign from Tatiana. Brandy was served, and the footmen also withdrew, and shortly after them Egbert and Chesnais 'on official business'. Auguste knew what his role was to be now – Egbert had made that quite clear. He was to be an *agent provocateur* among these black-dinner-suited gentlemen: Jacob, Pierre, George, Robert and Bertrand.

"*Messieurs*," Auguste began, "as you all probably know, I have been given a mission by His Majesty, since he could not be here himself. He, as I do myself, feels it is unlikely that Louise murdered Mirabelle and then killed herself, although new evidence makes that entirely possible." He sent a silent plea for forgiveness to the purveyor of this 'new evidence' at present blissfully at Balmoral, unaware of his involvement. "Even so, His Majesty would still wish to know the background to the crimes, and now the police have left us, I have to ask your help. I am particularly sorry to do so in a place of such poignant memories for Robert."

"Surely poignant is hardly accurate?" Bertrand observed.

"And why not?" Robert demanded.

"He means Mirabelle blackmailed you into marriage," Jacob drawled, "and that you hated Louise."

"Hated? I loved her. I loved them both."

"You took Mirabelle as your wife for love alone, did you, Robert? Surely you cannot expect us to believe that?" Bertrand asked, appearing slightly amused.

"For what else?"

Bertrand toyed with his brandy. "If not blackmail, perhaps for money?"

"No," Robert answered curtly.

"The challenge to a duel is still on, Robert," said Jacob. "I left it for a while for obvious reasons, but I still feel strongly."

"I'm sure you do, Jacob. You always were an annoyingly persistent little gnat and still are. How Louise and Mirabelle used to laugh at you."

"I doubt if either of them had much cause to laugh in August," George said gruffly.

"Nor I," Bertrand said. "For me at least this day brings painful memories. Robert may have hated Louise, but I loved her."

"You lie on both counts," Robert said. "You may have done at first, but it soon passed. You had no objection to her *amitié amoureuse* with me, until it threatened your career."

"Gentlemen!" George weighed in, shocked at this display of Gallic temperament.

"Why, dear old George. And what were your feelings for Louise?" Robert mocked. "Where did you go that afternoon after Auguste passed us? I saw you setting out along the path that would take you to Le Hameau. Did you and His Majesty have a session *à trois* with Louise?"

"You're no gentleman, sir," shouted George. "You dishonour the King of England."

Robert roared with laughter. "He needs no assistance from me."

"Robert," Bertrand interrupted. "Not in public, *if* you please, and not in connection with my wife."

"This is not public," observed Jacob. "This is a gentlemen-only discussion." He winked at Auguste.

"Quite," Pierre said.

Robert shrugged. "If you believe I slept with Louise all those years for any reason other than love, then you're crazy."

"You didn't love Mirabelle – or Hélène," Jacob said viciously.

"Was Louise blackmailing you too, Robert?" Pierre asked.

"Are you claiming, Pierre, that even if Robert did not kill Mirabelle, he could have murdered my wife because she was blackmailing him?" asked Bertrand.

It was Robert who answered. "Aren't you ignoring the fact, Bertrand, that as regards Louise, there is *no* evidence that I did anything but love her, or of any blackmail attempts, and that others in this room also had good reason to kill her, including, my dear sir, yourself."

"What possible reason could I have?"

"Two at least spring to mind," Robert replied quietly. "Jealousy and fear for your career."

"Alas, motive – even were you correct – is insufficient to convict me, Robert."

"Damned rum thing, though, your pretending to be a footman," George pointed out.

Auguste interrupted. "I think we're missing the point, gentlemen. It is Mirabelle's murder that is central to what happened here that day. She was indeed threatening others besides Robert who, once he had married her, had no reason to kill her. She was no threat any longer as his wife. However, as I am sure that the answer to both crimes lies in the Paris of the nineties not in the present, I suggest we talk freely about it."

"Gentleman to gentlemen?" asked George uncomfortably.

"Of course," murmured Robert. "Even Pierre can, I suppose, be included in that definition."

"Very well," George said, "I don't mind telling you I was dizzy with Paris life. I wanted to live there, marry there. England was finished, I thought. I've never forgotten the time I first saw Louise dance. La Dervicheuse – she was like a whirling flame, hypnotic, and when" – George looked round defiantly – "she seemed to like me, I thought I was the luckiest fellow around. I wouldn't want Winifred to hear me say that, of course," he added hastily.

"Or myself?" Bertrand asked.

"No, naturally. Not that there was anything improper, you understand." George went scarlet. Free speaking was one thing, tactlessness quite another.

"I do indeed." Bertrand remained imperturbable. "I married Louise in December 1895 and the only gentleman whom she mentioned as having been part of her life was Robert. He had, she explained, forced her into a liaison to which she had agreed because she had to send all the money she earned back to her family. Then he married someone else. Most honourable, Robert."

"The true facts don't change, whatever you *say*, Bertrand," Robert replied mildly.

"I agree with George," Jacob said. "It was exciting in Paris then, particularly for an art student. In England, art lacked inspiration, but in Paris it was branching out in new directions. I drew Louise and – er – she seemed to like me too, and then I saw Hélène. She let me paint her, but nothing more. I was twenty-one, but she thought of me as a mere boy; she had other admirers, that was clear. And one of them was Robert. He had a title to offer her, money and a home, and all I had was a possible career some way in front of me."

"Are you saying Hélène married me for money?" Robert asked.

"No. She was greatly in love with you, but it remains a fact that you could offer her more than I."

"Inspector Rose tells me that in fact Hélène was very rich," Auguste said.

Bertrand laughed. "How very convenient, Robert. *Now* I understand."

"I did not know that when I married her." Robert was still unruffled by Bertrand's taunts.

"Of course not," Bertrand mocked.

"Pierre?" Auguste asked.

"Jacob and George are English, and they saw a different Paris to mine," he replied without his usual bluster. "They saw the excitement and entertainment. I saw it as a place to make a living. I haven't the advantage of a count's title, but in the Republic of France that shouldn't have mattered. I found it did. You needed connections then, and you still do."

"You were in Paris throughout the nineties?" Auguste asked.

"No. I was there between ninety and ninety-four, the Zidler years of the Moulin Rouge. I had no money to begin with, so I thought I'd start a photography business based on postcards of Zidler's girls. It was my brother Michel who took the photographs, and I ran the business side. He had great artistic talent, and we talked of getting into Paris society once we had made enough money to establish ourselves at a good address."

"Ah, money again," Robert sighed.

"*Alors*, Michel fell in love with Louise – and that was that." Pierre ignored the interruption. "No matter what Bertrand thinks, we need to speak plainly. Louise seduced him. No other word for it. He was married, with two small children, but he lost all reason."

"I understood, Auguste, you wished us to talk about Mirabelle and Hélène, not Louise," Bertrand said coldly.

"It's all the same story," Pierre retorted, "and I wouldn't be telling it if matters weren't obviously coming to a head. Michel killed himself in ninety-four, and there I was, left stranded. I couldn't take a decent photograph in those days, Zidler was leaving and his successor didn't like me. Hélène was the only person to help me. She said she'd talk to Robert and ask for his help in introducing me to society. She felt sorry for me. She knew what it was like to be poor. Or so I then assumed. Robert, of course, refused."

"How cruel of me," Robert murmured. "Was there any particular reason I should help an ungifted photographer to make money from my friends?"

"It was about that time I met Mirabelle," Pierre ploughed on doggedly. "She suggested that I should learn to take photographs, then move away to the Riviera where it was cheaper and there was a ready market for – er – photographs. I did well there, and looked round for the next step. The Lumière brothers had started their moving pictures in ninety-five and by ninety-seven films were getting very popular. There were specialist opportunities, shall we say, films for gentlemen only. I made a few in the south, did well, and was ready to come back to Paris and leave films behind me. I met Mirabelle again in Cannes, and she gave me one or two introductions to their Paris friends."

"Haven't you left something out?" Robert mocked. So that was where the postcard had come from, Auguste thought. The consommé was clarifying, at last.

Pierre glared at him. "No."

"Monsieur Danielle?" Auguste tactfully turned the conversation.

"We haven't heard from Robert yet," Bertrand replied. "Nevertheless, if you wish, I will speak, though I have little to relate. I married Louise in late ninety-five and was not a frequenter of the Moulin Rouge. But Robert was, and of the Jardin de Paris. Later I came to know Robert better – and Hélène. Poor girl. Not a happy marriage in my opinion. I shall be most interested to hear Robert's view."

Robert laughed. "And so you shall. Hélène was, as you say, Auguste, very rich, though I did not know this until just before we were married. She was a precious thing, a work of art, all spirit, all heart, all talent, and I loved her. I am sure that Louise must have given you a different picture of Hélène, Bertrand, but that is my remembrance of her. She was fragile and consumption took her away from me."

"With the help of a little arsenic?" Bertrand enquired.

Robert stared at him. "May I ask what proof you have of such an outrageous statement?"

"Alas, none. However," Bertrand's voice began to rise, losing control at last, "perhaps Louise did. Though she was no blackmailer, that is why you hated her, and conspired with Mirabelle to kill her. Or did you kill Mirabelle too? Whether you did it or not, you most certainly killed my wife."

"I loved Louise," Robert shouted. "Can none of you understand that? I adored her. If she had proof of anything it was that. It was you, driven by jealousy, who hated her so much. You who persuaded her into coming to the Trianon, then followed her here to murder her. You who planned to blame me for it. You who—"

"Killed Mirabelle?" Bertrand finished for him.

"Yes, and I can prove it."

Bertrand stared at him, white-faced. Then he rose to his feet. "Indeed? In that case, gentlemen, you must excuse me. I have a confession to make to Inspector Chesnais."

As the footman opened the door to the *salon*. Auguste saw Tatiana sitting by the fire. It was obvious she had not been having an easy time with Alice and Winifred. Entertaining two ladies, one of whom could only chatter about Marie Antoinette, and the other to whom all mention of France and the French was anathema, could hardly have been relaxing, particularly today. Alice was in the midst of informing them about the exciting new novel by the Baroness Orczy about the adventures of the so-called Scarlet Pimpernel in rescuing aristocrats from the fury of the Revolutionary mob. The Scarlet Pimpernel was of course an Englishman.

"Where is Monsieur Danielle, Auguste?" Tatiana asked. "Will he be joining us?"

"I doubt it," Robert replied for him. "He is at this moment confessing to the murder of his wife – and of mine."

"Was he being blackmailed too?" Winifred cried out in excitement, drawing a puzzled look from George.

"I've always thought Danielle's public claims of integrity too good to be true," Pierre said with satisfaction. "It's obvious that woman – Louise – forced him to marry her, because she had something on him."

"My dear Pierre, everyone was accusing me of being a victim of blackmail a short while ago. First by Mirabelle, my poor wife, and then by Louise," Robert pointed out.

Pierre looked round the room. "Whether she was a black-mailer or not, several of us here had good reason to loathe Louise. Danielle has done us a favour."

"I don't understand." George frowned. "How could both Louise and Mirabelle be blackmailers, and both be killed at about the same time and place. Rather a coincidence, isn't it?"

"Round and round the maze," Jacob commented brightly. "I'd like to reach the centre. If Danielle killed them both, enough of the whys. *How* did he do it? So far as I can gather, he merely disguised himself as a footman. Kindly explain, *mon maître chef.*"

"Monsieur Danielle *also* impersonated one of the officers in the garden."

"*Mon dieu*, I thought that was a ghost!" Pierre said sarcastically.

"Ghosts," George said. "That reminds me—"

"Not *now*, George," Winifred said sharply, her eyes on Auguste.

"I do not know what Monsieur Danielle is telling Inspector Chesnais," Auguste said, "but it could be this. When Louise told him that she intended to go to the Petit Trianon, he decided on his plan to be present, though, he hoped, invisible to her."

"I told you it was a ghost," Pierre chortled.

Auguste ignored him. "He put the opium in her cup or glass, in his capacity as footman, but unfortunately Mirabelle saw him and told him so as she went to the garden. He seized a knife, took up his position as court guard in the grounds, and then murdered Mirabelle. He changed back to livery in the Trianon, made great play of helping Robert with the cake, then followed him on foot back to Le Hameau, to check how Louise was. She was not present and, satisfied his plan had worked, he left."

Tatiana was staring at him aghast. "But—"

To Auguste's relief, Egbert and Chesnais entered at that moment. His delaying tactics had worked. Behind them was Bertrand Danielle.

"What's he doing here?" Robert asked sharply, rising to his feet.

"I have come to enjoy the entertainment," Bertrand replied.

Robert's eyes darted from one to the other.

"Monsieur le comte," Chesnais stepped forward, "I have to arrest you for the murder of your wife, Comtesse de Tourville, and Madame Louise Danielle."

"There are," Egbert explained the following day in Tatiana's home, where Bertrand, Pierre, Alice, George, Jacob and Winifred had gathered, "two central pivots to this case. The first is that Mirabelle was a blackmailer, the second is that Robert did indeed adore Louise."

Robert's wild protestations of innocence for Louise's death rang once more in Auguste's ears.

"He murdered her, however," Bertrand stated flatly.

"He has admitted killing Mirabelle," Egbert continued, "but denies murdering Louise. He also denies putting opium in either of their glasses or food."

"Naturally," Bertrand murmured. "Louise's ghost would be far from pleased if he admitted to killing her even by accident."

"I'm inclined to agree," Egbert said. "The count confirmed that Mirabelle had been blackmailing him for years over Hélène's death. When his money ran out, she demanded marriage, and he talked it over with Louise. It was her plan, so he claims. He would murder Mirabelle on the lawn, while Louise kept up a loud and one-sided quarrel inside the Petit Trianon to provide an alibi. In the event, Louise was not in the Trianon, but suffering the early symptoms of opium poisoning. Robert had no choice but to return to the château."

"Why?" asked Winifred.

"His clothes were heavily bloodstained," Auguste explained. "His cloak, which he had taken off on the lawn, concealed them while he returned to the château. It was easy for him to change, for he had a bedroom there, having slept in the Queen's bedchamber."

"The château was searched," Tatiana objected.

"Robert had rid himself of the incriminating clothes. He packed them into a hamper, and took it to his motor car as planned. Louise should have been with him, but of course she

237

was not, and Robert had to find some other reason hurriedly for his late arrival. The cake was ideal, but unfortunately he did not recognise the footman as Bertrand Danielle."

"Equally unfortunately, although my earlier statement was accurate, it did not convey the entire truth," Bertrand said blandly. "I cannot think how it happened. I returned to the first floor by the terrace steps, having passed Mirabelle alive, and came down the staircase in order to go to the kitchens. I then stated I met Robert coming out of the kitchens with the washing tub about four o'clock. Both statements were true, but there was a ten-minute gap between my movements, accurately though I described them. I came down the staircase, and searched the old guard room for Louise. As I emerged, I met Robert coming in the main entrance and turning towards the stairs. He was huddled in his cloak and hat, and did not even glance at me. I was curious about his demeanour, and thinking Louise might be involved in it I followed him upstairs and waited for his reappearance. I was startled when he then went into the kitchens, and once again followed him. I believe he originally told Inspector Chesnais that a chef and a footman bore witness to his movements, but no footman came forward *then*. It was I."

"Doesn't seem like reliable evidence to me," George answered weightily, as if speaking for English justice.

"You are correct, Mr Ladyboys. Fortunately, I was intrigued by a hamper I saw inside Robert's car as I put in the washing tub; and opened it while Robert was cranking the car. I managed to extract one of the blood-stained gloves Robert had been allotted by George to wear as the Running Man. Gloves, I might mention, that are far too small for me to have worn." He spread open his large hands.

"Why didn't you speak earlier?" Alice said indignantly.

"We've all been so worried, and you knew all the time who the murderer was."

"I regret that very much, madame. I have tendered my apologies to Inspector Rose here, and to Inspector Chesnais. I can only explain my lapse of memory by my wish to see Robert squirming on the point of a pin as he had tortured me for many years. For him to know that his life depended on my statements alone, was an exquisite pleasure for me. He did indeed love Louise; unfortunately so did I, and of the two of us, it was Robert who absorbed all her affections. Love does not always blind one to the imperfections of the beloved, and I was well aware that Louise's morals were non-existent. I still loved her, and Robert murdered her, whether he admits it or not. Mr Didier can no doubt explain better than I how it happened."

"I believe," Auguste took up the story, "that Robert intended to kill Mirabelle with opium, and that the knife was a last-minute desperate thought when he reached the lawn and found Mirabelle unaffected by, instead of comatose with, opium. He had by mistake put the opium in Louise's coffee, not Mirabelle's."

"How?" Jacob asked. "I was between them, and you couldn't mistake one for the other."

"The crowded room and the mirrors caused it," Auguste explained. "A mirror generally reverses the image, but there are odd results when you get mirrors at right angles as they were in that corner. As you approach the corner from one angle, the mirror image that attracts your eye is a double reflection. It was Robert's misfortune that the room was crowded, and he looked in the mirror as he walked across to the table, but being in a hurry chose the wrong image on which to rely. He had very little time to poison the coffee and, from behind, the hats and Louise's fair wig hid their faces. He therefore relied on what he had seen when crossing the room. Louise on the left, Mirabelle on the right, according to his judgement. He assumed the positions should be reversed for a mirror image, not realising that this was a double reflection and thus was true to life. It was a simple – and for him, terrible – mistake."

"I may be to blame," Jacob said soberly. "Unwittingly, of course. I visited Hélène shortly before she died – of consumption I was told. She was very ill, but she gave me something. A locked diary, which she wished me to give to her best friend in the event of her death. At the funeral, I carried out my promise, and gave it, still locked, to Mirabelle. Looking back, I feel that may well have contained all the confirmation Mirabelle needed that Robert was slowly poisoning Hélène."

"You couldn't have known, Jacob," Alice said consolingly. "You acted in good faith, just like Queen Marie Antoinette when—"

"We have prepared a light luncheon in the dining room." Auguste interrupted quickly. "If you would all like to accompany me . . .?"

George coughed. "Just a moment, Auguste."

"Yes?"

"Hate to mention it, but what happens to the wager now?"

Auguste blinked. "Robert has been arrested for murder."

"I know it seems out of order," George replied apologetically, "but I like to get things straight. What's the form, do you suppose? Suppose this was a two-horse race, and one horse didn't turn up?"

"Then you have won, George," Winifred said triumphantly.

"No, old girl. I like to win fair and square. As a matter of interest, Auguste, *did* you see any ghosts yesterday?"

"*Did* you, *chéri?*" Tatiana asked innocently.

Auguste cast Tatiana a look of agony, but it was ignored. There was no escape. "I believe so."

George looked sad. "So I would have won, and so would His Majesty."

All the majestic terror that Bertie's name could inspire in him seized hold of Auguste. He scrabbled in his mind for a solution. What would he do if the *côtelettes de Souvaroff* were burnt? What if the spun sugar collapsed on a *pièce montée*, what if he dropped *le rôti* on the floor? Every *maître* chef had disasters; every *maître* chef had to cope with them out of the inventiveness of panic. How could he say to His Majesty that he would have won the wager but unfortunately he, Auguste Didier, had had a hand in its having to be called off.

Inspiration came to him.

"Not necessarily, George. The hunt for ghosts on the tenth of August was abandoned halfway through, and the wager was restaged on the fifth of October. The terms of the wager were, I recall, that the ghosts of Marie Antoinette and her court would be seen at the Trianon."

"And were they?" Alice asked breathlessly.

"Unfortunately not. I saw the ghost – if ghost it was," Auguste added diplomatically, "of the Comtesse Du Barry, mistress of King Louis XV."

He led the way to luncheon, ignoring the heated debate that was breaking out behind him.

Auguste tossed and turned. The night was long, and sleep would not come. His mind churned round in half sleep, half nightmare, informing him that the *rognons* he had eaten for dinner were disagreeing with him, and that it would take him into the kitchen to dissect why this should be so. Ingredients were examined, one by one, and found to be impeccable. He was in the scullery now, washing the dishes, examining his left-over plate for incriminating signs of opium. In vain. He must finish the work in the scullery. Every *maître* chef should wash dishes once in a while, to return to the roots of his art. Glasses first, glasses free of opium. Then the cutlery, then the plates as the waters of the case grew murkier and murkier. In his sleep he gave a loud cry, waking Tatiana up.

"What is the matter?" she asked anxiously.

"I cannot wash the *knife*." He gave a howl of anguish.

"Go to sleep, *ma mie*."

He woke in the morning with a crystal-clear mind, washed in the refreshing waters of sleep. If their assumption as to Robert's having intended to kill Mirabelle with opium was correct, how did Robert happen to have a knife about his person, when he walked towards Mirabelle from his position as Running Man, having expected to see her comatose or dead? There was still a question mark over the case, although it was a question mark to which he was now sure he knew the answer.

"My love, I have someone I must see today," he told Tatiana at breakfast. "May I drive the car?"

She looked horror-stricken. "Not today. I have someone to see also."

"My darling, you shall have any new car if you wish, if you would take a *fiacre* today."

"Thank you, Auguste, but—"

Auguste was out of earshot, intent on his own mission, and only slightly conscience-stricken. If his theory was correct, he would be just in time. Half an hour later he walked into the Basilique de St Denis. He studied the plan of the church, and hurried up the right-hand aisle. Should he go first to the crypt or the Louis Philippe chapel? He chose the latter, for it was nearer, and there, on her knees in devotion, he found Alice. She was not facing the altar, however, but the ornate stone kneeling figures of Louis XVI and Marie Antoinette.

"Madame," he said quietly, and Alice opened her eyes.

"What are you doing here?" she asked crossly.

"You did kill Louise, didn't you?"

"No. How can you say such a terrible thing, *here*?"

"In mistake for Mirabelle," Auguste added.

"I didn't mean to kill Louise, or Mirabelle either." She was indignant that he should think so. "It was an accident. I was very upset about it. I thought if I took a little laudanum with me I could put it into Mirabelle's coffee so that she would fall asleep on the lawn. Then I could take her place as Marie Antoinette. I must have got the wrong cup, just as you said Robert had, and put too great a quantity in. I didn't mean to kill *Louise*, I truly didn't."

"Did it mean so much to you?"

"Of course." Alice seemed surprised at the question. "The Queen was my ancestress. I had the *right* to play her."

"To her it all seems quite logical. She's unbalanced, to say the least, and laudanum preparations vary greatly in strength," Auguste said for the umpteenth time to Tatiana after a gruelling day spent at Sûreté headquarters with Egbert and Chesnais. Egbert was still there, calming Pierre down, but Alice had seemed somewhat nonplussed at his agitation.

"Auguste—"

"Nevertheless, her actions resulted in Louise's death."

"*Ma mie*, I want to tell you about *my* day. I have something exciting—"

"Is it outside?" Auguste asked, resigned to the inevitable

long discussion on the merits of a new car outside their
door.

"No. It won't be delivered for some months."

"Is Monsieur Bollée constructing especially for you?" This
sounded even more expensive than he had feared.

"No. I'm building it."

Suddenly Auguste's concentration was fully on her. "Constructing it yourself? Is that safe, my love?"

"It's been done for thousands of years."

"Motor cars or women building things?" Auguste was lost.

"The latter. But it's not a motor car."

Epilogue

"What about the wager, Auguste?"

Egbert sipped a brandy after dinner. Tatiana had ad-journed with Edith to discuss babies, and Auguste had spent a considerable time with Egbert pontificating on the joys of future fatherhood to which Egbert had patiently listened. Edith had been flushed with pride at the success of her celebration meal culled from the delights of Mrs Marshall's cookery books and based on Mr Pinpole's meat. Auguste felt he might never rise again from the dual onslaught, and only by fixing his mind very firmly on future delights could he overlook the battle that seemed to be in progress in his digestive system.

"It was decided, Egbert, that as only the Comtesse Du Barry appeared, the result should be a draw."

"No such thing in a wager, is there?"

"There is in this one."

"What about ours?"

"Ours?" Auguste repeated blankly. Then realisation dawned. "Egbert, my apologies. I had entirely forgotten."

"As I see it, our wager was a draw too. We were both right. You were right about Robert whose motive lay in the past with Hélène Mai, and now we know about Alice, I was right about there being a motive in the present. Jealousy."

"So our wager is off."

"No, it isn't," Egbert said firmly. "I want that meal from you, so to be fair, I'll cook a meal for you. How's that?"

"Delightful," Auguste replied weakly. The battle inside his stomach reached crisis point.

"Oh Egbert, that *will* be fun," said Edith, entering the parlour in time to overhear. "I can give you some excellent recipes from Mrs Marshall to please Auguste. He did so admire her Little Bombs of Pheasant *à la Royale* at dinner."

"Splendid, my dear," Egbert said cordially. "And, Edith, make sure Mr Pinpole delivers his usual fine meat."

The menus and recipes for both these memorable occasions were:

Auguste's banquet for Egbert and Edith Rose
Mushrooms au vin
Cod au crème d'écrevisses Maisie
His Majesty King Edward VII's Chicken
Petits pots de crème d'orange
Canapés à la Bismarck

Egbert's meal for Auguste and Tatiana Didier
Highbury Soup
Spiced Fillets of Salmon
Mr Pinpole's Boiled Mutton with Caper Sauce
Edith's chocolate pudding
Stilton cheese and celery